I0721345

DESERTED

The Duel, Book 3

Mary Lancaster

© Copyright 2023 by Mary Lancaster
Text by Mary Lancaster
Cover by Dar Albert

Dragonblade Publishing, Inc. is an imprint of Kathryn Le Veque Novels, Inc.
P.O. Box 23
Moreno Valley, CA 92556
ceo@dragonbladepublishing.com

Produced in the United States of America

First Edition June 2023
Trade Paperback Edition

Reproduction of any kind except where it pertains to short quotes in relation to advertising or promotion is strictly prohibited.

All Rights Reserved.

The characters and events portrayed in this book are fictitious. Any similarity to real persons, living or dead, is purely coincidental and not intended by the author.

ARE YOU SIGNED UP FOR DRAGONBLADE'S BLOG?

You'll get the latest news and information on exclusive giveaways, exclusive excerpts, coming releases, sales, free books, cover reveals and more.

Check out our complete list of authors, too!

No spam, no junk. That's a promise!

Sign Up Here

www.dragonbladepublishing.com

Dearest Reader;

Thank you for your support of a small press. At Dragonblade Publishing, we strive to bring you the highest quality Historical Romance from some of the best authors in the business. Without your support, there is no 'us', so we sincerely hope you adore these stories and find some new favorite authors along the way.

Happy Reading!

CEO, Dragonblade Publishing

Additional Dragonblade books by Author Mary Lancaster

The Duel Series
Entangled (Book 1)
Captured (Book 2)
Deserted (Book 3)

Last Flame of Alba Series
Rebellion's Fire (Book 1)
A Constant Blaze (Book 2)
Burning Embers (Book 3)

Gentlemen of Pleasure Series
The Devil and the Viscount (Book 1)
Temptation and the Artist (Book 2)
Sin and the Soldier (Book 3)
Debauchery and the Earl (Book 4)
Blue Skies (Novella)

Pleasure Garden Series
Unmasking the Hero (Book 1)
Unmasking Deception (Book 2)
Unmasking Sin (Book 3)
Unmasking the Duke (Book 4)
Unmasking the Thief (Book 5)

Crime & Passion Series
Mysterious Lover (Book 1)
Letters to a Lover (Book 2)
Dangerous Lover (Book 3)
Merry Lover (Novella)

The Husband Dilemma Series

How to Fool a Duke

Season of Scandal Series
Pursued by the Rake
Abandoned to the Prodigal
Married to the Rogue
Unmasked by her Lover
Her Star from the East (Novella)

Imperial Season Series
Vienna Waltz
Vienna Woods
Vienna Dawn

Blackhaven Brides Series
The Wicked Baron
The Wicked Lady
The Wicked Rebel
The Wicked Husband
The Wicked Marquis
The Wicked Governess
The Wicked Spy
The Wicked Gypsy
The Wicked Wife
Wicked Christmas (A Novella)
The Wicked Waif
The Wicked Heir
The Wicked Captain
The Wicked Sister

Unmarriageable Series
The Deserted Heart
The Sinister Heart
The Vulgar Heart
The Broken Heart
The Weary Heart
The Secret Heart
Christmas Heart

The Lyon's Den Series
Fed to the Lyon

De Wolfe Pack: The Series
The Wicked Wolfe
Vienna Wolfe

Also from Mary Lancaster
Madeleine
The Others of Ochil

CHAPTER ONE

A NOTE OF hysteria tinged the laughter of the younger ladies in the drawing room. Which was an entirely inappropriate position in which to be discovered by the gentlemen now returning from the burial of the late Duke of Cuttyngham.

His Grace had died suddenly in a duel.

Sophia Wallace, very recently engaged companion to the widowed duchess, hastily tried to rearrange her expression into something more suitable. She dared not look at the duchess or at Lady Hera, Her Grace's stepdaughter, in case the mirth sparked back into life. Already Lady Hadleigh, sister to the late duke, was glaring at all three of them in outrage. Well, Lady Hadleigh had not understood the joke.

With some curiosity, Sophia watched the gentlemen enter. First came Mr. Anthony Severne, cousin to the late duke, slightly pompous and solemn and approaching middle age. A fleshy man followed on his heels with an expression of exaggerated sorrow— Lord Nimmot, whom the duchess detested. Then came Lord Hadleigh, vaguely harassed as usual, and a tall, elegant man with a smooth, handsome face and a supercilious air.

Dear God, it's him!

From sheer instinct, Sophia tore her gaze away from him, as though if she did not see him, he could not possibly be there. She could pretend she was mistaken, that she had never met him...

Yes, that was an excellent idea. He need never know she recalled anything about him, and he was hardly likely to notice a mere companion.

The noise in the room suddenly seemed too loud. She knew a few other gentlemen must have come in after him, including the new young duke, for she heard his uneven tread and the tap of his stick across the parquet floor. But she kept her attention deliberately on the duchess or on the drawing room furnishings.

The room must have been oppressively opulent at the best of times. Now, suitably trimmed with black crepe around the mirrors and paintings, and the glass cabinets of priceless if ugly treasures, it was utterly gloomy and anything but welcoming. It was, she believed, decorated to the taste of the late duke, whom Sophia had never met. She fixed her gaze on the solitary vase of white lilies on the table that separated the young, widowed duchess from Lady Hadleigh.

Inevitably, the funeral guests all approached Her Grace first and bowed, murmuring words of condolence that the duchess received graciously, though without any pretense of excessive grief. The late duke, Sophia gathered, had not been a very lovable man. Lord Nimmot flicked one curious glance at Sophia, standing as invisibly as possible behind the duchess's chair, as befitted a mere companion, before he moved on to address Lady Hera.

And then *he* was before the duchess, and Sophia could not breathe for the thundering of her heart and all the old indignation and remembered humiliation. She had to hold herself rigid to conceal every feeling, including fury. While *he* stood there like the personification of aristocratic propriety, in his immaculate black coat and black cravat.

Even while he spoke softly to the duchess—dear God, that distinctive, disturbing soft voice!—there was still a haughtiness to his posture, as though he were looking down his long, aquiline nose at lesser mortals. His eyes were a hard gray with just a hint of icy blue. They had looked different in the moonlight, almost silver, although the lean, sharp bones and smooth planes of his face were the same. As was his mouth, which at first glance was long and thin until one realized its exquisite shape and the devastating tenderness of which it was capable…

To Sophia's irritation, the duchess gave him her hand, and of course he bowed over it with easy elegance.

"It is good of you to come," the duchess murmured. "Might I speak with you later on?"

"Of course," he replied.

The duchess gestured with one had toward Sophia. "My companion, Miss Wallace."

Damnation! Why did she have to draw his attention to her? But while Sophia stopped breathing altogether in panic, the cold, indifferent gaze passed over her face without recognition, and he inclined his head with the civil disdain due to one of such inferior station.

"Lord Frostbrook," the duchess murmured, and he passed on to Lady Hera.

Sophia exhaled at last. *Frostbrook?* she thought wildly. *Dear God, he is an earl! Which clearly has not made him a gentleman!*

Worse than that, had Lord Frostbrook not been the duke's second in the duel that had killed him? She might have known he was Giles's enemy too—Giles Butler being the man who had shot His Grace in the stupid duel.

Giles. For several moments, she tried to calm herself with thoughts of Major Giles Butler, whom she had known and loved all her life. It was Giles's laughing, if absent, face that had helped her cope with her grief when each of her parents had died suddenly, and then with the awfulness of her new home with her cousins in Dorwich. Giles, who had been away from England for so long, fighting in Spain and France with the Duke of Wellington. Giles, whose very occasional letters had been precious islands of gladness in a sea of misery. And who, even when home, had not come to visit her, let alone rescue her, until he had killed the Duke of Cuttyngham in a duel and fallen in love with the duchess.

Stupidly, Sophia had always imagined Giles would marry her. They had been betrothed in their cradles by their mothers and grown up as friends, though by adolescence they had agreed they would never follow through with such a foolish arrangement. She had never told Giles she had always been secretly in love with him.

Damn him, too, she thought wearily. *Damn them all...*

Somehow, she managed to make stilted conversation with one of the neighbors. The duchess drifted away toward the buffet and the supercilious figure of Lord Frostbrook, who stood there alone. Deliberately, Sophia looked the other way.

Finding Lady Hera beside her, she risked asking, "Was Lord Frostbrook a great friend of your father's?"

Hera shrugged. "I would not have thought so, though he came to the tiresome autumn balls at Cuttyngs. They had yachts in common. And politics, probably. My aunt would quite like me to marry him, since he is an earl and rich."

Sophia regarded her warily. "Would *you* like to?"

Hera considered quite dispassionately. "There is something attractive about him, and of course he is absurdly handsome. But no. Frostbrook is a rake of the first order, by all accounts. Also adept at avoiding the traps of the matchmaking mamas. Women seem to like him, though. I quite like him myself. He can be very charming when he chooses."

"He seems unpleasantly cold and haughty to me," Sophia said with secret relish.

Hera shrugged. "Some of the time. His friends call him Frost for a reason, I suppose. Though they are odd traits for a confirmed rake, are they not?"

"I wouldn't know," Sophia said hastily. He had not seemed so cold and forbidding at their first meeting... Which she would *not* think about here.

Shortly after that, the neighboring landowners departed with muted thanks and condolences, and the solicitor announced the reading of the will, in which, apparently, Lord Frostbrook was mentioned. With the duchess's permission, Sophia used the moment to flee. No one else noticed.

She did not go far, for her nerves demanded instant peace. She walked into the library, which she already knew was the domain of the new duke, apparently a gifted academic. Even he, careless of conventions and civilities, could not leave the reading of his father's will for the next half an hour.

Shaking, Sophia dropped onto the first chair. Such fury with a stranger over a minor event that had occurred more than six months ago was not like her. She had felt angry and humiliated at the time, but it had hardly been a life-changing occurrence. There were worthier causes for her ire. Such as her cousins. And Giles. And the duchess.

She veered away from Giles and the duchess with a wave of guilt and discomfort. The letter she had purloined this morning felt like a lead weight around her neck, even when it resided in her own bedchamber nowhere near her. For Sophia, Giles was unattainable now. But then, for Giles, so was the duchess.

And she was thinking about them only to avoid thinking of *him*. Lord Frostbrook, whom she had encountered only once, under shocking circumstances that she would never tell anyone, and which she profoundly hoped he had forgotten, along with her face. After all, they had met in moonlight and there had been wine on his breath.

A shiver of guilty pleasure vibrated through her. She could picture the scene now, the gracious house, in the grounds lit by a hundred lanterns. She could almost hear the music drifting outside from the ballroom amidst the laughter and chatter of the fashionable, the riot of color and glittering jewels. She remembered the scents of early autumn and the swish of fallen leaves at her feet. And *him*, the most beautiful man she had ever seen, with the hard yet humorous eyes and the devastatingly sensual lips…

She closed her eyes. *How dared he?* Her fists clenched, but just for these moments, she could not, or would not, dampen the memory with anger. She let herself remember.

NATURALLY, SHE HAD not been invited to the Dawsons' ball at Fairly Park. But Cousin Amelia had accompanied her son William and daughter Allegra. They had all been very excited because among the guests was to be a highly eligible earl. Allegra had had a new gown, and her mother's pearls to wear.

Sophia had waved them off with genuine pleasure. No doubt she would be expected to act as lady's maid upon their return, but in the meantime, she looked forward to several hours of uninterrupted sleep.

Which, of course, she never got, for almost as soon as she had cleared up and retreated to her tiny bedchamber next to the servants' stairs, an urgent message arrived from Allegra.

"You put the wrong fan in her reticule," said Millie the kitchen maid.

Sophia stared at her. "I gave her the fan she asked for."

"Well, now she wants a different one."

Sophia regarded her. "She doesn't want you to take it to her, does she?"

"I'm not posh enough to be a lady's maid."

I'm family, not a servant! But there was no point in railing against her lot, or even lowering herself by answering the maid, who was already blushing hotly with embarrassment.

"I don't suppose they sent the carriage for me along with this message?" she asked, with no real hope.

"No, miss. A stable boy from Fairly Park rode over with the message. He's gone now."

This was no longer thoughtlessness. This was deliberate cruelty. And her only weapon was to pretend she neither noticed nor cared. Millie retreated. Sophia did not even trouble to glance in the mirror. She simply found the required fan, seized her cloak, and left the house, taking the front door key so that at least she wouldn't wake Millie or Cook to let her back in. Then she began the hour-long walk to Fairly Park.

It was a pleasant, moonlit night, and had she not been so exhausted in body and spirit, she might even have enjoyed it. But it had been two years since her father's death had led to her being ejected from her home by the distant relation who inherited the entailed property. She had intended to seek a position as governess or companion, but a cousin of her mother's had come to the rescue, offering her a home with his mother, his sister, and himself. In return, he said, all they would expect was a little companionship.

And she, lonely and desperate, had walked into the trap. William West was a pompous bully, his mother a wasp-tongued hypocrite with psalms on her lips and naked ambition in her heart. Allegra was a thoughtless child brought up to believe she could have whatever she wanted. The family, apparently, could not afford all the servants required to staff their pleasant house, let alone the expensive dresser Allegra had set her heart on, or an ordinary lady's maid for her mother. Sophia was expected to fulfill all these roles and more, for the privilege of a roof over her head.

Some people in Dorwich thought she was Mrs. West's housekeeper; some imagined her a lowlier servant. She had been introduced to no one, never dined with the family when they had guests, and was invited nowhere.

By the time she trudged over the fields and woods to Fairly Park that evening, her spirit was in rebellion, although she could see no simple way out. She had food and shelter, which was more than many. And she still had the increasingly distant possibility of rescue by Giles, who had been betrothed to her when they were babies. Or even by his family, if only they would come and visit her. On the other hand, although she wrote to them, pride prevented her from telling them what her life was truly like in Dorwich.

Although the weather was now fine, it had rained earlier in the day, and by the time she approached the big house, her skirts were splashed with mud, and her hair was coming loose from its pins. The brisk exercise also made her perspire uncomfortably, plastering stray locks to her neck and forehead. Grumpily, Sophia pulled the hood of her cloak further forward and shoved her hair beneath. Then, avoiding the guests who had spilled onto the terrace at the back of the house, she skirted around to the main drive and marched up to the front door.

It was too late for new arrivals, too early for anyone to be leaving, but she was vaguely aware of a man in evening dress strolling in the same direction. She didn't care. She knew Allegra would expect her to deliver the fan to her in person but she had no intention of doing so.

She swept up the front steps so quickly that she took the footman guarding the open front door by surprise. He sprang forward in alarm, blocking the path of whichever disreputable servant imagined they could use the front door.

Sophia, who on principle had no intention of using a servants' entrance to oblige Allegra's spite, did not hesitate. Looking the footman in the eye, she kept coming. As he puffed out his chest and prepared to forbid her, physically if necessary, she slapped the fan into his chest. His fingers grasped it from instinct.

"Deliver that, if you please, to Miss Allegra West," she snapped. "Good evening."

She turned on her heel and marched back down the steps. A dark figure detached itself from the shadows.

"Magnificent," it observed in a soft voice that somehow managed to reach through her temper and into her veins. "You got the domineering footman and the inconsiderate mistress in one hit."

"I don't know what you are talking about," she said flatly. And made the mistake she never quite recovered from—she looked at him.

She had to glance up, but the moon shone down, and there was enough light from the house and carriageway to show her the most beautiful man she had ever laid eyes on. And yet his face was utterly masculine, even hard, with cheekbones like blades, all firm, strong lines and sleek symmetry. Her breath vanished. Her insides felt like liquid.

She missed her footing, and his fingers, long, elegant fingers, closed over her arm.

"You are exhausted and need to rest," he said abruptly. "There is a seat just on the corner here."

In truth, she had been exhausted before the walk, which her ill nature had turned into a forced march. She allowed herself to be led around to the stone seat, where much less light penetrated. She thought that was a good thing. At least she wouldn't be able to see him. Which made repelling rudeness much simpler.

"You need not wait," she said dismissively as she sank with relief onto the bench.

"I need not, but I want to." Amusement lurked in the beguiling voice. "I find things much more entertaining out here."

"Then why come to a ball?" she demanded.

His eyebrows flew up. "A very good question. Duty is the short answer."

"Then you are falling short," she pointed out as he sat down beside her.

"Everyone needs a respite. Have you come far?"

"Far enough."

"Then you clearly need an escort home."

It would have been laughable if her throat had not suddenly closed up. A sharp tongue was all she had left.

Deliberately, she turned her head and looked into his shadowed face. His eyes gleamed, oddly brilliant, and his good looks only made everything worse. "What's wrong? Are there not there enough maids to bother in the house?"

He blinked. His breath caught, though whether in laughter or outrage was not clear. "You think I *bother the maids*?"

"I am glad to say I have no idea and can only judge according to the evidence before me."

"Why did I not think of that?" Now, it was definitely laughter in his voice, unexpectedly engaging, even tempting. "Perhaps you would come inside and explain your theory to a few matchmaking mamas of my acquaintance?"

She stared at him. "You *want* such a reputation?"

"If it will curtail the marriage lures. I would much rather be free—and not, before you ask, in order to *bother the maids.*"

"I annoyed you," she said with a little crow of victory that caused him to smile. Butterflies danced in her stomach.

"On the contrary, I enjoy novelty. And would accept much worse insults if they would make you smile like that again."

"Like what?" she asked suspiciously.

"Like the sun breaking through cloud. Like every golden treasure rolled into one. Be still, my beating heart."

Now she knew he was making fun of her. "That too could be arranged," she said, and stood. At once, he stood with her, banishing the rest of her scold, for it brought them too close together, and every inch of her was suddenly aware of every masculine inch of him. She could feel his warmth, smell his skin…

"You don't believe me," he mourned.

"Of course not," she managed, "and I have no time for games."

"One should always have time for games, but in fact I meant every word. May I not escort you home?"

"You will muddy your dancing slippers."

"I am such a brave fellow that I don't care."

In spite of everything, an involuntary laugh broke from her lips, winning an answering smile from his. Remarkably, his eyes smiled too, and the butterflies in her stomach dived lower. It was all nonsense, of course, and she did not trust him an inch. But he did intrigue her, if only because he took the trouble.

Perhaps her eyes betrayed her, for without warning, he leaned nearer. So close that she could make out the sensual shape, the very texture of his lips. That fascinated her, and the next instant, his mouth touched hers, soft and caressing. Stunned, she had no idea what to do. But he did.

She had never imagined a man's kiss could be so delicate or so sensual, moving on her mouth like silken temptation, while his fingers closed lightly around her nape, holding her head steady and gently massaging so that she gasped and twisted her head in pleasure. No less tenderly, he deepened the kiss, and she hung helpless in heat and bliss and…

He drew back barely enough to untangle their lips. His breath had quickened, and she smelled the wine on it. "Please, let me take you home," he said huskily.

Reality flooded her like a bucket of cold water, and with it came shame and fury. He pressed nearer once more, but she stepped smartly back out of his hold.

"Under no circumstances," she managed, relieved her voice worked and did not tremble like the rest of her. "You are mistaken in every one of your assumptions. If you dare to follow me, I shall scream. I believe embarrassment is the worst punishment for men like you."

With that, she stalked off, sure that she had finally silenced him. And it seemed she had, for he did not follow. Only his soft, surprised laughter seemed to drift after her in the suddenly cold breeze, completing her fury.

Some six months later, in the young Duke of Cuttyngham's library, she felt again those brief moments of intrigue and pleasure, and the long, angry walk home. She understood better now why she had been quite so furious. It was not so much his insulting presumption or even the way he had made her feel. But for those few moments with a mere stranger, especially for the space of that blinding kiss, she had forgotten all about Giles and her hope that he would revive their betrothal.

Well, she had extricated herself in time—just—and no one knew of that instant of temptation except herself. And possibly him. But there was no hope of Giles Butler. His heart belonged to another who would surely break it. And she, for the time being, would go on being companion to the woman who held it.

The door pushed open, and she jumped to her feet, ready to return to her duties. But it was not a servant summoning her to the duchess. It was *him*. The Earl of Frostbrook.

Chapter Two

AT LEAST THOSE moments alone, remembering and understanding, had provided her with some strength. Her hands might have been inclined to clench, but she could meet his gaze and hold her expression to one of bland surprise. She had no idea how good a friend he might have been to the late duke. He might have been used to wandering the house as he chose, but he owed the duchess and the new duke more respect than that.

"Might I help you, my lord?" she asked.

One perfectly arched eyebrow lifted. "It is *possible*," he allowed with undisguised doubt, "Miss…"

"Wallace," she supplied.

"Of course." He inclined his head very slightly. There was no sign of the amusing opportunist who had intrigued her at Fairly Park. But then, here he was sober and had just attended his friend's burial. There was no trace of warmth or even humor in the wintry gray-blue eyes, and his posture, while not exactly stiff, was certainly haughty, if not downright supercilious. Clearly, he considered himself as immeasurably above the duchess's companion as he was above Allegra's put-upon "maid".

"Miss Wallace," he repeated. "Her Grace's very recently engaged companion, betrothed, I understand, to a Major Butler."

Her heart lurched. "Battle," she corrected him, for this was the name and the story she and Giles and the duchess had concocted to account for the duchess's time jaunting about the country largely alone with Giles.

He shrugged his elegant shoulders very slightly. "My apologies. They sound so similar."

"Only if you slur your words."

"Which you have never done."

Her eyes flew to his once more, but he was already walking away from her toward the nearest bookshelf.

"It is unusual," he observed, "for a betrothed lady to seek a paid position."

"If you say so."

He took a book from the shelf and turned toward her with a small, glacial smile. "You are quite right. It is assuredly none of my business. But you should be aware, Miss Wallace, that Her Grace is not without protectors."

Good grief, he is warning me off! Only with difficulty did she bite back an indignant retort. By the time she had recovered enough to speak civilly, he had already bowed infinitesimally and walked out of the room, abandoning the book on the nearest table.

DINNER THAT EVENING was a tense affair. Although the family was joined for the night by Lord Frostbrook and Lord Nimmot—who had been bequeathed, respectively, a horse and a set of rare books—the new duke had made it perfectly clear that he wanted everyone, including his aunt and uncle Hadleigh and his cousin Anthony Severne, gone by the following morning.

Lady Hadleigh, who did not like the duchess and had already been bested in a clash of wills with her, was also resentful that the new duke took her part. Anthony appeared merely a little sorrowful. But then, according to the duchess, he had been left nothing at all in the will, despite the fact that the duke had apparently relied on him, or at least made use of him, for years.

Seated beside Lord Nimmot, whose puffy, lecherous eyes were all too often fixed on the duchess, Sophia found herself more or less ignored, although Lord Hadleigh did address a few amiable if offhand words at her. Lord Frostbrook, on the other side of the table, never once glanced at her, directing most of his remarks to the duchess, or to Anthony Severne on his other side.

Although the food and the wine were as excellent as they always seemed to be at Cuttyngs, Sophia ate very little and was highly relieved when the duchess declared the ordeal over by rising from her place.

"You will forgive me if I retire early. I do thank you for supporting us at this time and beg you to make yourselves at home this evening. Good night."

Sophia, on her feet with alacrity, at once followed her to the door, though Lady Hadleigh was apparently taken by surprise and clearly added it to her list of grievances, as it was customary for ladies to leave the table with their hostess. She took her time, and Sophia, for the sake of precedence, felt obliged to wait for her to exit the room before her.

Naturally, the men had all risen and bowed. But rather to Sophia's surprise, Lord Frostbrook forestalled the footman by opening and holding the door for them. The duchess cast him a quick smile, almost as though she liked him. Lady Hadleigh nodded graciously. Sophia walked past with her head down, but to her surprise, he followed her from the room and caught her arm with one hand while closing the door with the other.

She snatched her arm free as though it were burned and glared at him.

"A moment only," he murmured impatiently, his gaze not on her but at the duchess, already hurrying for the stairs. "Tell her to lock her door."

Her eyes widened. So he too suspected Nimmot of more than worship of the duchess from afar.

"I already have," she said.

Even more surprising, he fell into step beside her. Lady Hadleigh had gone into the drawing room. Perhaps Frostbrook was heading to a cloakroom, for it was customary for the gentlemen to remain at table a while longer with port and brandy and manly conversation, and he had not bidden his host good night.

"Were you present at the duel?" he asked abruptly.

She stared at him. "Me? Of course not. Whatever makes you imagine that?"

He did not answer directly. "Her Grace has asked me about it. Specifically, about Major Butler's part in the quarrel. Do you know something I do not?"

"Not about the duel," she said sweetly. "It was you who was there, I understand, presiding over ritual murder." She veered left toward the staircase, without a word, leaving him standing in the gallery alone.

SOPHIA COULD NOT even begin to go to bed. She paced her bedchamber, as though trying to escape the uncomfortable thoughts and guilts that pursued her.

Her words to Frostbrook had been less than wise, since as well as insulting him, she had basically accused Giles Butler of murder.

Of course, he *had* been the duke's opponent in the duel, and His Grace had undeniably died with Giles's bullet in his body. But the duke had issued the challenge, and Giles had intended to miss him. Dr. Rivers, the physician who had attended, seemed to have some doubts about how the duke came to die so immediately of so minor a wound. According to the duchess, Rivers even suspected the duke had been taken ill and actually stumbled into the path of a shot that would otherwise have missed him altogether.

Frostbrook's question and her own unwise answer had led her into a difficult discussion with the duchess, one where Sophia had been forced to acknowledge that she had not even asked about Giles's prospects. She had merely nursed her misery and her jealousy, while Rosamund, the duchess, had already written to Wellington and was moving heaven and earth to see that Giles did not suffer unduly for what had been a tragic accident.

Sophia had ended by saying bleakly, "I may have loved him longer than you have, but I don't love him *more*, do I?"

"I don't think you can," the duchess had replied unhappily.

Their feelings for him were not equal. The duchess seemed to be implying that, given the impossibility of Giles marrying her, he might well return to Sophia. Sophia doubted she could bear to be second best. But more than that, she would be settling, too. Her love for Giles was rooted in the past, in childhood friendship and present unhappiness, where the image of him as her white knight charging to her rescue had only ever been fantasy. She did not know the man he was now, any more than he knew her.

That brought its own pain, another acknowledgement of foolishness and weakness. A letting go that left her adrift.

Footsteps mingled with her own, although the sound was more distant, in the passage. She paused. So did the stealthy footsteps outside. She heard a faint clunk, as of someone trying to open a door—the door opposite Sophia's, if she was not mistaken. The duchess's.

Impulsively, Sophia crossed her own comfortable chamber, listening to the rattle of the door, which grew increasingly frustrated. Thank God the duchess had taken advice and locked it. Sophia snatched up her shawl and threw open her own door.

Just as she had suspected, Lord Nimmot stood there, bent over as though he would peer through the keyhole. At least he was dressed. He jumped upright, spinning to face her, his cheeks puce with the effort and the annoyance of being interrupted.

"Are you lost, my lord?" she asked in a stage whisper. She pointed along the passage. "Your chamber is in the west wing, on the other side of the main staircase."

"Of course it is," he replied testily, although also in a loud whisper. "Her Grace invited me for a glass of sherry. To offer comfort, no doubt, since Cuttyngham was a friend of mine."

Lying toad. "You must have misunderstood. Her Grace is exhausted, and we cannot allow anyone to disturb her. Good night, my lord."

He glared at her, clearly unwilling to give up this chance.

She smiled. "Shall I ring for a servant to call His Grace? I expect he is still up."

"Thank you, no," Nimmot said between his teeth. He snatched up his candle from the shelf in the passage. "I am well aware where to find His Grace."

He stalked off, clearly seething. Worryingly, it was not the locked door that deterred him from forcing attentions on the duchess. It was the promise of humiliation and scandal if he tried.

Vile man. Sophia turned back into her bedchamber, though her heart sank at the prospect of another hour or so pacing the same space. She would have gone out for a more energetic walk in the fresh air, were she not afraid Nimmot would come back and somehow break into the duchess's room.

A sardonic smile twisted her lips. She could not dislike Rosamund Severne. Nor could she help feeling responsible for her, and not solely for Giles's sake, either. So, she would stay awake here for another hour, though she would stop pacing and instead admire the gardens and the surrounding countryside by whatever moonlight was shining on them tonight.

She went and pushed up the sash as far as it would go, then sank onto the cushioned seat below and stuck her head out of the window until the night air blew against her face and hair. She breathed in and out again with quiet pleasure, but had not even registered the scenery visible beneath the moon and stars before her breath caught with the sudden certainty that she wasn't alone. She dropped her gaze.

A perfectly groomed male head poked out of the window immediately below her own and twisted around to look up at her. Lord Frostbrook.

For an instant, she was speechless while her heart recovered from the shock. Then she frowned, for she knew the guests were quartered in the west wing. "Which room are you in?"

"I don't know. It has a billiard table."

She hesitated, recalling that he had at least had the decency to warn her against Nimmot's designs on the duchess. She leaned out, lowering her voice even further. "Do you happen to know if Nimmot has gone to bed?"

There was a moment's silence. From his own light and hers, she saw now that he was in his shirt sleeves, without his cravat. The strong column of his throat seemed to rise in shadows from the depths of his snowy-white shirt.

He said, "Wait." And his head disappeared.

She used the time to admire the sky, the rolling fields, and the glittering river flowing eastward toward the sea. He made no sound on his return, but she still knew the moment he reappeared.

"Yes," he said quietly. "Was he bothering her?"

"The door was locked. I sent him away with a flea in his ear."

"What an admirable companion."

She regarded him doubtfully, unsure if he was mocking her.

"Compliment," he answered, just as though she had asked. "Gratitude is not required."

"Good," she replied, hoping she didn't sound as suddenly uncertain as she felt. She hurried into speech. "Did you know the late duke well?"

"We were political allies, not bosom friends."

"But he was a reactionary old—"

"So am I," he interrupted mildly.

She frowned. "Why?"

She fully expected an icy set-down. Ladies, let alone ladies' companions, were not meant to be capable of understanding politics, and she had already insulted his own. But, in fact, he appeared to think about it.

"I like order," he said at last.

"Even the same old order of poverty and powerlessness enjoyed by the vast majority of the population?"

"A radical in our midst," he observed. "Are those Major Butler's—forgive me, Major Battle's—politics?"

"No," she said baldly, though actually, she had no idea of Giles's beliefs.

"Well, if he has any sense, I daresay he will convert."

She scowled down at him. "What exactly do you mean by that?"

"I beg your pardon. Was I slurring?"

She had to bite back the involuntary laugh. Now, at last, he was like *him*, the stranger at Fairly Park, and that brought back a world of danger, even if he didn't know it. Or her.

"No, my lord. You are alarmingly clear."

"Pray don't be alarmed, ma'am. I believe both you and Her Grace may retire undisturbed and unmolested."

She was almost disappointed to be dismissed. Which was ridiculous as well as irritating. She was no child to be sent to bed, and certainly not by him. On the other hand, he had been helpful.

"Thank you," she managed.

He waved one elegant hand. "Think nothing of it. Good night."

"Good night," she said civilly, and shut the window before drawing the curtains.

As she prepared for bed, she was very aware that he could still be in the room beneath, gazing out of the window. And instead of being irritated, she recognized those exciting little butterflies in her stomach with some surprise.

⤜⤜⤜✷⤛⤛⤛

IN THE MORNING, learning of Nimmot's attempt at her bedchamber door, the duchess insisted on going down to breakfast to face him before he departed. Her aim was to prove both her disdain and her lack of fear, and Sophia admired her style. For someone who was so down-to-earth and friendly, she could become almost frighteningly haughty in the blink of an eye.

Almost like Lord Frostbrook, also encountered in the breakfast parlor with Nimmot and the family. Immaculately dressed and groomed as always, he was the personification of icy propriety—the man who had once attempted to seduce her while in his cups, and then forgotten her. Who had seconded the late duke in his fatal duel, yet exerted himself to look to the widowed duchess's safety. Who liked order and manners, and yet took off his coat to play billiards alone and look out at the night sky as she did.

He rose and bowed as she entered behind the duchess, but he did not look at her, and all his remarks were addressed to Her Grace.

The young duke made one of his brief, abrupt speeches of thanks and dismissal, and stamped off, leaning on his stick. Sophia blocked out Lady Hadleigh's bitter complaints until the duchess, having calmed the waters on her stepson's behalf, bade farewell to her guests and departed. She seemed to be wound so tightly that she would break.

"Do you ride, Sophia?" she demanded as they climbed the stairs.

Ten minutes later, Sophia descended once more in one of the duchess's old riding habits. It had not been dyed like the mourning clothes and was a little too large around the chest, but the burgundy color was pretty. It was years since she had ridden at all, and she was both nervous and excited about doing so now.

At the foot of the stairs, her foot faltered, for Lord Frostbrook strode across the entrance hall, a greatcoat over his arm and a valise in his hand.

Catching sight of her, he bowed. "Miss Wallace."

To her surprise, he waited for her, delivering the coat and valise to his valet, who took them out of the open front door. Somewhere in the house, Lady Hadleigh's petulant voice held forth. From outside came the quick yet heavy crunch of footsteps, of servants bearing luggage across the gravel terrace, and the snort of a bored horse eager to be on its way.

"My lord," Sophia replied civilly. "I wish you a pleasant journey."

She halted a yard away from him and curtseyed under his cold gaze. To her surprise, he held out one languidly graceful hand. She did not want to go near him. Now was not the time to be reminded of a kiss he had long forgotten. As though he saw her hesitation, his lip curled, and she could not bear his contempt. She stepped closer and laid her hand in his. His long fingers curled lightly around hers.

"Goodbye." Determinedly, she looked up to meet his gaze. He was too tall and too physical, and somehow he now stood much too close. The faint, elusive scent she associated only with him crept into her senses. His thumb moved casually on her skin, and she felt it right down to her toes like a lover's caress. She could not breathe. She needed to back away from him, yet she seemed held in place by some invisible thread, and he appeared to be waiting for something.

His lips twitched. "What?" he said softly. "No farewell embrace? Not even, as the Scots say, for auld lang syne?"

She stared at him in shock. *Did* he remember her?

He leaned closer, and her heart tried to dive into her stomach. His breath tickled her ear, making her gasp. "I own to disappointment," he whispered.

Upstairs, a door banged, and with a jolt, sense returned.

She curled her lip. "Really? I thought you would be used to that."

Laughter, not anger, caught at his breath as he released her and stepped back. He swept out of the door while she gazed helplessly after him, her mouth no doubt unbecomingly agape with the knowledge that he really had remembered her after all.

CHAPTER THREE

THE COMFORTABLE TRAVELING carriage of Aaron Loman, Earl of Frostbrook, carried his lordship down the sweeping Cuttyngs drive and through the impressive wrought-iron gates to the road. He was still smiling, since there was no one else to see and the girl really did amuse him.

He had recognized her even before he entered the drawing room yesterday. Glimpsed through the open door, there had been the same distinctive laughter in her face, along with a familiar determination to banish it. By the time he entered the room, she had been seated sedately beside but a little behind the duchess, and she was looking anywhere but at him. Which had confirmed his suspicions.

She had the same thick blonde hair that had looked almost silver in the moonlight, long-lashed, direct blue eyes, and something in her distinctive posture that was both graceful and grumpy. Surely, brushed and dressed in smart mourning clothes that were too big for her, this was the delightfully disheveled maid from Fairly Park.

Of course, there had been a few disheveled women in his life since then, all providing much more intimate pleasures. He had barely thought of her. And yet he had remembered well enough to recognize her. There had been a rare sweetness in her untutored kiss… But he was not a man who valued sweetness.

He was, however, a man used to spotting frauds and flim-flammers, and for the duchess's sake, he was suspicious of the transplanting of "Miss Wallace" from Fairly Park to Cuttyngs as Her Grace's companion.

It was Nimmot who had first mentioned her, with vicious contempt. "Some goddaughter of the duchess's sister-in-law, or some such complicated relationship. In need of a position while her betrothed returns to the Continent to fight. But there's the bizarre part, Frostbrook—her betrothed is a Major *Battle*. What did this Butler look like? The one who killed the duke?"

Frostbrook had stared at him. "Like a thousand other infantry officers. And you do neither the duchess nor yourself any favor by causing distasteful rumors and lies." The duchess had always inspired his pity and his protection. The first time he had seen her acting as nominal hostess at a Cuttyngs ball, she had been a bewildered seventeen-year-old bride, neglected and blatantly despised by her husband, who had made no secret of the fact that he married her for breeding purposes.

Frostbrook curled his lip in contempt. The late Duke of Cuttyngham had been a political ally in the House of Lords, but a thoroughly unpleasant man. His death was probably a blessing for his widow. But where did the companion fit in?

She spoke like a lady. Her diction never slipped, and she was clearly well-educated. Her manners were perfect, too, except when talking to him, which he rather liked. Very early on at Cuttyngs, he recalled she had been like that at Fairly Park too. He had been too disguised to notice at the time. But he doubted she had ever been anyone's maid. No wonder she had been so insulted by his ardor, to say nothing of his amorous proposal.

Perhaps he should have left the matter alone. He had meant to when he rose that morning, for he sensed her innate decency, and she was clearly looking out for the duchess. She was worthy of consideration at the very least. And yet confronted by the half-defiant, half-proud lady, he had suddenly decided to discover if she was as indifferent as she pretended. Desire had taken her by surprise at Fairly Park, and it had been irresistible to find out if he affected her still. That he did aroused him further. And yet toying with such a woman was beneath him. His lovers were always women who understood how the game was played, not virtuous maidens whose precarious existence depended on their reputations. Sophia Wallace was one woman he could never have, and he ought to put her out of his mind.

What he should be really thinking of was a wife.

But he wouldn't. Not until he really had to. For the moment, he was more inclined to think of avoidance strategies. And he was unusually content to beguile the journey to London by remembering the pulse beating at the base of Sophia Wallace's graceful, enticing throat when she had thought he might kiss her. And smiling at the stunned expression on her face as she realized he remembered her after all.

Arriving at his London house in the late afternoon, he was not best pleased to be informed that his mother awaited him in the drawing room. Sighing, he handed his greatcoat and hat to Palmer, his butler, and went directly to see her.

"You needn't look like that," she said tartly as soon as he entered. "I am staying with Lady Widdicombe, not putting you out in the slightest."

"You could never put me out," he said patiently. "I have asked you many times to use Frostbrook House as your own."

"And each time, your voice was as cold as cut glass."

"I shall smile next time. You do not need an invitation, and I never issue one in any voice that I do not mean to be accepted." He bowed over her hand then bent and kissed her cool, scented cheek. "If you are staying with Lady Widdicombe, have you come to join me for dinner?"

"Of course not. I have come to see how things are at Cuttyngs. How is the poor duchess?"

She had met "the poor duchess" twice and both times dubbed her a little dab of a thing unable to fill her predecessor's shoes. Since this was what the late duke had intended—not through any love of his first wife, but as a means of isolating his second—her opinion was not unusual. Though Frostbrook suspected that their next meeting might surprise his mother. The little duchess had grown teeth and resilience and was rather charming besides.

"She is coping," Frostbrook said politely, taking the seat opposite her, "and was asking after you. I believe she means to write, if she has not already done so. What is it you really want to know?"

Irritation sparked in her eyes before she hid it. "I have decided to hold a party at Wellis Manor."

Wellis was one of his lesser estates in Surrey, useful largely because of its proximity to London. Brookwood, his primary seat, was further north, in Lincolnshire.

"In the summer?" he asked with polite interest.

"At the end of the month. Just a two-night break from the hectic gaiety of the Season."

"It isn't so hectic, though, is it? Half the *ton* has gone to Brussels to lionize Wellington."

Her eyebrows rose, a supercilious gesture he recognized as very similar to his own. "Must you criticize?"

"No," he said in surprise. "I didn't. I merely made an observation. You may hold as many parties as you wish at Wellis."

"One will suffice for this year. I shall need you as host."

He eyed her. "Shall I be treated to a parade of simpering debutantes of excellent birth, virtue, and accomplishment?"

"I would hardly invite debutantes of any other kind," she retorted.

"Yes, but will there be any *interesting* people?" he inquired.

Her lip curled. "Like you, Frostbrook?"

"God, no," he said at once. "I am more than tired of my own company. I only tolerate it because of alternatives like the simpering debutantes."

"Then you refuse me?"

He counted slowly to five. "No, Mother. Of course I do not refuse you."

Although she left shortly afterward, his spirits had already dived. He did not want a damned wife. Particularly, he didn't want a damned wife selected by his mother. And yet, wearily climbing the stairs to his bedchamber, he knew he had avoided marriage for long enough. He needed to get it over with. Take the first well-bred girl who did not get on his nerves. And was not proposed by his mother.

He wondered how well-bred Sophia Wallace was, and the smile returned to his lips. Just for a moment, he allowed himself to contemplate it, a few visions flashing through his mind, quick exchanges of words and passion. And his mother would hate her. An added incentive.

But no, he could not do such a thing to Sophia. There was already a deep sadness about her. He didn't know what caused it, but he did recognize it. Besides which, she was engaged to this Butler fellow—not Battle, whatever she said—who might well be hanged for the murder of the Duke of Cuttyngham. No wonder she was sad.

He had never been comfortable with the prospect of Butler paying with his life for a tragedy forced on him by Cuttyngham himself. Dr. Rivers, who had attended the duel as physician, believed there was more to it, that Butler had not actually done the killing. The wound was too slight, and the death too quick. And the duke might indeed have staggered into Butler's safe line of fire, from whatever cause.

If it would make Sophia Wallace smile and be happy, he would do his best to see that Butler was saved for her. Although even if charges against him were dropped, it was true he had little control over the forces of Napoleon Bonaparte.

ONE OF THE hardest things Sophia had ever done was to confess to the duchess that she had hidden Giles's letter from her. She had taken it from the post table the morning of the funeral, because she had recognized the writing, because she was jealous, because she did not want Rosamund further hurt by the impossibility. A whole jumble of reasons that made no sense beside the only fact that mattered—that Anthony Severne, the late duke's cousin and friend, had set law officers to Harwich to prevent Giles from escaping the country. Even though neither the duchess nor her stepchildren, including the new duke, wanted Butler pursued.

Undecided, the duchess had been loath to interfere further in Giles's life. And so Sophia had opted for honesty, and given Rosamund Giles's letter, in order to make up her own mind with all the available facts, including Giles's love.

Inevitably, the duchess had gone haring off to Harwich, this time taking her maid with her, and the second best traveling coach. Her paid companion had waved her off with genuine good wishes. Bizarrely, Sophia had been left behind to chaperone Lady Hera, a distant, but oddly engaging girl of unexpected wit and intelligence. Together, they began to clear out the dower house on the edge of the park and order the necessary repairs to the roof and stonework, with the intention that the duchess could live there on her return.

Then, more bizarrely yet, Lady Hera confided that she was going to Lincolnshire to take up a paid position as companion.

Sophia scratched her head at this. "You want to be someone else's companion? While the *actual* companion is left with no company?"

Lady Hera laughed. "You have Victor."

Victor being Hera's brother and the duke. "That is another thing. It will cause talk if I continue to live here with Victor."

"Who cares?" Hera said. "He likes you, and you aren't scared of him. Between you and me, I am glad he will have company. Just until Her Grace returns."

Sophia, who was by no means certain Her Grace would ever return, asked instead, "Why are you doing this?"

"I want to," Hera said lightly.

"I took the post with Her Grace because I needed to. I have to support myself. You don't."

"It is not a matter of support. It is…starting again. Being useful. Learning about myself. Do you think I am mad?"

"No," Sophia said. "But I think you can come home whenever it bores, annoys, or exhausts you."

"And you cannot," Hera said quietly.

"On the other hand, since I came here, I have not been bored or exhausted at all, and only very slightly annoyed, so I have no intention of complaining. I'm just not sure what I am doing here anymore."

"Whatever it is Her Grace brought you for," Hera said shrewdly. "Besides, I would be very grateful if you would look in on Victor from time to time, make sure he speaks occasionally to someone who is not a servant."

The unlikely suspicion that Hera was actually matchmaking crossed Sophia's mind and was thrust aside. Victor Severne was Duke of Cuttyngham, rich, dramatically handsome, and formidably clever. He would not lack for marriage prospects.

The day that Hera departed for Lincolnshire, Sophia came to a decision and went in search of the duke. He was not difficult to find. When he was not riding around the estate with his steward, he was nearly always in his library.

"Sophia," he said informally, lifting his rear off the chair and dropping back into it again by way of courtesy.

"Your Grace." She took the chair he indicated and looked him in the eye, mostly to stop his attention straying back to the page. "With Lady Hera gone, it will cause talk if I remain here."

His brow furrowed. "Her Grace wants you here."

"She did not foresee your sister's departure," Sophia said

tartly. "Sir, we are not related, and it is not just stupid people who make tattle and scandal out of nothing. I propose that I remove to the dower house, at least until Her Grace returns."

"The dower house? Is it habitable now?"

"A few rooms are. It also means I can keep a closer eye on the work."

"That is true," he allowed. A glimmer of a shy smile shone in his dark eyes, and she thought he would make some lucky woman very happy. "But you will come over and drag me out for tea some days?"

She smiled back. "Most days, if you wish. Then it's settled. I shall move my things over today."

LITTLE MORE THAN a fortnight ago, she had lived as a servant in her family's house, with one tiny room to call her own and no energy or spirit to enjoy even that. Now, she lived alone apart from two maidservants thrust upon her by the duke, in a gracious six-bedroomed house. Admittedly, it was generally full of carpenters, plasterers, and painters, but there was always somewhere to find peace.

On top of that, she rather liked running the household, which was so different from that of her cousins. There, Cousin Amelia had been in charge and Sophia had been more servant than even housekeeper, constantly at the beck and call of everyone. At Cuttyngs, she was given respect. She actually enjoyed organizing the order of the work at the dower house and generally looking after everyone. She included the duke in this. Each afternoon, she would walk over to the big house and join Victor for tea. He would emerge from the library and limp his way to the drawing room to drink tea and eat scones and receive Sophia's report on progress in the dower house.

Their meetings were cordial, impersonal, and occasionally

amusing, for His Grace was quick-witted and entertaining when he stopped scowling long enough. She guessed he was in pain a good deal, but knew better than to ask him about it. Tea with His Grace helped remind her why she was here—employed by the dowager duchess—and let her keep her promise to Lady Hera.

Only once, on the third day after Hera's departure, did things stray toward the personal. As Victor limped into the drawing room, he carried a letter in his free hand. He set it on the table between them while the servants brought in the tea and Sophia poured.

Only when they were alone, and each had taken a sip from their elegant china cups, did Victor say abruptly, "Were you aware Her Grace had made the acquaintance of Major Butler?"

Sophia's heart gave a little lurch of guilt. Her gaze fell to the letter on the table. Was it in the duchess's hand? It didn't matter. The situation had changed since she had agreed to Rosamund and Giles's mad plan, and she owed this man the truth. In fact, she suspected his stepmother had already told him.

"Yes. I believe they met by accident, and when they heard of the duke's death, they came to me for help to avoid any scandal."

"Why?" He was not rude, but he was, suddenly, just a little formidable.

"Because Major Butler and I are old friends. Our mothers even betrothed us in the cradle, somewhat optimistically."

"Indeed. It seems he is now going to marry my mother! Stepmother."

Something tore at her heart. She did not know if it was happiness or pain.

"Why?" the duke demanded.

"I believe they fell in love," Sophia said as lightly as she could. "One cannot always plan these things."

"Will he look after her?" the duke growled, and Sophia gazed at him in surprise. There had been very little sign of it before, but he appeared actually to care for his stepmother, or at least feel protective toward her.

"Yes," Sophia said. "To be honest, he is so devoted to her that I almost expected him to bring her straight back here at risk of his own arrest. He is not doing so, is he?"

"No. She appears to have gone with him to Brussels. This"—he gestured to the letter—"was begun in Dover and sent from Ostend. I presume they mean to marry." He gave a short bark of laughter. "It will certainly give the tabbies something to get their claws into."

"It is a pity he is the man who killed your father," Sophia allowed.

"And that she is in such a damned hurry. Sorry." He raked his hand through his untidy hair and shrugged. "Oh well, why should she wait? She wasted enough of her life in this house." He raised his teacup like a glass of brandy in a toast. "Good luck to her, I say."

"And I," Sophia said, with only the faintest hollowness to her voice. Though it was odd how little she felt now that she knew that Giles was definitely lost to her. But then, she had known it in her heart even before he met Rosamund. Had he ever loved Sophia, he would have called on her as soon as he returned to England. She tried to pull herself together. "Do you want me to leave?"

He blinked. "Why should I? You are overseeing work I cannot be bothered with. And besides, Her Grace sends you her regards and says she will write to you once she is settled. She may want your companionship over in Brussels."

"I suppose that would be exciting…" Although would she really want to live with Rosamund and Giles? The idea was both funny and sad, and yet a little thrill passed through her at the prospect of traveling to another country. She drew in her breath. "Will you go?"

The duke's lips twisted in self-disparagement. "No. How is the dower house today?"

With the difficult moment thus overcome, she returned to the dower house as usual, made plans for the following day, and pottered a little in the garden she was trying to revive, before enjoying a solitary dinner.

The space and the peace she found at Cuttyngs had their inevitable effect on her, and as the days passed, she began to relax, not into past tragedy or future anxiety but into present contentment. In all, she could not believe her luck. It could not last forever, but the first attack took her by complete surprise.

She had just picked a few flowers to make into a posy, meaning to take it up to the big house to brighten the duke's library, when she heard voices in the hall. One of them belonged to Alice the maid. The other was male.

Good Lord, has His Grace actually come to me for tea?

She had suggested it yesterday, for the duke never visited anyone except his estate workers and tenants, and even then she suspected he never dismounted, let alone entered their homes. She knew this bothered Rosamund, the duchess. The duke was almost morbidly self-conscious of his lameness, largely on account of his father's constant, bitter jibes. He was apparently aware that his father hid him away through shame, so Sophia could only imagine what effort it cost him to go out and about on the estate. Hera had apparently helped teach him the basics of riding during their father's absence, and he had taught himself the rest. Now, he looked very well on a horse, though she suspected mounting and dismounting were awkward for him.

Sophia was so delighted he had made the effort to call on her, which she saw as a new step forward for him, that she hurried across the morning room from the French doors, the flowers still in her hand, to greet him.

But when she stood in the doorway, already smiling, her visitor was striding toward her with no trace of a stick or even a limp.

Not the duke, but her cousin William.

Chapter Four

"Yes, *I*," William uttered with a curl of his lip. He was not a particularly tall or handsome man, but he had developed a certain air of command, no doubt from throwing his weight around Dorwich. "Did you think I would not find you?"

Sophia sighed. "I hoped. Alice, some tea, if you please."

Turning, she walked back into the room and laid the flowers on the table as she passed.

"So now you order servants around?" he sneered, clearly furious to find her so comfortable.

"My dear cousin, I have been ordering servants since I could talk, and even then I did so with more grace than you ever spoke to me from the moment I first entered your house."

"You cast my charity in my face!"

"Oh, get off your high horse, William," she said impatiently. "We both know I saved you more money than I ever cost you, so let us have done with pretense. What brings you here?"

She sat in her usual place, waving her hand to show William he might sit if he chose. He did not notice, for he was gazing around the room with some displeasure. The morning room had needed no repairs, merely some fresh decoration, which it had received. The carpet was a little old but well beaten, and it showed its quality and bright colors, as did the curtains and the sparse furnishings. The room was a little bare, perhaps, but it was undeniably comfortable and tasteful, and he clearly hated that.

"You, of course," he answered at last. "I have come to take you home."

"Don't be silly, William. I have been engaged by the duchess."

"If that woman really was the duchess—"

"If she was not, what am I doing here at Cuttyngs?" Sophia asked.

"More to the point, *where is she now?*"

Sophia regarded him haughtily. She had nothing to say, but since he was already in full flight, she doubted she could have got a word in if she had tried.

"Exactly! I know Her Grace is not in residence, for I asked for her at the main house before I asked for you, supposing only that you must have misled the duchess, if that is who she really is! The duchess is away from home, so what the devil is her so-called companion doing here?"

"Preparing the dower house for Her Grace," Sophia said smoothly. "I am pleased with progress so far. But then, even you must admit my skill in organization."

A muscle twitched at the corner of his eye. "Of course I do. But more to the point, Sophia, you are my family, and it is not fitting that you take employment. You must come home to us."

"No, I must not."

"Why? The duchess will not keep you when you are married. If you really imagine this officer will marry you on his return."

"Then I shall stay with the duchess. Allow me to be clear, William. Wild horses could not drag me back to your house, where I received not even the basic courtesies due to a servant, let alone any warmth or consideration. I would rather scrub floors for the duchess and be paid accordingly than return to your drudgery. Ah, here is tea."

He blinked several times, as though trying to adjust to her manner while Alice set the tea tray on a table in front of Sophia. There were only a few biscuits on a plate to have with it, as though the servants were well aware that this was not a welcome visitor.

"Thank you, Alice," Sophia murmured, and the girl departed again, leaving the door open.

Sophia poured a cup, even added milk and sugar as she knew he liked it, and then held the cup and saucer out to him.

He met her gaze, and she knew suddenly it would be a clash of wills. He would not rise to accept the cup, and she had no intention of taking it to him as she had done dozens of times in his house. Here, she was treated as the lady she was, and he could do likewise or remain thirsty.

She allowed several seconds to go by before she set the cup back down on the table, pushing it aside it order to pour the second cup for herself.

"I trust your mother is well?" she asked politely.

William swallowed. She almost saw him decide to change tactics. "Actually, no. She misses you. We all miss you."

Sophia sipped her tea and smiled. "Engage a housekeeper. Or even a maid. One less gown for Allegra would probably pay for them."

"For God's sake, Sophia, do you have to be so vulgar?"

"I am only giving you the benefit of my advice. But we need not talk about it at all." She sipped her tea, comfortable with the silence because she knew he found it both frustrating and infuriating.

At last, he rose and snatched up the cup and saucer from the table.

"Take a biscuit," she encouraged him.

He glared at her, and she knew he would have liked to sit down without one. But the habit of accepting anything he had not paid for was clearly too strong, for he took two biscuits and placed them in his saucer before he sat down.

"You must miss your own things," he said abruptly, gazing at the dyed black gown borrowed from the duchess. Sophia had altered this one to fit her better, and even so, its quality shone through.

"No," she replied. "You may give Millie the few clothes I left behind."

"Sophia!" He leaned forward, suddenly serious. "We had not realized you were so unhappy. You arranged things so well for us, we thought you enjoyed it. If we were mistaken, I can only apologize. Humbly. Only come home with me and things will be different. You need not lift a finger. Mother will take you calling with Allegra, if you wish. A new gown, a bonnet or two, I daresay…"

"Stunned as I am by your generosity, I gratefully decline."

"You are embarrassing the family!"

She laughed and set down her finished tea. "What family?" she asked.

"Ours, of course!"

"There was no *ours*, though, was there? There was your family and there was me, grieving for mine."

"For God's sake, Sophia, I have already apologized and promised it will be different. Your point is made, and we can forgive each other as families do. Now go and pack what you wish to take and let us go home."

He gulped down his tea, pocketed the biscuits, and stood. "Now."

She regarded him with amusement from her chair. "Goodbye, William."

It was like a red rag to a viper. His expression suddenly ugly, he strode up to her, seized her by the arm, and yanked her out of the chair, so quickly that her knee bumped painfully against the table in front of her.

"Enough!" he said between his teeth. "I am the head of your family, your guardian, and you will obey me and come home. After this scandalous masquerade, you will be grateful for the roof over your head and for any acknowledgement whatever from my mother. Moreover," he continued, dragging her across the floor toward the French window, "you will damned well *stay* at home, even if I have to marry you to ensure it."

At that, her stunned brain finally reacted. She dug in her heels and pulled back so suddenly that he catapulted into her. She wrenched her arm free, far too angry even to be frightened. William, his color high, opened his sneering mouth and reached for her again—just as a soft, yet incisive voice spoke from the doorway to the hall.

"Dear me, have I stumbled upon a mismanaged seduction?"

Oh, God, it had to be him, at this precise moment…! She wanted to close her eyes so that she would not see his contempt. But pride jerked up her head, and even while the heat of anger and shame surged into her face, she forced herself to turn and look at the Earl of Frostbrook.

Naturally, he was immaculately groomed and dressed in a smart blue morning coat and buff pantaloons that he filled to perfection. His boots were polished and entirely free of mud, his cravat snowy white and intricately folded. What the devil was he even doing here? He strolled gracefully across the room toward them, his expression one of mere amusement, and yet somehow his presence filled the room.

William must have sensed the same thing, for she could hear his quick, shallow breathing, and he said nothing at all.

"Allow me to assist," Frostbrook drawled. "Firstly, I do not favor the piratical approach. It will almost certainly go instantly awry, and really, good manners proclaim that one does not drag a lady across the room like a sack of potatoes."

So he had seen that part, too. How long had he been there?

While William's mouth fell open, Frostbrook halted a mere foot or so away from Sophia and held out his hand. "One must show her the deference due to her sex."

Almost blindly, Sophia laid her hand in his and could not understand the immediate comfort when his fingers lightly clasped hers. More than comfort. Awareness, pleasant, insidious, and so very welcome.

"A little adoration never goes amiss," Frostbrook added,

bowing reverently over her hand, and then, to her amazement, brushing his lips across her fingers. "Only then might one suggest a pleasant walk among the flowers, which cannot, of course, compare to the beauty that is, hopefully by this time, on one's arm." He laid her fingers upon his sleeve, and she let them stay there mainly because she had no idea what else to do. "You perceive the difference, I trust?"

His voice now could have cut glass. His gaze had locked on William's, his eyes hard as agates, his mouth a shapely sneer.

William, blushing a fiery red, was reduced to bluster. "You entirely misunderstand the situation, sir, for—"

"I do hope so," Frostbrook interrupted coldly, and finally, with awe, Sophia realized he was defending her. Protecting her. *Her.*

The same realization must have reached William too, for he blurted indignantly, "I am not seducing her, sir! She is my cousin, and I am taking her home to her rightful place with my mother and sister!"

"She does not appear to wish it," Frostbrook observed.

"She is willful and even wicked, sir. I need only refer to her misrepresentations to Her Grace, her cavorting about the country with some half-pay army officer, her lies—"

"Yes, yes," Frostbrook said impatiently. "So why on earth do you want her back?"

That threw William so utterly that Sophia inhaled a quick breath trembling on laughter.

But he recovered quickly. "Duty, sir," William declared. "She is of my family. I am her guardian, and I can brook no defiance. I can see that you mean well, but I take leave to tell you she is not your concern and this family matter none of your business."

Frostbrook smiled, very slightly. "Do you?" he said softly. "And you are?"

"Mr. West, sir," Sophia said, finding her voice at last. "William, Lord Frostbrook."

William, whose color had faded to pale, flushed hotly once

more. "I believe we have met."

"I don't recall it," Frostbrook said. "But certainly, I think it might be best if we do not meet again. If you have a complaint concerning your cousin's presence at Cuttyngs, you may write to Her Grace the duchess. Or the duke may receive you at the main house, although I would doubt it."

The dismissal was obvious, and William clearly had no authority here, whatever his family connection to Sophia. But he would not give up.

"Sir, my mother requires her, and my carriage awaits."

"Indeed, then allow me to escort you."

"I shall not put you to the trouble," William said between his teeth.

"It will be no trouble for His Grace's footmen," Frostbrook said gently.

"Sophia!" William said desperately.

"Please give my regards to Cousin Amelia and Allegra. Goodbye, William."

Behind his helpless anger lurked an almost laughable astonishment. He could not quite understand how it had come to this, but he had no choice except to bow jerkily and stalk past Frostbrook and into the hall, where Alice waited with his hat. Sophia knew this, for she hastily disengaged herself from Frostbrook and ran soundlessly across the floor to make sure he left.

"Thank you, Alice," she said in relief as the front door closed behind him. Slowly, she turned back into the room. Lord Frostbrook stood perfectly still where she had left him. "What if he does not go?" she wondered aloud.

"The duke's servants and my own are making sure he does."

She frowned, trying to grasp the meaning of his words. "Why are you here?"

"His Grace sent me to fetch you for tea. You may thank me later."

"I suppose I do thank you," she allowed, "although it would

have been more satisfying to eject him myself."

"How was that going?" he asked politely.

She scowled and opened her mouth to blister him.

"As I say, your gratitude can wait," Frostbrook murmured. "Is that boor really your cousin?"

"William West. You will have seen him, if not spoken to him, at Fairly Park. You may even have danced with his sister."

"The scatterbrained Allegra who cannot remember to bring her own fan to a summer party?"

"Oh, she remembered it. Unfortunately, once she got there she discovered some rival lady in possession of one exactly the same, so naturally she could not use it."

"Naturally," he agreed. "And your place is this household?"

"As you heard," she said, walking to the teapot to hide her humiliation.

"Cousin in theory only?"

"And in practice the drudge you met delivering my cousin's wretched fan. You will understand why I accepted Her Grace's offer of a position in her household."

"Most timely," he agreed, and she cast a quick, suspicious glance at him. She could tell nothing by his demeanor. "Perhaps you would like a cup of tea? Is it still warm, or shall I ring for a fresh pot?"

Was he making fun of her? "It's fine," she snapped, sinking into the chair William had dragged her out of and surreptitiously rubbing her bruised knee. "But if you would like some, ring for a fresh cup."

"Thank you, I would not."

She was annoyed to find her hands trembling as she poured. Damn William, he had cut up her hard-won peace. She set down the pot firmly, and to her surprise, Lord Frostbrook added a lump of sugar and a splash of milk.

She said, "I do not care for sweetened tea."

"It helps with shock, or so I am told. How did you come to be living with such unpleasant cousins?"

She swallowed. "My father's property was entailed. The male relation who inherited it did not wish the added burden of an indigent, unmarried girl. I would have taken any position I could find, but only the Wests offered me a home. My father's will had made William my guardian, and he seemed eager to have me. I missed my parents. I went."

She turned her face aside from his scrutiny and drank the sweet tea.

"Are you not yet one and twenty?"

"I am two and twenty, though I fail to see why it matters."

"Perhaps your cousin has charge of your affairs until you are five and twenty or married?"

"I have no affairs!"

"Then why is he so eager to have you under his roof that he will drag you off—"

"Like a sack of potatoes," she reminded him.

"As you say. I believe I even heard the most ungracious offer of marriage I have ever imagined."

She grimaced. "That was new. They must be more financially embarrassed than I had thought if they truly cannot afford a real maid."

His gaze was alarmingly steady on her face. "Quite." He stirred, picked up a biscuit, and sniffed it before replacing it on the plate. "Tell me, have you ever been to the George Inn in Essex?"

She blinked, as much at the sudden change of subject as at the actual question. "I don't believe so. Why, what happened there?"

"A duel, among other things."

She opened her mouth, then closed it again, searching his face. "Giles and the duke's duel?"

"Indeed."

"Why on earth should you imagine I was there?"

"Where exactly did you meet the duchess and Major Butler before you came to Cuttyngs?"

Her hackles rose. She answered sharply, "In Dorwich, when they came to my cousins' house to find me."

"Then you and Her Grace had not, in fact, been chaperoning each other almost since she left Cuttyngs?"

She pressed her lips together in silence and stared at him defiantly. "Neither Her Grace's movements nor mine are any of your concern."

"Probably not," he agreed, taking the wind out of her sails. "In fact, now that I have met the inestimable Mr. West, I have doubts you could ever have escaped his house for long enough to reach the George Inn. Without help."

"Why should you even imagine I was there?" Though had he not asked her once before if she had witnessed the duel?

"Because some woman was. And you are apparently betrothed to Major Butler."

She gazed at him, trying to grasp his meaning, and then laughed, genuine amusement cut with sudden pain. "You imagine an assignation between us?"

"You are right. It makes no sense."

She finished the tea, glad to see her fingers no longer shook, and rose to her feet. She paused. "Why does this woman matter? The one you say was at the George Inn?"

He stood and shrugged. "She probably does not. Dr. Rivers, the physician in attendance at the duel, is looking for evidence to clear Butler of murder. Several of us saw a young woman watching the duel from a distance. None of us know who she is, but it is possible she knew or saw something that might help."

"Help?" She regarded him in disbelief. "You want to help Major Butler?"

"I have no objection to helping Major Butler," he drawled. "Or anyone else, providing it does not put me out. Shall we inflict ourselves on His Grace?"

Oddly, although there was nothing in his face or voice to imply it, she could almost imagine she had hurt his feelings.

"Has Dr. Rivers inquired at the inn for this woman?" she asked as they walked out into the hall.

"No. I believe he has gone north to visit his family before

taking ship to join the army in the Low Countries."

"How far is the inn from here? A day's travel?"

"Probably."

"Then *I* could go and inquire." The prospect was suddenly exciting, but it inspired no similar eagerness in Frostbrook's haughty face.

"To save your gallant major?"

"If he can be saved," she said evenly. *But he is not mine.* Did that hurt? She could no longer tell. He was with Rosamund, and they were going to be married.

"Or perhaps the duke could escort you?" he mused as she seized her bonnet from the hook in the hall.

It took a moment before she grasped his meaning. Her fingers paused on the faded ribbons of her hat while furious color flooded into her face. Even then, she was aware that her anger was worsened by hurt, because he had defended her from William, and just for a moment she had imagined an unlikely yet curiously welcome friendship. And now this, suggesting the duke escort her to the wretched inn that he had brought up in the first place, as though that had always been her intention in suggesting she go. As though she were encroaching and engineering a closeness with the highly eligible nobleman, when all she had done…

She drew in a shaking breath and jerked her gaze up to his. "Are there any ways in which you have not insulted me?"

He raised one eyebrow. "A few. Though my suggestion was more of a query than an insult."

"To see if I were pursuing the duke?" she said furiously. "Taking advantage?" She turned on her heel. "Be so good as to tell the duke I will call another day when he has no guests to embarrass him. Good day."

She swung on her heel and stalked toward the stairs, almost weeping with angry disappointment. More than anything, she wanted—*needed*—to be away from him. And yet suddenly he stood right in front of her at the foot of the stairs.

"You are very prickly," he observed.

She glared. "And you are very rude!"

"Ruder than Mr. West?"

"Debatable."

His eyes glinted. In anyone else, she would have called it a twinkle. In Frostbrook, it was too subtle, more provoking than a sharing of humor. And yet it was curiously beguiling. She wanted to look away and could not.

"We could agree on interfering and over-careful," Frostbrook offered. "In my own way, I am trying to be dutiful to the late duke's family. You probably know that *he* never was."

She tilted her chin. "And you don't know me from any other scheming hussy."

A slow smile began to curve his lips. He was devastating. "Then come and scheme with us over tea. Or wine. Or dinner."

He had spoiled her grand exit. Now it seemed like a mere tantrum, especially when he offered her his arm. She could not even scowl at him without appearing graceless.

She laid her hand on his arm. "At least you have never treated me like a sack of vegetables," she allowed.

CHAPTER FIVE

I T SEEMED SOPHIA Wallace always surprised Frostbrook. From the sharp-tongued maid he had almost imagined her to be on their first encounter, who refused to flirt and who had revealed a depth of sweet, un-awakened passion before fearlessly sending him about his business to the unlikely companion pretending not to know him. To the vulnerable young woman, struggling in the arms of another man…

He could not deny that had given him a bad moment. Despite his inevitable suspicions on discovering she had remained at Cuttyngs unchaperoned, the sight of her with another man had twisted something deep and unpleasant inside him. He hated to see that man on overfamiliar terms with her. He had watched with icy control as this man had snatched her up so intimately. Only when, piercing his unprecedented jealousy, he observed her pull back in fear and anger, had his paralysis broken and he had intervened, masking his own shame and the depth of his fury with her boor of a cousin.

She had remained so self-possessed throughout that it had hurt to recognize she was not. That she was a vulnerable woman alone who had been threatened and all but assaulted before he had troubled to put a stop to it.

Perhaps it had been his own vulnerability rather than his suspicions that made him keep questioning her. Or even the dangers of the outrageous idea haunting the back of his mind as he contemplated his mother's party next week. But as they walked together along the path to the big house, he was conscious mainly of wonder, because he had almost made her cry. It felt like a new responsibility, and, even more amazingly, not one he was in any hurry to shake off.

"Your cousin has left," the duke greeted her in the drawing room. "I presume he has no legal right over you?"

"So do I," she said wryly.

"Don't you know?" The duke scowled as she poured tea and passed it to him with the ease of familiarity.

"No," she admitted, passing another cup to Frostbrook without looking at him. "My father apparently made him my guardian, but I am of age and have nothing to guard."

"I'll have my people look into it," the duke said.

"Please don't trouble. I suspect Lord Frostbrook has seen him off and he will now give up. His lordship tells me you and he are trying to trace a woman who might have witnessed the duel?"

"It is worth a visit to the George. Frostbrook is going to drive over there tomorrow."

"It will cause less talk if another woman makes the inquiries," Sophia said.

"It might," Frostbrook agreed, and when the duke glanced at him in surprise, he said, "I can drive Miss Wallace."

The duke scowled. "Not unless you can be back before dark."

"I am a nobody," Sophia said dryly. "No one minds about my reputation."

"They will if you're with *him*," the duke retorted. "Besides, Her Grace will mind."

Sophia opened her mouth to object, then closed it again.

"I shall take good care of her," Frostbrook said mildly. "If there is any problem about our return, I shall simply take her to my sister, who resides only a few miles from the George."

"I'm sure your sister will be charmed," Sophia said with sarcasm.

"Actually, she probably will. Do you accept my escort?"

She regarded him. "If you promise not to overturn the carriage."

The duke let out a crack of laughter.

"I have not done so recently," Frostbrook said. "I suppose I am too plodding to have accidents."

⟫⟩⟨⟪

"LIAR!" SOPHIA THREW at him, some twelve hours later, as his team thundered along the road at what seemed to her breakneck speed. She clapped one hand to her head to keep her bonnet from flying off, and clung with the other to the side of the curricle.

Frostbrook laughed. Had she ever heard him laugh before? Only teasingly. This was much more full-throated and committed, and the sound was peculiarly exhilarating. Or perhaps that was due to the sheer speed of the magnificent horses, and the sway of the well-sprung curricle as it hurtled along the road, passing carts and carriages and riders with equal ease.

After the first few miles, he adopted a more moderate pace, out of consideration not for her, she suspected, but for the still-lively horses.

"Do you always travel at such a pace?" she asked, half expecting he was merely trying to ruffle her.

"When I can."

"Why?" she asked.

He looked surprised. "I like it." His hard eyes gleamed. "Don't you?"

She laughed before she meant to. "Perhaps. Up to a point."

"I still shan't overturn you," he promised.

They changed horses midway through the morning. The new animals appeared to be his own, too—a matching team in both pace and appearance. She assumed that he kept horses at the posting houses along all the main roads. When they resumed, in a matter of minutes, he gave the horses their heads once more, sweeping around bends and over hills with happy abandon. She would have thought him reckless, except that he was always in control, managing his team with the lightest of touches and almost casual skill. But there was strength in his light hands, and the horses responded instantly to his slightest command. When he used the whip at all, it barely tickled them. She approved of that, too, though of course she did not tell him so.

Around midday, they again turned into a posting inn, and he suggested they halt for luncheon.

"I was hoping you would say that," she confessed, for her stomach was rumbling.

A frown flickered across his smooth brow and vanished. "You must tell me whenever you wish to stop for any purpose, for I probably won't notice otherwise."

As the ostlers came running, he issued his orders to them while climbing down and coming around to help her alight, a courtesy she had grown unused to. But Frostbrook, it seemed, commanded every courtesy. The innkeeper himself showed them into a private parlor and immediately supplied them with lemonade, tea, and a very tasty pie newly baked by his wife.

Frostbrook behaved like a perfect gentleman, neither stiff nor over-casual. He had traveled, in spite of the recent wars, and shared his impressions of scenery and customs that made her long to see these places, too. They touched on music and literature, and she discovered that while she did not always agree with him, she could see his point of view. He never overruled her opinion as feminine misunderstanding. She began to like him. Which was probably why she finally felt able to ask, "Why are you helping Giles Butler?"

She only recognized the warmth in his eyes as it cooled. "It isn't necessary to wish to marry him in order to discover the truth," he said coldly.

Irritated, she wanted to make some witty, careless retort. Yet what came out was: "I don't want to marry him either."

His eyebrow flew up. "I thought you were betrothed."

"Our mothers betrothed us in our cradles. We never took it seriously. I might have preferred it to William's house, but Giles preferred the army." *And now he prefers the duchess...* She could not bring herself to say that, whether for her own sake or Rosamund's.

His eyes might have been expressionless, but they seemed a little too piercing as they held hers. "Do you mind?"

"No."

"Then he won't call me out for driving around the county with you?"

"Not from Brussels."

"Then I have another few weeks to live."

"Don't joke," she said quickly. "He never meant the duke to die. Or even to hit him."

"So Rivers tell me. He is too eager to be shot by the French instead. I suppose there is at least purpose in that."

She narrowed her eyes. "Are you despising Major Butler?"

"I am philosophizing," he said severely. "Don't interrupt."

In spite of herself, she laughed, and shortly after, they set off again with a fresh team of horses. And less than an hour later, they approached the George Inn.

Frostbrook was clearly recognized. The ostler called him "my lord," and the innkeeper bowed profusely.

"Two mugs of small beer, if you please," Frostbrook requested. Since the coffee room was empty, he ushered Sophia into a chair and sat beside her. The landlord signaled to the tap boy, and Frostbrook continued at once. "You recall the last time I stayed at your house? It was very busy."

The landlord scowled. "Full of soldiers and noblemen who should know better. Begging your pardon."

"I see you remember the duel."

"How could I forget it? With His poor Grace lying dead on that very table? Not a pleasant thing for my customers!"

"Worse for His Grace," Frostbrook pointed out.

The landlord agreed to it.

"I don't suppose you saw the duel yourself?" Frostbrook asked him.

"Of course I did not! I already told Dr. Rivers that before he left."

"But you know exactly who stayed here that night. I was present at the duel, and I saw a young lady there, some distance back toward the inn. She was watching through the trees."

"Doesn't seem right to me."

"No, none of us should have been there, according to the law. However, it is important that I speak to this lady. Is she here?"

"Weren't none of my staff," the landlord pronounced.

"That isn't what I asked," Frostbrook said gently.

Immediately, a nervous look overtook the innkeeper's face. "Well, there were only one female guest, and she left a couple of days after the rest of you."

"Does she have a name?"

The landlord took a deep breath. "She's a gentle young lady and don't have an easy life. I'd hate her to be upset."

"So would I," Frostbrook said. "Unless she had anything to do with His Grace's death."

The man's eyes widened in horror. "With his death? Of course she had not!"

"I still need her name."

Their eyes clashed, but inevitably, the innkeeper's fell first. "Rainey," he said reluctantly. "Miss Olivia Rainey."

"Was she here alone, or with someone?" Frostbrook asked.

But the innkeeper was already backing away. "I'm sure I couldn't say, my lord. She had her own room and kept to it while the soldiery was about."

He vanished into the depths of the inn, and the boy brought their mugs.

"I don't think we'll get much more out of the innkeeper," Sophia said ruefully. "He clearly likes her or feels some kind of obligation toward her."

"Or to whoever she was with," Frostbrook pointed out.

"What is it you suspect? That she was the duke's mistress and might know about whatever illness made him stagger into Giles's pistol ball?"

"Something like that. At any rate, I would like to talk to her."

"Then, if you will excuse me, I shall inquire of the innkeeper's wife where I might find the cloakroom."

Ten minutes later she returned, refreshed and triumphant. "Farnton Heath," she said, sitting down. "I have no idea where it is, but that is apparently where Miss Rainey resides."

His eyebrow lifted. "How did you manage that?"

"I told the innkeeper's wife I was concerned for her. Apparently, so is the innkeeper's wife, who seems to be fond of her."

"Then she knows her well?" Frostbrook said.

"I presume that's why she and her husband wish to keep her out of your wicked clutches."

"My clutches are not wicked."

"But in this, your name was not as valuable as the Duchess of Cuttyngham's. I'm afraid I said I was doing her bidding."

"Resourceful. Miss Rainey must be here a good deal if they are so attached to her. Did you discover why she comes?"

"She receives letters here, perhaps every two or three months over the last few years. Usually, she comes alone, stays a night, two if there is no letter waiting for her. Sometimes one turns up while she waits."

"And that was what she was doing the night of the duel? Collecting post?"

"Yes, but she stayed several nights."

"Alone?"

"So far as I can gather. They know of no connection between her and anyone else who stayed the night of the duel. I didn't like to ask about the duke in particular, since I'm supposed to be here on the duchess's behalf."

He leaned back in his seat. "Interesting. I wonder why her post is delivered so far from her home?"

"To keep it secret from her neighbors?"

"Why?" he asked.

Sophia met his gaze. "Shall we go and ask her?"

"Why not?" he said, and finished his ale.

⊱⊱⊱⊰⊰⊰

THE VILLAGE OF Farnton Heath was off the beaten track and some distance from the George.

"How did she travel to the inn?" Sophia asked.

"With difficulty, I can only imagine," Frostbrook replied, urging his horses on over the appalling road that was more a rutted mud path. "No wonder she needed a night to recover between journeys."

It was late afternoon before they arrived in the village of Farnton Heath, which seemed to be set in poor farming land. An inquiry of the ancient blacksmith sent them to a cottage at the end of the main road.

The cottage was not large, but it seemed to be in good repair, with a pretty garden and an apple tree.

Two boys of around ten, who had followed them from the blacksmith's shop, stood in the middle of the road, gawping admiringly at the horses. Frostbrook beckoned, and the boys trotted up at once, although their expressions were somewhat fearful.

"Hold the horses and you can have sixpence each," he offered.

"Coo," said one boy, reaching up immediately to stroke the nearest soft nose.

Frostbrook handed Sophia down and opened the garden gate for her. The boys, more interested in the horses, ignored them. Frostbrook rapped the polished knocker and stood back, allowing Sophia to take the lead.

The door was opened quickly by a middle-aged woman in a

mobcap and starched apron. At sight of Sophia, and behind her, the elegant figure of Lord Frostbrook, her jaw showed a tendency to drop. Clearly, she was not used to visitors of quality.

"Good afternoon," Sophia said affably. "Are we correct in believing this to be the residence of Miss Rainey?"

The woman's gaze flickered to Frostbrook, to the boys holding the waiting horses. "Who wants to know?"

"My name is Sophia Wallace. I am companion to Her Grace, the Duchess of Cuttyngham."

The woman's jaw dropped.

"Is Miss Rainey at home?" Sophia asked.

"Aggie, who is it?" came a voice from the left of the entrance hall, and an instant later, a young woman walked into view. She too paused at the sight of her visitors, her eyes widening in clear surprise.

The first woman, Aggie, said, "The lady says she's from the Duchess of Cuttyngham."

"Then they had better come in," the young lady said quietly. And she was a lady. Her gown was neither new nor fashionable, nor even of particularly good material, but she was neat and curiously dignified. She spoke with the well-modulated voice and crisp accents of the well born or well educated, and her curtsey, while brief, was perfect in grace and depth.

She led them across the short hall into the parlor from which she had just emerged and turned to face them.

"I am Sophia Wallace," Sophia said at once. "This gentleman is Lord Frostbrook, a friend of the late duke's."

"Olivia Rainey." The young lady, who was certainly no older than Sophia and possibly a year or so younger, showed no sign of being overwhelmed. "Please, sit and tell me what I might do for you. Aggie will bring tea in a moment."

The parlor was a little rustic for fashionable tastes, but there was a decent carpet, thick curtains, and four comfortable chairs.

When everyone had duly taken a seat, Miss Rainey regarded them expectantly. Although outwardly calm, her fine, dark eyes were troubled, even turbulent. Sophia, who suddenly had no idea where to begin, cast a quick glance at Frostbrook, whose expression was bland to the point of boredom. No help from there, then.

She took a breath. "Our hope is that you might be able to help us discover exactly what happened on the day the Duke of Cuttyngham died."

The faintest twitch of her brow betrayed Miss Rainey's fresh surprise. Why had she thought they were here?

"You must know he died in a duel in the woods near the George Inn," she said quietly.

"What led you to attend such a distasteful event?" Lord Frostbrook asked, his pleasant voice and manner quite at odds with the blunt words.

Miss Rainey colored. She was, Sophia thought, a remarkably pretty girl. She found herself hoping Miss Rainey had not been the mistress of so unpleasant a man as the duke appeared to have been.

"I did not attend," she replied. "I observed."

"May we know why?" Sophia asked. "Forgive me, are you somehow connected, related, to His Grace?"

The ghost of a smile flitted across Miss Rainey's face and vanished. "Somehow. The relationship is distant and, you might say, on the left-hand side."

"You are illegitimate," Frostbrook stated.

Sophia scowled at him. "That is hardly Miss Rainey's fault."

His eyebrow lifted. "I am curious as to whose fault it is."

"Why?" Miss Rainey asked. "Forgive me, my lord, but I cannot see how it concerns you at all."

"Oh, it doesn't," Frostbrook assured her. "Unless it bears on why you attended—I beg your pardon, *observed*—the duel. And what, in fact, you saw."

"There were several other, closer observers. I cannot think why you have come to me. Nor why you are picking over the scandal."

Sophia made a decision and sat forward. "Lord Frostbrook was one of those closer observers. He was the duke's second. The duke's opponent was a friend of mine, an army officer who is now facing a murder charge."

Miss Rainey's gaze flickered between then. "You are, in effect, from opposite sides?"

"We are on the side of truth," Frostbrook said smoothly. "I was there when the duke provoked the quarrel. I know he did not mean to make it a killing affair. And the officer's seconds swear he meant to shoot wide. Yet somehow, the duke died. The duchess and the officer's friends want to know how that can have happened."

Unexpectedly, Miss Rainey sprang up, walking quickly to the window. Frostbrook rose with her, waiting politely for her to turn and face them once more, which she did after only a few moments. No doubt the memory upset her.

"I saw them pace away from each other and watched them turn and take aim. Both the pistols fired. The duke fell, and the officer dropped his weapon and ran to him. There was a doctor already there, and...and the duke's seconds, yourself included, I presume, although I do not recognize you. You were all too far away. I only knew the duke because of his opponent's uniform."

Her fingers were clenched against her skirts as though the memory distressed her. Sophia, feeling the echo of it, understood.

Frostbrook said, "I understand you cannot be familiar with dueling etiquette, but did anything seem odd about this duel to you? The timing? The order everything happened? The posture of the duelers?"

Miss Rainey had the courage to consider it. "There seemed to be a lot of standing around at the beginning, and at the end everything happened so quickly that it seemed all to be in the same moment."

"When the shots were fired?" Frostbrook prompted.

Miss Rainey frowned with concentration. "It must be all muddled in my mind. The shots were fired together, and yet in my mind, I see the duke begin to collapse the instant *before* he fired. Before either of them fired."

Sophia's breath caught, and she glanced triumphantly at Frostbrook, who leaned his shoulder against the mantelpiece and crossed his long, elegant legs. "That is what Dr. Rivers saw."

"But not you?" Miss Rainey asked.

"My attention was on Butler—the officer. I suspected he was aiming just a little wide of the duke and was judging that we would all brush through the idiocy without trouble when I realized Cuttyngham had collapsed. It certainly could have happened as you and Rivers saw it. Would you be prepared to give evidence if the case comes to court?"

Again, Miss Rainey spun away from them, hiding her face. "If my father permits."

There seemed only one obvious question, though it stuck in Sophia's throat. It was too intrusive.

Frostbrook said softly, "Why did you go the woods that morning? Did you know about the duel?"

Her back still to them, she nodded. "I knew. I don't know why I went. I just felt something was wrong."

"I'm sorry," Frostbrook said with unexpected gentleness. "Was the duke your father?"

Her shoulders shook, but when she turned back, it was amusement, not grief, that lurked in her eyes. "No, my lord. His Grace was not my father."

"Then you did not go the George to meet him? Or on earlier occasions to collect his letters?"

Color stained the skin along the length of her cheekbones and spread outward. "No. I never heard that the duke was aware of my existence. His cousin, Anthony Severne, is my father."

CHAPTER SIX

"WHAT DOES IT mean?" Sophia wondered aloud half an hour later as they bowled back along the village street. "Is it of any importance to our concerns, or just to her and Anthony Severne?"

"Cousin Anthony," Frostbrook murmured. "Almost a fixture at the late duke's side. When last seen, he was clearly trying to become the same for the new duke, but Victor's having none of it. For now, at least."

"Lady Hera doesn't like Anthony," Sophia admitted. "She says he is sneaky. Moreover, a Cuttyngs groom, whom Her Grace particularly dislikes, appears to be in Anthony's pay and helping him to arrest Giles Butler. We overheard them in the stables." She glanced at him. "That is the real reason the duchess left again. She has gone to warn Giles."

Slowly, he turned to face her, letting the horses find their own way. She could tell nothing from his expression, though he seemed to be making some kind of judgment from hers. But he said only, "Olivia Rainey seemed to have no knowledge at all about Major Butler beyond the fact that he shot the duke. She does not appear to share her father's thirst for vengeance against him."

"Anthony must have paid for her education, and for the cottage," Sophia mused.

"Tight-fisted commoner," Frostbrook said on a sneer.

Sophia blinked. "You keep your own illegitimate children in better style?"

"I would if I had any, which I don't." He paused. "To my knowledge. But such is not a proper conversation for a lady. Let us turn to more immediate matters. I have no desire to drive through the night back to Cuttyngs, though I will if you wish it. I suggest instead that we inflict ourselves upon my sister, who lives only an hour or so from here."

"But she will not want me, and I have nothing with me!"

He shrugged. "She will lend you what you need, and of course she will like you." He cast her a sardonic glance. "Don't take it too personally. She likes everyone."

"She would have to be very good-natured indeed to put up with an unknown woman with no chaperone or luggage, traveling alone in the company of her brother!"

"The company of her brother does count against you. But it will arouse her compassion, not her ire. Unless it is with me, and I am impervious."

"Even if she is so agreeable, she must have a husband."

"He is agreeable, too. Has to be, really, with my sister and all those children."

Sophia blinked. "How many does she have?"

"Dozens," he replied. "They get under one's feet and all over one's clothes. Like sand. Or mud. Shall we return to Cuttyngs after all?"

DUSK WAS FALLING as Frostbrook finally pulled up his horses at Landry House, an impressive Queen Anne-era pile, as he described it. Grooms materialized almost instantaneously to deal with the horses and curricle, and the butler stood on the doorstep, beaming in welcome.

"Welcome, my lord. Madam. What a pleasant surprise."

"You mean an unexpected intrusion," Frostbrook said sardonically, "but I brought Miss Wallace to smooth things over with my sister. Miss Wallace, this is Pickard, who holds the entire household in the palm of his hand. Are they in the drawing room, Pickard? We'll announce ourselves."

"Very good, my lord," Pickard agreed, taking their hats and outer clothing and passing them immediately to the hovering footman. No comment was made on their lack of baggage.

While Sophia gazed around the gracious hall—smaller and less grand than the one at Cuttyngs, but somehow more appealing—Frostbrook placed her hand on his arm and guided her up the sweeping staircase to a set of double doors on the landing. Here, Sophia hung back, suddenly wary of what kind of welcome she would receive. She had been so lulled by Frostbrook's assurances and the irresistible image of children dangling off his limbs and exquisitely tailored clothes that she had almost forgotten how she must appear to his sister.

A penniless young woman traveling alone with a rake of Frostbrook's reputation…

For a moment, his eyes gleamed with a rather wicked understanding. Then he threw open the doors and walked in before her.

It was a pleasant, domestic scene. A gentleman with spectacles fixed to the end of his nose sat on one side of the fireplace, his coat unbuttoned and his cravat loosened, reading from a worthy-looking tome. He was thin as a pole, his hair receding at the temples. On the other side of the fire sat a very plump, pretty woman, flicking idly through the pages of a magazine. A merry smile lurked on her face, as though she had just stopped laughing.

They both looked toward the door at the same time. The gentleman's book dropped to the floor. The lady emitted a squeal of excitement and waved both arms as though she would have flown across the room in welcome if only she were able.

The gentleman, grinning, rose to his feet and strode to them, holding out his hand. "Frost! An unexpected pleasure, as always."

The genuine welcome took Sophia by surprise. She could not recall ever seeing anyone at ease in Frostbrook's company before.

"I apologize for the unannounced descent upon you," he said, shaking hands. There might even have been a shred of warmth in his sardonic tones. "Allow me to present Miss Sophia Wallace, who is the Duchess of Cuttyngham's companion. Miss Wallace, my brother-in-law, Sir Humphrey Landry. And my sister, Lady Landry, who can no longer stand up. Are you increasing again, Jude?"

"Don't be beastly," Lady Landry said comfortably, heaving herself to her feet. "Just because I choose not to stand for a mere brother, however well he thinks of himself. How do you do, Miss Wallace? Welcome to Landry House. Have you dined?"

"Actually, no," Sophia replied, "but having been bumped across most of Essex, I find I have no appetite."

"There, I said you were beastly," Lady Landry threw at her brother. "Come and sit by the fire, my dear, and Humph will bring you a cheering glass before tea arrives. And we can gossip about my brother's iniquities."

Sophia, remembering to check for stray children before she sat, realized she had seen none since she had arrived.

"Where are the hordes?" Frostbrook inquired.

"In their beds," Sir Humphrey said, offering Sophia a glass of wine, "at least in theory. So what are you doing gallivanting about the countryside unchaperoned at this hour? Lost a wheel? Horse gone lame?"

If there was a barb in his questions, it was aimed at Frostbrook, not Sophia. But interestingly, the earl's face did not turn all cold and supercilious at the challenge.

Instead, with a hint of ruefulness, he said, "Trying to solve a mystery. We pursued it too far to have any hope of returning to Cuttyngs before dark, but I had already decided we should inflict ourselves upon your hospitality." His lips quirked. "And your propriety, of course."

"What if we hadn't been here?" Lady Landry demanded. "What if we had been in London?"

"You're not," Frostbrook pointed out.

Her ladyship scowled. "I still think you ought to take a little more care of a lady's reputation."

"Actually, the decision was mine," Sophia said mildly. "Reckless, perhaps, but well intentioned."

Lady Landry regarded her doubtfully, as if she didn't quite know what to make of that. Then, unexpectedly, she smiled dazzlingly.

Sir Humphrey, having served everyone, sat down again. "Tell us about this mystery, then. What troubles you, Frost?"

Sophia thought he might turn the question and change the subject, but instead, he said, "The Duke of Cuttyngham's duel."

"Poor, silly man," Lady Landry said. "How is the little duchess?"

"Relieved, I should think," Frostbrook said. "More practically, she is concerned for Cuttyngham's opponent in the duel, who faces a murder charge."

"Risks of dueling," Sir Humphrey pronounced.

"To be fair, he was in an unenviable position. Before a room full of people, Cuttyngham insulted Butler's late commanding officer. Butler should have kept his mouth shut, of course, but he retaliated with an over-truthful description of the duke's intelligence and reasoning, and Cuttyngham challenged him. Neither party meant to make it a killing affair, and yet Cuttyngham fell with a pistol ball in his shoulder."

"What is the matter with men?" Lady Landry demanded of Sophia.

"Where to begin?" Sophia murmured.

"The physician who attended him," Frostbrook continued, "also a man, didn't believe the wound should have killed him, or at least not so immediately. It was relatively minor and had no time to become infected. In fact, the doctor thought he might have died even before the ball hit him, falling into Butler's line of fire, which should, in fact, have missed the duke if only he'd stood still."

"Sounds dashed unlikely," Sir Humphrey observed.

"Particularly since we can find no evidence that Cuttyngham *was* ill," Frostbrook allowed.

"But now we have found another witness who saw what Dr. Rivers saw," Sophia added. "And Lord Frostbrook does not dispute the order of events."

"How could he?" Lady Landry demanded, then widened her eyes once more. "Oh, no. You were Cuttyngham's second, weren't you? Why did nobody tell me that?" She glared at her husband, who blinked apologetically.

"They don't normally tell us anything at all about duels," Sophia pointed out, "which is probably why the idiocy continues against all sense as well as the law of the land."

"Still, I am surprised the duchess sent you out alone with my brother in this cause," Lady Landry said thoughtfully.

"She didn't," Sophia said. "It was our own idea."

"Doesn't she mind your absence?" Lady Landry asked.

Sophia opened her mouth to reply before she recalled the dangers to Rosamund's reputation. Although if she were with Giles, surely that horse had already bolted. She cast a quick, wild glance at Frostbrook, whose lips twisted.

"The duchess has gone abroad," he said smoothly. "For her peace of mind, no doubt."

Perhaps it was fortunate that they were interrupted by the arrival of footmen bearing tea trays, and the subject was changed.

"Oh, have you been roped into Mama's wretched party at Wellis Manor?" Lady Landry asked her brother, as he took a cup of tea from her and passed it to Sophia.

He wrinkled his nose, which Lady Landry clearly understood.

"I thought you must have been," she said wryly, "for she did not demand Humph's presence as host."

"You mean, you two have wriggled out of it?" Frostbrook asked.

"Sadly, no. We thought about it, but the prospect of watching the hunt was too intriguing."

What hunt? Sophia wondered, bewildered.

"Do I want to know who?" Frostbrook murmured to no one in particular. "No, probably not."

"You might need to for purposes of self-defense," Lady Landry said. "Because this is to be a three-pronged attack. But perhaps you have a plan?"

Frostbrook met her gaze. Despite Sophia's puzzlement, the brother and sister appeared to understand each other perfectly. Behind the blandness of his smile, Sophia thought she saw a trace of defiance. "Perhaps I do."

"They are talking about a party organized by their mother," Sir Humphrey informed Sophia, "the Dowager Countess of Frostbrook."

Lady Landry turned to her. "A party of guests for a two-day visit to enjoy the cool of nature—and a ball, of course—at Wellis Manor, which is only a couple of hours from London. At this stage of the Season, it is actually quite a good idea."

"Yet you do not wish to go?" Sophia asked.

"Oh, *I* want to go. Frostbrook does not. Mama is always plotting to marry him off to some diamond of the first water, but so far he has always won free."

Sophia frowned. "It hardly seems kind to the poor girls thus paraded and humiliated," she blurted.

"But kinder than actually marrying them," Frostbrook drawled.

Was there a faint tinge of color along the sharp blades of his cheeks?

Sophia, already blushing for her loose tongue, muttered, "I'm sorry. It's none of my business. I never had a Season in London, but 'the Marriage Mart' always sounds utterly demeaning."

"It is," Frostbrook said.

"No, it isn't," his sister argued. "I met Humph in my first Season, and I would never have met him at all otherwise. But how is it, Miss Wallace, that you never had a Season?"

"Judith!" Humphrey protested. "Not our business."

"I don't mind," Sophia assured him. "My family were middling people, country gentry, not the sort to assume a Season in London a necessary step in a young lady's life. I did not feel it a loss. And then my mother took ill, and balls and parties were the last thing on anyone's mind."

"Of course not," Lady Landry said, quick compassion in her kind face. "So how is it you come to be the duchess's companion?"

Sophia could not resist a quick glance at Frostbrook. His family were beguiling, too easy to talk to, and yet she didn't know them. But he did not even look at her, let alone guide her. He seemed…distracted.

"It is a recent post," she said at last. "Since His Grace died."

"And she went abroad without you?" Lady Landry said in surprise.

"She did not wish to leave Lady Hera unchaperoned," Sophia said. "But with Hera now visiting in the north, my only duties have been to prepare the dower house at Cuttyngs, in case Her Grace chooses to reside there."

"Leaving you free to pursue the matter of the duel," Lady Landry murmured, "but still without *fun*." She glanced at her husband. "Humph?"

Sir Humphrey gave a smile and a faint shrug.

His wife beamed. "Exactly. Miss Wallace, you must come to my mother's ball."

Whatever Sophia had expected, it was not that. "Oh no," she said at once. "I am not invited."

Lady Landry waved that off. "I'll write ahead and tell her I'm bringing a young friend. She is bound to have a male in reserve to make up the numbers."

Sophia felt herself floundering in sudden panic. "You are too kind, ma'am, but I should not be comfortable—and besides," she added with sudden inspiration, "I have nothing suitable to wear."

In fact, she had nothing of her own at all. Even the black gown she wore now was dyed and altered from the duchess's cast-offs.

For a moment, Lady Landry looked disconcerted. "Not insurmountable," she declared. "My woman is wonderful at alterations, although the difference in our sizes is quite…daunting. I suppose we could try threatening my modiste in London for an urgent order…"

"Absolutely not," Sophia said in alarm. "I have no money, no desire, and no use for a ball gown!"

"I believe I can help," Frostbrook said.

His sister glared at him. "No, you can't, Aaron!"

"All we need do is pass through London, stop briefly at Frostbrook House, and go on to Wellis."

"On no account!" Lady Landry exclaimed. "She is better wearing my altered things than cast-offs belonging to your—"

"They are not cast-offs of anyone," Frostbrook interrupted with a mildness that still cut through his sister's bluster like a knife. "I apparently bought them in error. Any slight discrepancy of size can be much more easily dealt with by your dresser."

Sophia stared at him. "How can you buy gowns in error?"

His face remained bland while his eyes gleamed. Sir Humphrey choked on his tea.

"Don't ask," Lady Landry commanded.

"There is nothing remotely unsuitable," Lord Frostbrook said. "I am a man of taste and discernment and absolutely no vulgarity. Ask anyone of the *ton*."

Lady Landry closed her mouth. "That is true," she said reluctantly.

"Actually, I'm afraid it makes no difference," Sophia said. "I shall not go, though I thank you for your kindness. I must return to Cuttyngs."

"Oh." Lady Landry looked deflated. Then she brightened. "But—"

"Don't badger the girl, Judith," Frostbrook said. "It is her choice."

LADY LANDRY HERSELF showed Sophia to her bedchamber, which was aired, comfortable, and warm.

"Thank you, this is lovely," Sophia said. "I only hope we haven't put you out or held you up if you are intending to travel to Surrey."

"Oh, we always intended to leave tomorrow, spend the night in London, and then go on to Wellis Manor in time for the party. So, we shan't need to leave at the crack of dawn in order to drop you at Cuttyngs first. If that is still your desire? Because we would love to have you with us. You are good for my brother."

Sophia blinked. "I am?" Unwanted heat was seeping into her face.

"He would not have brought you here if he did not like you. Though, given his reputation, I should probably warn you against him."

"Given his reputation, I'm surprised you accepted my presence at all."

Lady Landry laughed. "Even Frostbrook would not inflict his ladybirds—or his mistresses of higher rank—upon his sister."

"Good grief, how many does he have?" Sophia blurted. "No, please don't answer that."

Lady Landry laughed. "I don't know," she confided. "But inevitably far fewer than gossip gives him. I do know he is not as black as he is painted. And to you, being a respectable, unmarried young lady, I should not even speak of such creatures at all. I have not shocked you, have I?"

"No."

"Good." Lady Landry sank onto the bed, as though testing it. A pile of linen lay beside her, including a nightgown and fresh chemise. Toothpowder and other toiletries were arranged on the washstand. "Because I do think it would be amusing if you came with us. To give Mama her due, her parties are always entertaining—she is a perfect hostess—and I guarantee you will enjoy it. Also, you would be doing my brother a favor."

Sophia's smile was a little twisted. "I think you misunderstand, my lady. Apart from our inquiries into the duel, we have no interest in each other's company. He is too polite to say so, but he does not want me there."

Lady Landry blinked. "Polite? *Aaron?* Only in the iciest way, and trust me, none of us would be in any doubt of his true wishes. He likes your company. And you would, in fact, be helping him a great deal if you came with us."

Sophia laughed. "I do not see how."

"By protecting him from Mama's latest matrimonial offerings, of course."

It took her breath away. Understanding opened up like a book, instantly read. And with it came not amusement or excitement but pain.

"I believe he is big enough to look after himself," she managed. "And so must the poor matrimonial offerings."

"Well, think about it," Lady Landry said, standing up. "Decide in the morning—at least before we take the Cuttyngham road. Good night, Miss Wallace."

"Good night, my lady," Sophia replied, calling on all her reserves of courtesy. "And thank you for your kindness."

⟫⟪

"I'm not sure if she'll come or not," Judith Landry said discontentedly as she climbed into bed beside her husband. "I said something wrong, though I'm not quite sure what."

"Don't interfere, Jude," Humphrey advised. "He has enough of that from your revered mama."

"Which is why Miss Wallace should come, to remind her—"

Humphrey turned his head on the pillow and regarded her. "No, Judith. What is the real reason you want her to come?"

Judith smiled sheepishly. "I like her. And when have you ever known him to bring any female to meet us? And don't repeat the nonsense about the duke's duel, because at best Aaron is killing two birds with one stone. He always meant to bring her here."

"I don't see why you would think so."

Judith slapped his wandering hand. "Yes, you do. He likes her, Humph. I've never seen him like any female before."

"That's because you don't associate with the kind of female he likes," Humph said. She scowled at him, and he relented. "Of course, Miss Wallace is different, and he is very subtly different with her. But remember the example of your lady mother, Jude, and don't interfere."

"Yes. Humph," she said meekly, and he laughed as he took her in his arms.

CHAPTER SEVEN

FROSTBROOK, STRIPPED DOWN to his shirt sleeves, was passing his bedchamber door toward the washstand when he heard a scratch on the wood. Suspecting it was Judith come to interrogate him, he painted a sardonic grimace on his face and opened the door.

His expression probably slipped, for it was not his sister but Sophia who stood there, a candle in her hand. Any amorous hope that might have sprung to life was squashed by her obvious hostility.

Sighing, he opened the door wide, and she brushed past him. He closed the door quietly and turned to face her.

"How have I offended you now?" he asked.

"Is that why you brought me?" she blurted. "To protect you from your mother's matchmaking?"

He sighed again and waved one hand toward the two arm-chairs by the fire. "You had better sit down."

"I don't need to sit to hear a yes or a no."

"But you did need to come alone to my bedchamber at midnight?"

Two spots of color bloomed on her cheeks. She did look rather magnificent when she was angry.

"You are right," she said shortly. "It is of no importance, and I believe you have already answered." She strode past him to the door, clearly determined to leave once more.

But he understood her only too well and cursed both his sister's interference and his own shillyshallying. He caught her hand before it touched the handle, and she immediately jerked it free, though at least she paused long enough to glare at him.

"Of course it is important, but the answer is no simpler than your anger with me."

"I am not angry with you," she snapped with such blatant untruth that he smiled.

Her eyes fell. She didn't know what to do, and for some reason, he could not take advantage. He moved away toward the dressing table, where Humphrey had kindly left a decanter and two glasses. He removed the stopper from the decanter and sniffed it, before splashing some brandy into both glasses. He held one out to her, and after a moment's hesitation, she came and all but snatched it from him before sitting in one of the chairs.

"Well?" she demanded.

He sat opposite her and sipped. "You think I am manipulating you, using you for my own purposes and probably laughing up my sleeve about it."

"It crossed my mind."

"So did the plan you mention cross mine," he admitted. "But at some point during our journey, I decided against it. I wouldn't have mentioned it if Judith hadn't."

"Because I couldn't carry it off? Or because I am too unpleasant to be with?"

Stunned all over again, he stared at her. "My dear girl, you have a very odd idea of both of us. You are hurt because you imagined we might be friends."

She looked away into the dying embers of the fire. "Don't be ridiculous."

"I thought we *were* friends. That's why I would have asked you to play my betrothed at this party—to teach my mother a lesson rather than to avoid determined debutantes that I have been skillfully sidestepping for years. Except, on our journey, I came to the conclusion it was beneath you to pretend such a thing."

He wished he could see her face, to know if she believed him.

"It is most certainly beneath me to wear your mistress's gowns," she flung at him.

A bark of laughter escaped him, and she gave him the benefit of her magnificent glare.

"Believe it or not, it is beneath me to offer them to you," he said. "Or to keep such things at Frostbrook House. The gowns I mentioned were ordered before I left for Cuttyngs, when the idea first came to me. They should be finished and delivered tomorrow. I expect them to fit you perfectly."

Her eyes widened, brilliant enough to sear him, deep enough to drown in, and lovely enough for him to enjoy the pain they caused him. Only he could not enjoy hers.

"Damnation, Sophia," he said irritably. "They might be inappropriate gifts, but they are not insults! Providing attire was the least I could do if you were prepared to do me this favor."

"And since I am not?"

He shrugged. "Who cares? If you don't want them, I'll give them to the maids, or some charity or other."

"You really have that amount of money to waste?"

"I am not a poor man. Nor, it seems, a wise one."

She searched his face seriously. "You thought it would be amusing?"

"I thought we might have fun. It might also give your Major Butler a kick where he needs it."

"He is not my Major Butler. He's Rosamund's. The duchess. They are going to be married. She told Victor."

His heart gave a twist of sympathy, while the rest of him rejoiced. She was not heartbroken. She had grieved his loss long before this. "Which means we have no one to be hurt by the charade."

"Except the poor girls whose hopes your mother has raised."

"It was always too late to prevent that. In any case, such

mercenary hopes don't interest me."

She regarded him. "Won't you have to marry some day? For the succession of the earldom?"

"I should, but I don't have to. I have twin brothers still at school."

For some reason that made her smile, and his breath seemed to vanish. "Do you really?"

"Really. If you are particularly unfortunate, you might meet them one day."

She sipped her brandy, apparently unconcerned by the heat of it trickling down her throat. "I was taught to dance," she said, "although I have not practiced in years. I never simper or giggle, have no small talk, and I am far too blunt to be appealing in Society. If that is the kind of betrothed you wish to flaunt before your mother, you may."

Oh yes, she could always surprise him. He leaned across the space between them and clinked his glass against hers. "To our happy betrothal."

SOPHIA WOKE WITH a feeling of reckless excitement that she had not known since childhood. Except this feeling wasn't childish at all, even though it stemmed from the fact that Frostbrook, whom she had always known was not as cold as he pretended, regarded her as a friend.

She had begun to understand that his icy, haughty demeanor was his armor, his defense against the people who wished to befriend him for his title, his wealth, his influence, or to marry him for the same reasons. His loneliness horrified her, even while she understood it. But the amusing, even self-deprecating man beneath—she had surely recognized him at their first encounter at the Fairly Park ball—was much more evident in the company of his sister and her amiable husband. And he had included her.

That was why she had been so hurt by Lady Landry's revelation, and why she had, on reflection, agreed to play his affianced bride. Such a worldly mother, who ignored the wishes and comfort of her son, deserved to be tricked and put in her place. If only Sophia could carry it off.

Aware of a presence in the room, she stretched beneath the covers and opened her eyes, expecting to discover a maid through the half-open bed curtains.

Instead, three children regarded her. Two were girls, perhaps six or seven years old, mirror images of each other. One of them held the third in her arms, a smiling baby of less than a year, though how much less Sophia did not feel qualified to guess. They all grinned at her in an encouraging kind of way.

"Good morning," one of the girls said.

"Good morning," Sophia croaked. "You must be Lady Landry's children."

"And you must be Uncle Aaron's friend. Mama said we would like you, so we came to see."

"I'm not very likeable first thing in the morning," Sophia warned.

"Does tea help?" asked the other girl.

"It does."

The girl turned, picked up a cup and saucer from the dressing table, and brought it to the bedside cabinet.

Sophia struggled upright, adjusted her pillows, and reached for it gratefully. "Thank you."

"We were helping Sally," the girl explained. "She's the maid who brings morning tea to the guests."

"I'm sure she is as grateful as I." After several blissful sips—the tea was still warm and just as she liked it—Sophia held the cup in both hands and regarded her interested visitors. "Uncle Aaron," she repeated belatedly. "Is that Lord Frostbrook?"

She was sure Lady Landry had called him by that name, and was disproportionately glad to hear the children use his given name also.

They nodded enthusiastically.

"He must be a great friend of yours," Sophia said, with more hope than expectation, but the children grinned happily, still nodding.

"We went to see him first," the girl with the baby said. "He made us go by winning the pillow fight."

"I expect he cheated. What are your names?"

"We're Heather and Harriet," said one twin without distinguishing. She hefted the baby, who was wriggling. "This is Little Humph. Or Humphrey on Sundays."

"Ah. The future baronet?"

"Oh, no, there's Art and Bart before him. Though personally I don't see why I can't be Sir Heather. I'm the eldest."

"It does seem unfair," Sophia agreed. "But that's the law."

"Sir Sophia would be good too," Heather said generously, betraying that she had already discovered her name. "Do you mind if I put Little Humph on the bed? He weighs a ton."

"He's safe," Harriet added, patting the bottom in question. Little Humph wriggled and chortled, and Sophia laughed, waving one inviting hand.

It was half an hour later before the maid came and shooed them out, with apologies to Sophia.

"It's fine," she assured the girl. "They are delightful."

"Breakfast will be served in about fifteen minutes, ma'am. Would you like me to help you?"

"No, thank you, I'll manage."

Within twenty minutes, she was washed and dressed and found her way to the breakfast parlor. Here she discovered not only Lord Frostbrook, Sir Humphrey, and Lady Landry, but also five children all but bouncing in their chairs.

"Miss Wallace," Sir Humphrey greeted her, rising to his feet. "Good morning."

"Good morning." She managed to curtsey while Lord Frostbrook and two small boys also jumped up, grinned at her, and then climbed back onto their chairs.

"This is the horde," Frostbrook said. "Horde, greet Miss Wallace."

"Good morning, Miss Wallace!" came the chorus.

"I have already met Heather and Harriet and Little Humph," Sophia said, smiling back at the baby in his high chair. She turned her attention to the other boys. "Art and Bart, I assume?"

"I'm Art!" said the larger. "You can sit beside me, if you like."

"No, she can't," Lady Landry said. "She can sit well away from sticky fingers, beside Uncle Aaron. Help yourself from the sideboard, my dear, and I'll pour you coffee."

In a household like this, children would normally eat in their nursery. It was highly unusual for them to join their parents at mealtimes, and Sophia rather liked that the Landrys saw no need to apologize for it. Besides which, the horde's liveliness was distracting and somehow made it easier for her to meet Lord Frostbrook again.

He held her chair for her when she sat, and she murmured thanks, avoiding looking at him in case she saw regret for their agreement last night. After all, he had decided against it once. She sipped her coffee, took a little egg onto her fork, and ate it. While the children chattered and laughed, she could feel him watching her.

This is silly. Either I trust him or I don't. Deliberately, she glanced up and met his gaze.

"Crying off already?" he murmured.

"Not unless you are."

A smile flickered across his handsome face, and her heart gave one of the odd little flutters that occurred all too often around him.

"No," he said, and raised his coffee cup as if toasting her.

They would do this, and it would be fun... A return smile trembled on her lips.

Lady Landry said eagerly, "Well? Have you made up your mind, Miss Wallace? Will you come to Wellis with us?"

"I will be glad to, if you are still prepared to take me."

"Hurray!" came the unladylike response. "Horde, you must go and clean up before you wave us off," she added as a plump young woman came in to retrieve the baby.

"You promised us a game of tag," Bart reminded his uncle as he slid off his chair.

"So I did," Frostbrook replied. "I'll see you in the garden in fifteen minutes."

Sophia regarded him with some amusement. There really was more to this man than met the eye.

Lady Landry was beaming. "There," she said smugly to her brother. "Aren't you glad I had a pleasant talk with Miss Wallace last night?"

"Yes, but so did I," Frostbrook said, "and we have improved on your plan."

Lady Landry's eyebrows flew up. "How?"

"We shall be engaged."

"That should stymie the countess," Sir Humphrey said with amusement. "Only, have you considered how breaking the engagement might affect Miss Wallace?"

"Yes," Frostbrook replied. "But I don't believe it will reflect badly on her at all. Jilting me will only add to her good character."

Sir Humphrey gave a hoot of laughter.

Lady Landry regarded her brother with affectionate contempt. "You are an idiot, sometimes."

"Indubitably." Frostbrook laid down his napkin and rose. "Hence my rash promises to your horde. You will excuse me?"

⁂

FROM HER BEDCHAMBER window, Sophia watched him running around the gardens below, catching his nephew or niece and making them shriek with delight before bolting off to avoid being re-tagged. It made her smile, because she could never have imagined the stiff, supercilious earl behaving in such a way.

A scratch at the door heralded Lady Landry, bearing a valise that she placed on the bed. "This is for you."

"Thank you, but I really don't need it. I have nothing to put in it."

"Take the things I left for you last night. I'm not sure what Aaron will have for you. Besides, some baggage will be expected of you at Wellis." Lady Landry moved to the window beside her.

For a moment they watched in silence as Frostbrook leapt over a flowerbed, pursued by Heather and Harriet from either side, and Art rushing him from the other side. He yelped and doubled back around a weeping willow tree, only to be caught by a triumphant Bart. He swung around, grinning fiendishly, and the twins spun on their heels and ran, squealing.

Lady Landry smiled. "That is how he used to be. All the time."

"Everyone grows up."

"Not like that."

Sophia glanced at her curiously. "What happened to him?"

"I think everything changed too suddenly. When he was thirteen, our older brother died, and suddenly, in among the grief, Aaron was my father's heir and people began to treat him differently. Not everyone, of course, but several boys at school who hadn't bothered with him before were suddenly his best friends. He was invited to their homes, toadied, if you like."

Lady Landry dragged her gaze away from her brother and children to meet Sophia's gaze. "As he grew up, girls of all classes hung around him, too, after his money or his wealth. It's the way of the world, but perhaps he was too sensitive. He took it all as lies. By the time my father died—Aaron must have been about eighteen—he had already adopted the pose you will be familiar with. It hurts him that no one sees his worth. He *thinks* no one sees his worth, only his title and wealth."

It was a troubling insight. But Sophia suspected it went deeper. "He thinks he *has* no other worth," she whispered.

CHAPTER EIGHT

THE JOURNEY TO London was varied and fun. The Landrys had a comfortable traveling coach and a lesser vehicle for baggage and servants. And Frostbrook insisted on driving himself in his curricle. Inevitably, everyone took turns to travel with him, despite his breakneck pace.

Sir Humphrey even took a turn driving the curricle, and when they all met up at the next stage to change horses, he enthused about the wonder of Frostbrook's horses. "Smooth as silk, give you my word, and receptive to the lightest touch. You should have a turn, Jude."

"I should not. I am much too indolent and I prefer the comforts of a well-sprung coach."

"Sophia?" Frostbrook challenged, for if they were to be betrothed, a little familiarity had to be introduced.

"I have driven with you before," she reminded him. "You cannot shock me."

"I mean to let you drive."

Her eyes widened. "I've never driven anything but a gig or a pony and trap."

"Now is your chance. The principles are the same, only the horseflesh is more obedient."

"Obedient?" she said doubtfully, regarding the stamping, pawing team being harnessed between the traces.

"Scared?" he taunted her.

"Petrified. But I'll do it. Just don't blame me if I overturn us all."

He helped her up to the driving side, then joined her before leaning toward her and gathering the ribbons. Sudden awareness distracted her.

"I'll start them off," he said, much to her relief. Accordingly, he guided the eager horses across the inn yard and out of the gate to the road, holding in check their frightening strength and spirit. And she gathered to herself the secret pleasure of his nearness.

Then, when the road was clear and straight, he let them go, and they flew along with the same exhilarating speed she remembered from their previous journey. It no longer frightened her. In fact, she laughed with sheer joy. So much so that even when he slowed the beasts and passed her the reins, some ten minutes later, she was not nearly as nervous as she had expected.

There was a novel thrill in guiding such beautiful horses, urging them to go faster or slower, avoiding the odd rut in the road, and swinging gracefully around bends. She loved the animals' instant response to her smallest movement, though mostly, she thought they did it all themselves.

"You are a natural," Frostbrook remarked. "I shall let you try my phaeton in town."

"We won't have time," she said regretfully. "But I can see why you prefer to drive yourself."

She would have stayed with him for the rest of the day, except she had no desire to betray herself, let alone encourage the strange thoughts and feelings that disturbed her in his presence.

At the last change of horses before London, they encountered acquaintances of the Landrys, who greeted them with apparent delight. The mother and daughter both fluttered around the rigidly polite Frostbrook. His eyes were weary.

Lady Landry—Judith, as she had become by then—introduced "my friend, Miss Wallace," which earned Sophia barely a glance from the daughter, and a longer, more assessing look from the mother. However, civilities were maintained, and they all looked forward to reunion at the countess's party at Wellis Manor.

"I was afraid you would blurt out the engagement," Sir Humphrey murmured to his wife as they prepared to set off once more.

"What, before informing my mother?" Frostbrook said. "We are not so ramshackle."

"Ha," Sir Humphrey replied.

Sophia had never been to London before, and the sheer noise threatened to overwhelm her. To say nothing of the unpleasant stench.

"It's the river," Lady Landry said, catching the involuntary wrinkling of Sophia's nose. "It gets progressively worse through the summer. By the end of July, anyone who can do so leaves town."

Criers of news and goods for sale competed with the loud rumble of thousands of vehicles and horses, people calling greetings and insults. The buildings and streets were so close together that Sophia did not know how anyone could breathe. Merchants and others in rich attire brushed shoulders with people so tattered and poor that she didn't know how they were still alive. Appalled, she didn't know how anyone could bear to live here, let alone to choose to come for amusement.

But gradually, they passed through to more salubrious areas, less crowded, less poverty-stricken, until they reached the wide, gracious squares of Mayfair, and the mansion on Brook Street that was, apparently, Frostbrook House.

Here, Lady Landry alighted with Sophia while Sir Humphrey took the carriage around to his own house. Frostbrook jumped down from the curricle while a footman ran down the steps to hold the horses' heads, and the grooms were summoned. Another footman collected their baggage and vanished down a narrow set of steps.

Lady Landry led Sophia into the house, greeting the butler

cheerfully by name.

"There will be four of us for dinner, Palmer," Frostbrook informed this impressive personage. "Show Sir Humphrey up to the library when he returns."

"Very good, my lord. I shall inform Cook. And I have taken the liberty of ordering tea in the drawing room."

"Thank you," Frostbrook said, ushering the ladies before him.

It struck Sophia that while she had observed him being uncivil, forbidding, and sarcastic with many people, she had never seen him be rude to a servant. Her cousins, she thought, could learn a great deal from this aristocrat they had once hoped to ensnare for Allegra.

"Ah…" sighed Judith, sinking onto the drawing room sofa—a rather beautiful piece of furniture in a charming and gracious setting. "Do you hear that? The silence of no children. Bliss." She frowned with sudden anxiety. "I hope they are not upset by our departure. And I'm sure poor Little Humph is teething. He will be inconsolable without his mama."

"I rather think it's his mama who is inconsolable without him," Frostbrook said.

"Don't be ridiculous." Judith sat back as the tea was delivered to the table in front of her. She reached immediately for the teapot.

"Edward," Frostbrook addressed the footman. "Were there parcels delivered here from Madame Celestine?"

"Yes, my lord," Edward replied woodenly.

"Bring them here to Lady Landry, will you?"

"At once, my lord." The footman seemed relieved, as though, like everyone else, he had imagined a less proper explanation for the gowns. No doubt word would spread that Lady Landry had overspent her allowance and was having things delivered to Frostbrook House to hide the evidence from her husband.

Two overburdened maidservants brought the gowns and parcels into the room.

"Oooh!" exclaimed Lady Landry, heaving to her feet. "Leave

them on the back of the sofa, if you please, and let me have a good look! You may go."

Lady Landry held up each gown in turn—a magnificent ball gown of ivory silk covered by gold net, two tasteful, exquisitely flowing evening gowns, four day gowns of assorted colors, and a riding habit of fine amber wool.

Speechless, Sophia felt her jaw drop. And that was before Judith turned her attention to the parcels containing spencers and shawls and gloves, walking boots and dancing slippers. And two boxes containing hats.

"I knew he'd forget the underclothes," Judith said with satisfaction.

"You missed the parcel beneath the riding habit," Frostbrook pointed out.

Judith scowled, and Sophia blushed.

"All this for two days in the country?" she said weakly.

"Well, you have to arrive, and leave, and pass the two days and evenings between," Judith said. "Actually, you've done very well, Aaron, though I suppose I should not be proud of you for developing such a skill with ladies' garments. Come, Sophia, let's take them upstairs and try them on. When is dinner, Frostbrook?"

"Whenever you wish it. Seven?"

"Eight, if she's to try everything on."

Judith's very superior maid was summoned to help them upstairs with everything, and Sophia spent the next hour and a half in a complete daze of wonder and guilty pleasure. She had never had so many new clothes at one time, and nothing new at all in the years since her father's death. She would have to have been inhuman not to love these clothes, all of which fitted her to alarming perfection, and managed to combine the taste she would have chosen, with a hint of the daring she would probably never have tried for, let alone achieved.

She gazed at herself in the glass, dressed in the second evening gown, which was a gorgeous shade of green-blue muslin, the color of a turquoise gem. Judith's dresser was ruthlessly brushing out and twisting up her hair.

Sophia gave a shaky laugh. "It will break my heart to give all this back."

"Of course, you will *not* give it back," Judith said. "What use will it be to anyone else?"

"Judith, I am a companion! These things are more suitable to the duchess than to me!"

"Then make the most of them," Judith said, standing back for a better appreciation of the whole effect. "You know, it goes against the grain to allow Aaron to feel smug, but I really think he is going to be impressed."

Sophia was too confused to know what she wished. She *wanted* to impress him, to see the warmth of admiration lighten his hard eyes. And yet the thought that it took hideously expensive silk dresses to do so—his choice of them at that—would be infinitely depressing.

❧

As HE HAD told Sophia at Landry House, Frostbrook had ordered the gowns on impulse when the notion of annoying his mother had first come to him. Exactly why he should have thought of Sophia in the role of his false betrothed, he did not know. He even tried to talk himself out of it and to ask a rather delicious actress of his acquaintance instead. But he knew Sophia would carry it off more convincingly, and she was, besides, better company. Somehow, he already knew that from their few brief and generally hostile encounters. To say nothing of her soft, heated mouth and his own perfectly genuine desire.

Sophia was lovely enough and different enough for his mother to believe in as his choice. And she would, besides, appeal to Judith and Humph. He could not inflict an actress, one of his own mistresses, upon them or his mother. And so he had decided to kill several birds with one stone. He decided to go and talk to young Victor about the unknown lady at Cuttyngham's duel, sound Sophia out about his mother's party, and then, hopefully, visit the George in her company and introduce her to Judith and Humph. But first, before leaving town, he had ordered the gowns she would need and which he knew she did not have. He had studied her, held her, and he was a good enough judge to make a decent guess at her measurements.

He had told her the truth at Landry House. At some point during the expedition to the George and their search for Olivia Rainey, he had appalled himself by his willingness to use her in such a way. She was far above such pretense, and he would not so demean her. Yet circumstances had forced him to seek his sister's help anyway, and she had the nerve to broach the suggestion to Sophia. And of course she had been furious on any number of levels when she had barged so recklessly into his bedchamber.

That, of course, had been when the other, even more daring plan had entered his head. But he was aware that her presence there was addling his wits with lust. He needed to think about it, and she needed to like him. Could he hope for more? She would not be swayed by fortune or title, and yet he could offer her a life of comfort and security, and a loyalty it seemed no one had shown her before. Her family had abused her; her betrothed had deserted her. Even the duchess had abandoned her in a house full of strangers.

And she liked Judith and Humph. She even liked the horde. That made him smile as, changing for dinner, he took the cravat pin from his valet and placed it unerringly.

"Perfect, my lord," Bridges, his valet, pronounced.

She is, Frostbrook thought with something like awe, *beauty, laughter, prickles, arguments, opinions, and all.* He never even thought of boredom in her company. "Thank you," he said distantly to Bridges, and went out. Like a schoolboy rushing to catch a sight of his first crush, he was desperate to see her again.

Frostbrook, don't be pathetic, he chastised himself. Then he forced himself to slow down, and strolled into the drawing room.

And knew without doubt.

She stood beside Judith's chair, accepting a glass of sherry from Humph and laughing at whatever he had just said, so Frostbrook saw her beauty at its dazzling best. Moreover, it was enhanced by the elegant, becoming style of her hair, swept softly up and twisted behind her head—all but one gleaming lock, which fell to her bare shoulder. And he had to admit he had judged the gown to perfection. The color of a turquoise, its graceful, simple style, suited her admirably.

And yet even as he acknowledged those facts and she turned to face him, the smile lingering on her lips, added color seeping into her cheeks, he knew it was not the gown or the hair. Or even her physical beauty, though it undoubtedly moved him. It was what lay behind the outward that he wanted with such power he could not breathe.

More than that, he knew with blinding clarity what he had to do.

SOPHIA KNEW THE moment he entered the room. A secret little shiver of awareness passed up her spine. She turned quickly to face whatever it was she would see in his eyes, whether indifference or admiration or even simple relief that she might be able after all to carry off the masquerade as his betrothed.

She was not prepared for the blaze that consumed her, scorching so that she felt naked and vulnerable and utterly desirable. Just for an instant, and then he blinked and the moment was gone, leaving her shaken and doubtful. Bewildered, almost panicked, she watched him advance the distance between them and hold out his hand commandingly.

It was her place, not his, to initiate any such hand taking, but she gave him hers anyway, as if there were no other choice. The fire she had imagined was gone from his harsh eyes, yet some fierce intensity lurked there still as he held her gaze and bowed over her hand.

His lips parted before he brushed them across her fingers and she melted from the inside out. She had not the strength—or the discourtesy—to snatch her hand free.

"What are you doing?" she blurted.

A gleam of wicked amusement lit his eyes. "Flirting. It is expected."

Her whole body seemed to be blushing, but at least he released her hand, which gave her the strength to retort, "There is no need here."

"No, he is right," Judith said unexpectedly. "You should practice, so you are used to it and don't jump a mile when he touches you. *Respectful* ardor is the thing, Aaron."

Sir Humphrey handed him a glass. "What a fine phrase. To respectful ardor."

I can't drink to that, Sophia thought wildly, only she was distracted by his long, slender fingers taking the sherry glass from his brother-in-law. Were they trembling? The possibility stunned her.

He clinked his glass against hers and caught her astonished gaze once more. "Respectful ardor," he repeated with self-deprecating humor. "I see the gown fits. And suits admirably. You look delightful."

"My lord, you don't have to—" she began in some distress.

"Come now, you are up to the challenge of so mild a compliment," he chided. "Anyone might say such things to you."

"I can't imagine anyone commenting on the fit of my gown," she retorted with a blessed return of spirit.

"Privilege of your betrothed," he said.

She swallowed. "They are all beautiful. Everything is. I can't accept them as gifts, of course, but I find I am grateful for the chance to wear them for a few days."

"As you wish."

Impossible to tell if she had hurt his feelings or amused him. But at least he had stopped the damnable flirting that she could not deal with.

He had not stopped, of course. The flirting crept in subtly when he placed her hand on his arm to take her formally in to dinner and held it there just a little too long; when he held her chair and leaned too close as she sat so that she felt the whisper of his breath on her nape. But there was nothing actually improper, let alone unpleasant, in his words or manner that any lady engaged to him could possibly object to. And he was right. If they were to carry this off with any conviction, she could not glare at him for every compliment, every touch. She just hadn't expected it to be so difficult. Or so secretly delightful.

Conversation was simpler. There was an ease of familiarity developed between them since leaving Cuttyngs, and she grasped on to that as to a lifeline. In fact, it was comfortable as well as enjoyable to be part of this company. She liked the Landrys, who were intelligent, amusing, and affable, and Frostbrook, in their presence, seemed a much less daunting prospect.

She didn't know whether to be relieved or sorry when Judith declared it was time to leave.

"Oh, I should pack up the clothes," she said, jumping to her feet, causing both men to rise with her.

"Sillers already took everything round to our house," Judith said as her husband held her chair for her to heave to her feet. "Shall we say ten o'clock tomorrow morning?"

"By all means," Frostbrook said. "I'll have them bring the curricle round at half past."

"I shall be ready at ten," Judith said with dignity.

"No, you won't," her husband said affectionately. "Thanks for dinner, Frost. See you tomorrow."

They walked together to the front hall, where, rather to Sophia's surprise, Frostbrook picked up a wrap and laid it around her shoulders. His hands lingered, light, unthreatening, and she inhaled the clean, distinctive scent of him, masculine and elusive like the man himself. It was another secret pleasure she allowed herself. She even glanced up over her shoulder with a quick smile of thanks. His head dipped and his lips brushed her cheek. Gentle, sweet, and rather wonderful. Even though it reminded her of that other kiss so long ago.

"Good night," he said softly.

"Good night," she managed. She was relieved she didn't stumble as she followed Judith out of the house.

CHAPTER NINE

"Y OU ARE NOT comfortable with my touch," Frostbrook said as they bowled along the road on the last stage of the journey to Wellis Manor. Naturally, she was in the curricle with him so they would be seen to arrive together, although they were always in sight of the Landrys' coach. "We can still call off the charade if you wish to."

Her gaze flew to his, to see if he wished to. Though his expression gave little away, she knew somehow that he didn't. Perhaps it was in the steadiness of his eyes, or the careful way he veiled them so as not to influence her. It seemed he was no longer quite so unreadable to her.

"I agreed to it, and I will go through with it."

"Not," he said carefully, "if it makes you unhappy."

She made herself think about it. "It does not make me unhappy. I am just not used to…attention."

"That is unjust, wasteful, and just plain wrong," he said.

She blinked. "It is the hand life dealt me. I am not complaining. I do not care to be fawned over."

Something moved in his eyes, a deeper veil. "Do I fawn?" he asked.

She shook her head, overwhelmed by the impossibility of telling him exactly what his "attention" did to her.

He said, "I had not thought, in our previous dealings, that I revolted you."

"*Revolted?*" She uttered the word in disbelief and had to drop her eyes before the sudden gleam in his. "Don't be silly."

He laughed, a curiously carefree sound from him. "No one but you has ever called me silly."

"An oversight, I am sure," she retorted.

"Why did you agree to the charade?" he asked.

She kept her gaze on the road ahead, wondering what she could say that was not *I would do anything for you.* At last, she drew in her breath. "It is not pleasant to be coerced, to feel you have no choice. I stayed almost three years in my cousin's house because I thought I had no choice. Sooner or later, your mother will come up with a way to counter your avoidance of her wishes. I am afraid she will find a way to take away your choices, or your honor."

He said nothing, although she could feel his eyes burning the skin of her face.

Then he said, "Thank you for believing I have any. Would you like to drive us through the gates?"

"Are we here already?" she asked nervously.

"Almost. Here, take the ribbons. I'll help you."

She slid nearer him and took the reins. The warmth of his thigh burned through the cambric of her new traveling gown where the blanket spread over her knees did not touch. One of his arms reached over her shoulder, and he lightly covered her hand, adjusting its grip. She was hemmed in between his arms, his gentle hands guiding hers where necessary as the horses slowed and swept through the open gates on their right. His touch was not uncomfortable at all. It was exciting and wonderful and she wanted more.

She risked a quick, smiling glance at him and saw it answered in his own glimmering eyes and the curve of his normally austere mouth. Her heart was shattering, and she was happy to feel the pieces fall.

But she had to watch the way ahead, pay attention to the

horses, for Frostbrook had released her hands and now sat straight beside her—probably too late to avoid being seen, but then, that was no doubt his motive in the first place.

The driveway led up to a charming old manor house, with a manicured lawn on one side and a riot of flowers on the other. A small group of ladies and gentlemen were taking tea on the front terrace beneath parasols. A couple of younger men were playing pall-mall on the lawn with some hilarity, though they paused to gawp at the passing curricle.

"Good God," said one. "Is that *Frost*? Being driven by a female?"

"Draw them round to the right," Frostbrook murmured in her ear, "and bring them to a halt."

Sophia was not sure she could, but as if they smelled their oats nearby, the horses behaved impeccably and halted at the front steps. Frostbrook did not wait for the groom before he jumped down, stroked the horses' necks in passing, and came to lift her down.

"Courage, my dear," he breathed, setting her on her feet and drawing her hand through his arm, even as he began to stroll toward the lady coming to meet them from the terrace. The countess, his mother. She knew her immediately by her proud posture and brisk, no-nonsense approach. There would be no affectionate reunion here.

Sophia and Frostbrook had to walk around the Landrys' coaches, and by that time, her hope of a private introduction to his mother was hopeless. But then, the earl had probably intended that the guests already present should hear exactly what they did.

"I had hoped you would arrive last night," the countess said by way of welcome. "I could have told you Judith would only hold you up."

"Mother," he said. "A pleasure as always."

"Hmph." Lady Frostbrook bore little physical resemblance to her son, except perhaps in the shape of her high forehead and her determined chin. Her gaze whipped over Sophia with barely a smile, to the coaches. "Judith! Come and introduce your friend."

"Allow me," Frostbrook said with a kind of restrained relish. "Mother, I am delighted to present Miss Sophia Wallace, who has consented to be my wife. Sophia, my mother, the Countess of Frostbrook."

The other guests, including those pretending not to listen and the men approaching with their pall-mall mallets, gave a collective gasp.

The countess remained rigid, her expression frozen rather like her son's. Only the thinning of her mouth and the two furious spots of color blooming on her cheeks betrayed her.

Sophia sank into a curtsey. "Lady Frostbrook. It is a great pleasure finally to meet you. I have to thank you for so kindly inviting me at such short notice."

"Miss Wallace," the countess said stiffly, with a bare inclination of the head. "I was led to believe you were my daughter's friend."

"Of course she is both, Mama," Judith said cheerfully, kissing her mother's unresponsive cheek. "You are looking well. Shall I take everyone inside to change before we join you?"

Frostbrook bowed somewhat ironically to his mother and with more panache to the company in general, and then, still holding Sophia's hand to his arm, sauntered toward the house behind the Landrys. Behind them, Sophia could almost feel the speculation and gossip bursting out, and the countess's helpless anger as her plans were thwarted.

"That could have been worse," Sir Humphrey murmured as they crossed the hall to the staircase.

"It will be, I'm afraid," Frostbrook said more quietly, for Sophia's hearing alone. "We caught her by surprise, and in company. If she catches you alone, refer her to me."

There was time for no more, as the housekeeper swept them up in breathless welcome. "We have put you in the blue room," she told Sophia. "It is next to Lady Landry's, but I'm afraid it is rather small."

To Sophia, who had lived for years in a chamber smaller than many linen closets, the bedchamber was perfectly adequate, and in truth, she was glad to be close to Judith. The bags Judith had given her were already in the room, so she hastily shook out the gowns and hung them up before splashing water over her hands and face. She was struggling into the blue afternoon gown when Sillers, Judith's maid, bustled in to the rescue, to fasten the gown and brush and re-pin her hair.

"Perfect," Judith pronounced, sticking her head around the door. "Come!"

Judith's willingness to aid and abet the masquerade—basically lying to her mother—was one of the things that made Sophia feel better about her own deceit, which was suddenly much more real now she was here. She had always imagined the countess to be an overambitious, meddling woman, but there appeared to be no warmth in her at all. Of course, she was angry at Frostbrook's announcement, yet in a manner that caused Sophia to regard her rather like the late Duke of Cuttyngham, whom she might never have met but who had so damaged his own children and his innocent young wife.

The woman may not have possessed His Grace's spite, but she seemed equally cold and unfeeling. Judith's warmth and general happiness was all the harder to account for. And Frostbrook's hard shell all the more understandable.

They found the guests still gathered on the terrace. A few more were playing pall-mall or strolling about the garden. Fresh tea had been brought, and the countess duly dispensed some for her daughter and Sophia.

A young lady sat beside the countess—a debutante by her youthful beauty and white dress.

"Good afternoon, Miss Brandon," Judith greeted her. "Allow me to introduce you to Miss Wallace."

"How do you do, Miss Wallace," the girl said politely, though her fine blue eyes were malevolent.

Ah, one of the rejected candidates for countess. "What a beautiful garden," Sophia said, imagining she had found a neutral topic.

"Indeed. I thought so when I first arrived."

Was that a barb? Implying it had lost its delight, because of Sophia's arrival? Surely, such a suspicion was morbidly oversensitive. In any case, Miss Brandon's eyes swept beyond her, suddenly soft and shy and smiling. Sophia did not need to be told that Frostbrook had arrived.

He sauntered into her line of vision, accepting a cup of tea from his mother and helping himself to a sandwich from the nearest plate.

"Miss Brandon," he murmured with a slight bow. "A pleasure to see you here. I'm glad you and your mother could join us."

Judging from the fixed glare of the dowager on the countess's other side, that was Lady Brandon.

"Frost, come and take a pasting at pall-mall!" one of the younger men called from the lawn.

Frostbrook raised his sandwich in acknowledgement and set down his cup.

"Oh, may I play?" Miss Brandon asked eagerly. "I would love to, only you will have to teach me, for I have never played before."

"Of course you may," Frostbrook said civilly. "There is little to teach. It's just a matter of training your eye and whacking the ball." He did not ask Sophia to join them, but he did glance at her with a quick smile that was seen by his mother as well as by Mrs. and Miss Brandon.

"She hasn't given up," Judith murmured.

"Who are the other candidates?" Sophia asked, wondering how much malice to expect from them.

"One is the quiet girl in pink at the next table."

"She looks as if she would rather be anywhere else," Judith said with a certain amount of sympathy.

"I expect she would. Her father's fortune was made in trade, so she is looked down upon in this company, although being a considerable heiress makes up for it. Mama would tolerate her at a pinch, but I suspect her main purpose here is to show Aaron what he'll be reduced to if he does not snap up Miss Brandon. Or the third choice, whoever she is."

Judith introduced her to a few other people, who were both amiable and curious, but the tea interlude was clearly finishing up to allow time for rest and recuperation—"And primping," Judith added *sotto voce*—before the more serious business of dinner.

As Sophia stood to return to the house, another carriage swept up the drive. In his role of host, Frostbrook abandoned Miss Brandon and the other pall-mall players to stroll over and welcome the new arrivals.

As the steps were let down, a man emerged and turned to help down an older lady and a lovely young girl. The blood froze in Sophia's veins.

Oh no. Surely, it cannot be… Almost blindly, she stumbled after Judith, then picked up her pace to keep Lady Landry's substantial figure between herself and the newcomers, while surreptitiously peeking to discover the truth.

Cousin William, clearly remembering his previous meeting with Lord Frostbrook at Cuttyngs, was looking horribly embarrassed as he introduced his mother and sister. He might even have murmured a few private words of apology or explanation about that encounter. Frostbrook might not have remembered him at all from his distant amiability.

Why did Sophia care that Allegra's beauty was fresh and lively and heartbreaking?

Lady Frostbrook made her stately way toward the carriage, and Sophia slipped unseen into the house.

"What is the matter with you?" Judith whispered.

"These are my cousins," Sophia said, "and they know perfectly well I am not engaged to Lord Frostbrook."

Judith turned startled eyes to her, then frowned. "How can they know? Have we not agreed it is a very recent engagement? Although you have known each other for some six months."

"I did meet him six months ago, but they don't know that. William has met his lordship before, at Cuttyngs…" Sophia trailed off, thinking that perhaps Frostbrook's manner then, dismissing the presumptuous cousin, might, in fact, support her story.

"It will work out," Judith said. "Although there might be a slight complication. I suspect the pretty young lady is my mother's third candidate for Frostbrook's hand."

WITH, ONCE MORE, the borrowed aid of Judith's dresser, Sophia was ready for dinner too early. She wore the second of the evening gowns donated by Frostbrook, an exquisitely cut dusky-pink muslin trimmed with delicate white lace, with matching lace threaded through her hair. But she barely noticed how she looked, so eager was she to talk with her fellow conspirators about the unexpected arrival of her cousins.

Accordingly, snatching up her reticule—another confection of pink and lace—she hurried along the passage to the Landrys' room.

Just as she was about to knock, her hand froze in midair, for the countess's unmistakable voice came from within.

"…you have not sponsored this foolish match to a nobody—"

"Oh, she is not a nobody, Mama," Judith said. "She may not have enjoyed Seasons in London, but she is undoubtedly a lady, and apparently a great heiress."

Dismayed by this lie on top of all the others, Sophia fled back toward her chamber before she was caught eavesdropping. On her own side of her door, she listened for sounds of Lady Frostbrook's departure and the swishing of her stiff skirts toward the stairs. Only after she had counted to ten did Sophia again risk approaching the Landrys' room.

Sir Humphrey's voice bade her enter, and she found the

couple in a cozily domestic scene, with Judith fastening her husband's sleeve buttons.

"He forgot them," Judith said with a smile. "You look lovely, Sophia."

"Thank you," Sophia said distractedly. "Why did you tell your mother I was rich?"

"It will make your stay pleasanter if she is brought to think of the engagement as a good thing."

"But I'll never keep track of all the lies," Sophia protested. "And my cousins know perfectly well I have not two pennies to scratch with!"

"Ah," Judith said, releasing her husband's arm with a wifely pat and turning toward her. "Well, apparently they are wealthy landowners."

Sophia stared. "No, they're not."

"That's what Mama believes."

A brief knock on the door heralded the entry of Lord Frostbrook, austerely elegant in black coat and pantaloons, his cravat a tasteful riot of snowy folds held in place by one jet pin.

"Good evening," he said. "What does Mama believe?"

"That my cousins are wealthy, and now that I am," Sophia said, pacing rapidly toward him. Realizing at the last moment what she was doing, she swerved back toward the window.

Frostbrook said dismissively, "Gossip. And Mother is hardly in the position of negotiating marriage settlements. But if that is what she believes about your cousin, it certainly explains why she invited them."

"How did she even meet them?" Sophia asked, spinning around to face her companions. "They are in no position to attend the Season in London."

"Apparently," Frostbrook said, "while West was trying to drag you away from Cuttyngs, his mother and sister were scraping acquaintance in London with one of my mother's bosom friends. Miss Allegra is a most striking young woman, and I believe a few words about the unhealthy air of Town, combined with a puritanical shudder over the constant round of pleasure, caught my mother's attention."

"Why does her ladyship always choose you such young females?" Sir Humphrey asked.

"They are more likely to be awed by my august presence."

Sophia swung away to hide her fury. Lady Frostbrook clearly undervalued her son and, worse, cared nothing for his happiness. Only for a good match in the worldliest of terms.

"You are perturbed by your cousins' presence," Frostbrook observed.

"I told Mama that Sophia is wealthy," Judith said apologetically. "Sophia is afraid her cousins will deny it and accuse her of lying—to me, if to no one else."

"I shouldn't worry," Frostbrook said. "You and they are hostage to each other's lies, and I hardly imagine the subject of money will come up at the dinner table."

That was true... "Have they acknowledged me as their cousin?" Sophia asked.

"I don't believe they noticed you," Frostbrook said. "I did not choose to put them right. Cousin William was so terrified in case I denounced him for his behavior at Cuttyngs that he almost gibbered while his mother said all that was proper. I shall have to go down now to play the genial host, and I think we may safely assume that you will be placed nowhere near me at dinner. But for the rest of the evening, are you prepared to play your part?"

"There is no point in my being here otherwise."

Only as his eyes hardened did she realize how he had construed her careless words. And, stunningly, they hurt him.

"I'll take that as yes," he drawled, with an ironic bow before strolling out of the room.

RATHER TO HER surprise, Sophia found herself much sought-after that evening. The guests gathered in the main gallery before dinner and were offered glasses of sherry and lemonade. Sophia, basking in the earl's smile and his mother's chilly greeting, chose the sherry, to strengthen her against the isolation and dislike she was bound to endure.

In fact, she was almost immediately surrounded by gentlemen, one of whom she had met at tea. The other two begged Judith for an introduction, and they all set about entertaining her.

Oddly enough, she *was* entertained, despite her distractions. They were witty and interesting and, rather than showing off, seemed eager to know her. It came to her at last that whether he knew it or not, these men regarded themselves as Frostbrook's friends. One confirmed it, just before they went in to dinner, by saying, "What a lucky fellow Frost is! Wish you very happy, ma'am."

Then, of course, she felt all the discomfort of her fraud, mixed up with her warmth that Frostbrook's friends were looking out for him. Frostbrook himself remained some distance from her, still greeting the latecomers to the gathering, though she noticed Miss Brandon was close enough to him to exchange the occasional word.

And then Allegra made her entrance. Her raven-black hair contrasting delightfully with the pure white of her gown, she looked lovely. She was also on her well-dressed brother's arm, while their mother walked behind—hardly strict etiquette, but it allowed Allegra to make quite the impression. A faint hush spread across the gallery as everyone turned to look. Allegra's dazzling smile was divided nicely between Lady Frostbrook and the earl.

Miss Brandon looked furious.

But Allegra's triumph was brief. There was no time for her to be surrounded by admirers, for everyone was already lining up for dinner as arranged by Lady Frostbrook. And the countess herself, a stickler for appearances, would have judged the Wests' arrival as discourteously late.

Another gentleman joined the group around Sophia and

bowed. He was the curate, she recalled. "I believe it is my good fortune to take you into dinner, Miss Wallace."

The others bowed to her, parting with amusingly expressed regret to take their own decreed partners into the dining room. Through the throng between, Sophia discovered all three of her cousins goggling at her in disbelief. Whether at her mere presence or at the size of her "court" was unclear.

She inclined her head graciously before turning with a smile to the awkward young curate.

Everyone knew their order of precedence, and Sophia and the curate were inevitably at the end of the line. Miss Brandon, a viscount's daughter, was on Frostbrook's arm at the front, and Allegra, with a middle-aged gentleman, somewhere in the middle. Judith was on the arm of one of Frostbrook's friends, while Sir Humphrey escorted the unhappy merchant's daughter, who actually smiled at him.

All became much clearer as they took their places at the table. Frostbrook had Miss Brandon and the merchant's daughter on either side of him. Allegra was close enough on the other side of the table to allow their eyes to meet should Frostbrook glance her way. Instead, when everyone was seated, he glanced once at Sophia and smiled.

It was too easy to smile back, especially when she had a role to play. But immediately after, without so much as a glance at any of her "rivals in love," she turned to the curate.

He was a shy man and a little awkward in company, so she did her best to make him feel comfortable and draw him out. He turned out to be a gentle man of dry wit and an already large family he clearly loved to distraction. Sophia liked him.

Every one of the plentiful courses was delicious. For Sophia, dividing her conversation between the curate and the gentleman on her other side—the youngest son of a local landowner—the time passed much more quickly and pleasantly than she could have hoped. Only then, of course, Lady Frostbrook led the ladies from the dining room to the drawing room, and Sophia knew the female claws would be out. Judith could not shelter her all the time.

And, in fact, Cousin Amelia seemed to have been waiting for her, for before they even entered the drawing room, Sophia found her arm seized in a grip of iron.

"Cousin," Amelia said fondly. "What a pleasant surprise to find you here." Her fingers dug into Sophia's flesh, hard enough to bruise as she all but hissed between smiling teeth, "What in God's name brings you here? Do you repay our kindness to you by trying to spoil Allegra's chances?"

Sophia smiled back with much more genuine amusement. "You mean with his lordship? Oh, Aunt, that ship has sailed. Do you not know Lord Frostbrook is engaged to me?"

The expression on Amelia's face was ludicrous and fiercely satisfying. Her grip fell away as though her fingers were suddenly too numb to grip. Sophia continued to the drawing room, though quite suddenly she noticed Allegra on her other side. Her face was so pale as to be white, apart from two spots of angry color.

"You lie, merely to upset us," she said in a lashing whisper. "When could you *possibly* have met the Earl of Frostbrook?"

Sophia smiled directly in her eyes. "Why, you brought it about, Allegra. I met him when I trudged through all that mud to the Fairly Park ball, on the night you demanded the other fan. I shall always be grateful to you for that."

She could never have imagined a sweeter revenge for the years of exhausting work, the humiliation and sheer loneliness they had inflicted upon her. But as she sailed into the drawing room ahead of them, only to be met by Judith and the merchant's daughter, who drew her into a huddle on the sofa, she found she was shaking. The encounter with her cousins might have been satisfying on one level. On another, she knew they would make her pay.

CHAPTER TEN

MOST OF THE ladies seemed unsure how to treat Sophia. Some must have heard Frostbrook announce their engagement, and the news would have flown around the rest—or at least those who had not arrived late like the Wests. But no one mentioned it to her, and to Sophia's sensitive ears, their conversation seemed a little awkward. She suspected Lady Frostbrook was spreading counter-rumors that the engagement would not last. She was correct, of course, but that hardly suited her son's purpose.

It was something of a relief when the gentlemen joined them in the drawing room. Frostbrook at once began to make his way toward Sophia, and Judith kindly vacated the place beside her in order to chat with old friends.

There were too many people around Frostbrook and Sophia for more than amiable generalities, but such marked attention must have been noticed.

Inevitably, the young, unmarried ladies were invited to entertain the party with their musical accomplishments. Frostbrook urged the merchant's daughter forward, much to the pride of her mama and the triumph of Lady Frostbrook.

"She is very good," Frostbrook murmured to Sophia when he caught her eye. "Are you?"

"No."

The girl sang a couple of charming songs and sat down to much appreciation, after which Allegra was nominated by Cousin Amelia. Frostbrook raised one quizzical eyebrow at Sophia, who bowed her head rather than reply that her cousin played like an angel and sang like a banshee. Perhaps someone had finally convinced her of this, for she played a very pretty piece on the pianoforte without singing a note, and then rose, saying kindly that she would like to give other ladies a chance.

"What about you, Cousin Sophia?" Amelia said maliciously. "Why don't you play for us?"

"Because I have a care for the company's ears," Sophia said mildly.

It won her a burst of laughter, which clearly annoyed all her cousins, but amused Lord Frostbrook. His mother, no doubt irritated by Amelia's interference, immediately asked Miss Brandon to play.

After a polite show of modest reluctance, Miss Brandon rose and glided toward the pianoforte, where she turned and bestowed a sweet smile upon Frostbrook.

"Perhaps you would turn my music for me, my lord? I have noticed you never lose the place."

Frostbrook rose. "Alas, I must regretfully decline. I have just promised Miss Wallace a breath of air on the terrace—from where we will still have the pleasure of hearing your music. Perhaps, Hornchurch…?"

A young man bounced to his feet with alacrity, and Frostbrook held out his hand to Sophia. She took it and rose, flushing to feel so many eyes upon her, whether openly or covertly. Placing her hand on his sleeve, Frostbrook strolled toward the French window that led onto the terrace.

Only as the breeze brushed her skin did she realize how oppressive the atmosphere of the drawing room had grown. Even out here, everything felt too close, almost expectant, as though a storm, real or metaphorical, was approaching.

Frostbrook did not close the door behind them, nor even

move out of the view of his guests until Miss Brandon began to play.

"She is very good, also," he allowed, drawing Sophia further along the terrace. "Naturally, she possesses all the ladylike accomplishments."

"But you don't love her," Sophia blurted.

"No," he said, halting and gazing down at her with unexpected intensity. "I don't love her. And it is time to give the company proof of our engagement. Respectful but undoubted proof."

Her heart jumped, for she knew what he meant even before his head began to bend toward her. His fingertips touched her cheek in a soft, tender caress, and suddenly she could not breathe. She remembered that distant kiss at Fairly Park, but mostly she longed for whatever was happening now, and for whatever reason. And she had agreed to co-operate.

She lifted her face to his, even parted her lips slightly, and closed her eyes. At the first brush of his lips, butterflies skittered across her stomach, and his mouth covered hers, holding her captive.

Every inch of her was aware of his tall, hard body so close to hers. She longed to press nearer, to be folded in his arms. But even as the kiss deepened, and he explored with sweet, unhurried delight, he touched only her lips and her cheek. She could do no less, cupping the slightly roughened skin of his face, yielding and blindly responding.

Wonder. She was lost in wonder, all but paralyzed as helpless pleasure sank into warm, heavy desire.

She had no idea how long it went on before a footstep scuffed the ground, and a male voice paused mid-word with a breath of laughter. And then a female squeak of shock.

Sophia's eyes flew open. Frostbrook's lips stretched, smiling on hers. And at last, she recalled their purpose here. To convince the company of the truth of their engagement. She had agreed to it, silently, but only now realized what he had done.

He had devastated her, stripped bare her emotions with one kiss. Especially not while he had retained his habitual coolness throughout. The kiss was skilled, practiced, calculatedly seductive, and yet he had kept it within the bounds of the "respectability" he had promised. No close embrace, no improper hands clutching her body. Preserving her reputation for when she jilted him.

"I will never forgive you for that," she whispered against his lips.

Something changed in his eyes, his never-readable eyes. How could she have convinced herself that she had begun to know him?

"For a kiss?" he breathed. "Or for ending it? We could risk another…"

They were alone on the terrace again. Someone else had begun to play the pianoforte, less expertly than Miss Brandon.

Sophia dropped her hand from his face as though she had forgotten about it and turned away from him to cool her burning cheeks. "Don't trouble," she said. "I believe we have done enough for one evening."

⇻⟫⟩⟨⟪⇺

FROSTBROOK REGARDED THE rigid back of his betrothed's head with wariness. Kissing her soft, silken mouth, so warm and so generous, had just become his favorite pastime. Ever. Her delicious response had all but unmanned him. But her entire being seemed to have changed in a heartbeat.

What would she never forgive him? Being discovered in the kiss? She must have understood that that was the whole point. Well, the whole point of kissing her here, where they were so likely to be disturbed, as they had been.

He had taken her by surprise. The sweet upsurge of passion from so chaste an embrace had taken them *both* by surprise.

He moved in front of her and leaned against the balustrade. Her body was stiff, her face so carefully expressionless that he knew she was hiding. He took her hand, and suspected she had to force herself not to snatch it back.

But he had to look after her. Tugging her with him, he moved casually back into the view of the drawing room window, where everyone could see him, but not Sophia, who stood with her back to the room, several inches to his right. There was little he could say with the window ajar, for he didn't know who would overhear. Still, with a faint smile on his lips, any watcher would imagine he was listening to her. In reality, he was feeling his way toward an understanding.

She was indeed hiding from him. Why would she do that unless she was hurt? Hurt by the kiss, by being seen and becoming the butt of gossip?

No. By *feeling* as she did when she imagined he remained cool and aloof, that this was all part of his plan.

A wave of hope, almost triumph, swept over him, because surely this meant she cared? His heart began to beat faster, but what he owed her now was comfort, not declarations that would seem only too false and for the benefit of others to hear. She gazed out at the garden, not at him, but her face was cooling in the breeze. The greatest gift he could provide her at the moment was his absence.

He glanced at the window and met Hornchurch's eyes on the other side. He gestured invitingly, and a couple of others strolled out on to the terrace while the very amateur music drifted out. They exchanged a few low-voiced remarks about the beauty of the moonlight. When Humph stepped out, too, Frostbrook wandered back inside, leaving his brother-in-law to look after her and protect her as it seemed he could not.

IN THE DISTANT days of his childhood, Frostbrook could never remember his mother coming to his bedchamber to wish him good night, even in the sharpest loneliness after his brother's death. But she came now, closing the door behind her.

"Mother," he said, and rang for his valet.

She looked annoyed, though she hurried straight into abrupt speech. "Who is she, this Wallace girl?"

"My future countess, who will require a little more respect from my family."

"Does she deserve it?"

"She is a gentleman's daughter, if that is what you mean, and the object of my unexpected affections."

"Then do I deserve that you humiliate me in such a way? To surprise me with this news in front of all my guests, when you knew, when *everyone* knew, I had invited Miss Brandon and the others—"

"For me to choose from, as though I were purchasing a new necktie? That, Mother, humiliates me and each of those poor girls you brought here to be looked over. They are not cattle, and neither am I."

She stared at him. "I am trying to help—"

"No, you are trying to control. While I have found my wife without your interference."

"Help," she corrected him with a surprising hint of pleading. "With my *help*, Frostbrook."

He smiled coldly. "Without it, Mother. You should go to bed. You will need all your strength for the ball tomorrow night."

For an instant, two spots of anger sprang up in her face, then her gaze fell. It was almost...defeat.

He pressed it home. "You will be kind to Miss Wallace, if you please. And welcoming."

"Since she is your choice, of course. As long as she will not...as long as she will be the countess the earldom deserves." She raised her gaze to his once more. There might have been capitulation there, or the beginnings of it. "Judith says she is an heiress. Which I suppose makes sense, since she is related to the Wests."

It crossed his mind to tell her that the Wests were so far from wealthy that they had turned their cousin into a housemaid. But something else had to be said that he needed her to understand.

"It does not matter to me if she is a pauper. She is the only wife I will ever choose." The glorious freedom, the sheer relief of truth, hit him like a blaze of sunshine in the midst of a storm, and, much to his mother's clear consternation, he laughed with pure joy.

At the same time, echoing his outburst of emotion, thunder cracked in the distance.

His mother, muttering about insanity and perverse behavior, stalked out of the room, leaving him mercifully alone. Still smiling, he went to the window, drew back the curtains, and opened the shutters. He liked storms.

The arrival of Bridges, his valet, with hot water for washing, disturbed him only briefly.

"Thank you, Bridges—that will be all tonight."

"Very good, my lord."

Bridges was always the perfect gentleman's gentleman. It was hard to remember, sometimes, that he had a large family of much less respectable, but occasionally very useful, professions. Frostbrook had employed them occasionally himself.

He opened the window to the elements, and a gust of wind took him by surprise. It was not raining yet, but a storm was definitely on the way. He could hear thunder rumbling about in the distance, see odd flashes of light in the sky.

The weather suited his mood—changeable, wild, elemental. Storms always affected them like this. As though the lightning woke something deep inside him and the thunder spoke to him, feeding the untamed feelings he normally kept so rigidly under control. It was a little like the release of physical pleasure, and God knew everything in him ached for that.

Watching was not enough. He closed the window, tugged off

his cravat, and threw it aside as he strode from the room.

He left by a side door that led onto a set of steps beside the kitchen garden. To the other side was the riot of flowers seen from the front of the house. And in front of him, lit by a sudden fork of lightning, was a cloaked female figure with bright silver-blonde hair.

His heart bumped, acknowledging the rightness of her being here, and yet he wondered what drew her, how the storm affected her. He moved silently up the steps but went no nearer, respecting her solitude, if that was what she wished.

The thunder crashed, close enough now to startle, and she jumped, stepping back, so that he saw her profile and realized she was smiling. He must have made some involuntary movement, or perhaps she sensed his presence, for she turned suddenly, just as twin forks of light split the sky.

She did not run. Instead she came nearer, and he went to meet her. He heard her gasp as the thunder crashed, catching at his nerves and vibrating deep inside him where the lust lay growling and aware. They stood side by side in silence, not touching, but at the next flash of lightning, her fingers threaded through his and clung, as though in anticipation, as though she needed to feel him.

The rain began as the thunder pealed. He wanted Sophia in his arms, writhing naked beneath him, more than he had ever wanted anything in his life before. There was a bizarre kind of sweetness in sharing this moment and yet touching no more than her hand. And he knew if he kissed her now, he would not stop.

And neither would she.

He could take her beneath the steps in a storm of bliss that would outpace anything the sky could offer.

Her cheek touched his shoulder. She did not seem to notice the rain. He made the mistake of looking at her, just as the lightning flashed, and every nerve crackled with an entirely different electricity. He bent his head, slowly, every inch predatory and aroused. And she made no move to draw back.

His mouth hovered over parted, trembling lips. He inhaled her fresh, distinctive scent, and something more exotic released by the storm, or perhaps her own desire.

God, he wanted her.

The rain suddenly gushed down, battering them, and he swept her down the steps into the shelter beneath.

Oh yes, he wanted her. But not this once. Forever.

With a groan, he pushed open the door, pulling her inside with him. His hands were clumsy as he locked and bolted the door. And then he strode away from her while his body shrieked in protest.

BY MORNING, SOPHIA had herself better in hand. The kiss haunted her, in a manner that was more delighted than outraged, and she was uneasy that she might have given away far too much of her feelings. But she had come to the conclusion that a man as experienced and confident as Frostbrook could not understand her feelings in any case.

She wasn't perfectly sure she understood them herself. Though she did acknowledge that Giles had never affected her like this. He was a friend she had known forever whom she had made into a knight in shining armor that would one day rescue her from her drudgery. It might have hurt that she was not the damsel he chose to rescue, but she could recognize that neither in reality nor in her wildest dreams had he ever excited her as Frostbrook did. As Frostbrook always had.

As for those strange, silent moments in the storm… She didn't even know why she had taken his hand, for she had planned to treat him with cool courtesy when next they met alone. But she had forgotten in her delight in the storm. Something inexplicable had passed between them, something as raw and elemental as the thunder crashing round their ears. Her body had seemed to hum with desires she could not understand, and when he bent over her so possessively, his mouth almost touching hers, she had been so sure he would kiss her. She had melted down to her very bones, yearned…

And then it—whatever *it* had been—was over. He had left her alone with the solitary candle on the nearby table, vanishing into the darkness, still without saying a word.

She had felt bewildered, disturbed, and yet…excited. Inexplicably happy. Life might seem to be spiraling out of her control, but at least it was fun. Circumstances had given her this time with Frostbrook to explore a different kind of friendship. She knew in her heart there would be pain, whether their friendship endured or not, but she could not be sorry for these days.

Accordingly, she joined the party that rode out the following morning to admire the gentle acres of Wellis Manor. Last night's storm had vanished as suddenly as it had arrived, leaving the ground somewhat soft and muddy but fresh and sweet-smelling. The morning sun was pleasantly warm, with a cooling breeze.

Sophia's cousins were not among the riders, although Miss Brandon was. Frostbrook, however, while remaining the perfect host, rode mostly beside Sophia, frequently pointing out landmarks to her, or the boundaries of the property.

"I am most admiring of the estate of which I shall be mistress," she assured him quietly, smiling for the benefit of observers. They rode a little ahead of the others, far enough to converse in private if they kept their voices low.

"I am glad you like it. There are charms to all my seats, although Brookwood in Lincolnshire is the largest. I think you will like it, too."

She blinked. "My lord, your make-believe is growing out of hand. I will never see Brookwood."

He turned his head to meet her gaze, one eyebrow raised. "You mean you would not come if I invited you?"

"With your mother as hostess?" she asked humorously. "Could either she or I survive the ordeal?"

"Oh, I think she is coming round," Frostbrook said. "She is almost contrite."

Sophia took leave to doubt it, but she only smiled and urged her horse onward. Apart from one occasion with Rosamund at Cuttyngs, it was years since she had ridden, and the pleasure was immense. Or perhaps the joy was simply in his company.

"Besides," he added, keeping pace with her some distance ahead of the others, though they were still in sight, "if we were married, you would not require my mother's presence."

Though something hurt deep in her chest, she forced herself to look around exaggeratedly. "My lord, no one can hear. You need not pretend to quite that degree."

"Why not? Does it offend you?"

"It would certainly offend your mother."

"I do not wish to talk about her."

"Just about the estates that would be mine if only we ever had any intention of marrying? Be careful, or I might forget to jilt you!"

To her surprise, he looked neither panicked nor amused, although a warm smile seemed to grow in his steady eyes. "Why don't you?"

"Why don't I what?" she asked, confused.

"Forget to jilt me. Marriage could be fun."

No, it wouldn't. It would be unbearable torture... "Not for you, it wouldn't," she managed.

"What makes you think so?"

"The very fact of this charade," she retorted. "You are going to great lengths to avoid marriage to one of the current or future well-born, beautiful, and accomplished ladies your mother lays before you. What on earth would you do if you found yourself about to be shackled to *me?*"

"Enjoy."

Don't make fun of me, please don't... "Unlikely for either of us," she retorted. "Although you would be well served if I took you up on your nonsense and insisted on marrying you."

"Why don't you?"

She stared at him. "Because we are pretending."

"Are you sure?"

Her heart beat too quickly, too loudly, and it hurt in ways she could never have imagined. She had almost dredged up a clever retort, but it stuck in her throat.

"It is possible you might come to love me a little?" he asked softly.

"Might you love me, too?" she snapped, determined to jolt him out of this bizarre, hurtful mood.

But he smiled, and nothing about him seemed hard or cold. "I might. I very much like kissing you, and since we are being frank, I want you very much."

Heat flamed through her body and into her face. Somehow, she managed to hold his gaze, to force mockery into her face, although she couldn't hide the bitterness in her voice. "So much that you would marry me? Oh come, my lord, what rot!"

A barely seen flick of his heel sprang his horse into sudden motion, galloping off the track into the woods. But she had no time to appreciate the respite, for it seemed he knew all his horses very well. Her mare leapt into action without any instruction from her at all. In fact, when Sophia pulled on the reins, she was ignored. The mare tossed her head and bolted after Frostbrook's horse.

It lasted barely a moment, for Frostbrook was in complete control of his mount. He pulled it to a halt only yards into the trees, then flung out his hand and seized the mare's bridle. She snorted but stopped in her tracks, clearly with no idea of going anywhere without her friend the stallion, and Frostbrook knew it.

He released the bridle and wheeled around to face Sophia, coming so close in that his knee bumped against hers. Before she could even guess his intent, he said, "Rot? Let us see, shall we?" And, leaning across from the saddle, he bent and swept one arm around her shoulders. Then he dragged her against him and kissed her, not with the careful, seductive tenderness of last night, but with a much wilder, harder passion that left her gasping.

This was what she had wanted, holding his hand in the storm…

With no hesitation, everything in her leapt to meet him. She didn't just like his embrace, she adored it and she wanted—*needed*—much, much more. Her breasts were pressed to his hard chest, causing all sorts of new sensations and desires that she had no name for. And her mouth, crushed beneath his, opened wide for him.

As quickly as it had begun, it ended. The breeze whipped playfully against her skin, and he straightened in the saddle.

"You see?" he said breathlessly, while he urged his horse back toward the track. "Marriage could be wonderful."

Then why did you stop? Why are you leaving me here…? Fortunately, she did not shout the words after him, and the mare was already following, as he had known would happen. And of course, everyone else, who probably thought her mount had bolted and Frostbrook had saved her, was waiting for them in concern. She had time to compose her expression, if not her heart. Presumably the odd angle of her hat and loosened hair would be put down to the bolting horse, too.

"Are you not used to riding in the country, Miss Wallace?" Miss Brandon asked, with entirely false solicitude.

"Nor anywhere else," Sophia managed.

"How does that come about?"

"Lack of practice," Sophia replied.

The younger girl smiled. "Like the pianoforte?"

Sophia smiled patiently. "Indeed, like the pianoforte."

"Do you not enjoy these things?" Miss Brandon asked maliciously.

"Yes, I do, but I have had so many other matters to attend to," Sophia said. "Do you have no other interests yourself, Miss Brandon?"

There was a pause. "I enjoy water coloring."

Of course she did. But Sophia did not laugh at her predictability. She was too busy wondering what on earth had just happened to her among the friendly, sheltering trees.

There was no further chance to talk to Frostbrook alone until they had returned and dismounted in the stable yard. He made a point of helping her, and his hands might have lingered on her waist, although surely that was for the benefit of any watchers. But then he walked into the stable to confer with the head groom, while the others, abandoning their mounts to the various stable lads, walked back toward the house.

Sophia began to trail after them, and then, with sudden decision, whirled back again and marched into the stables after Frostbrook. He stood by the open door of the stallion's stall, having some deep discussion with the groom while he stroked the beast's withers.

He saw her at once and moved toward her. "Miss Wallace?"

"Do you have a moment, my lord?"

"For you, I have many."

"Stop it," she said intensely.

He took her arm and drew her back out into the stable yard, which was now deserted as the horses were taken inside. "Stop what? I thought we had agreed to flirt?"

"Not when there is no one to impress. I want to know what you are about. Not so much last night, but this morning. No jests or subtleties—simple honesty, if you please."

He stopped and looked down at her thoughtfully. Butterflies flitted across her stomach. "Honesty? Very well. I have changed my mind."

It should not have hurt. "You wish me to break off our engagement now?" She tried to smile. "Perhaps you have been too amorous for my sense of propriety."

"Oh, I hope not," he said, unexpectedly fervent. "But I don't believe you can have been listening earlier. I am proposing we make our engagement real."

Her mouth fell open, and she deliberately closed it again. She probably looked like a goldfish. She certainly felt as helpless.

"Why?" she asked at last.

"Because I like you. Because you don't seem to *dislike* me. Because I can give you security, and you can bring me great pleasure. I hope to be able to do the same for you." A fascinating smile, hot and predatory, flickered across his face and vanished. "They have become something of an obsession with me—you and the pleasure."

Her whole body flamed. But she was far too flummoxed to be angry, as she suspected she really should be. "But I am no one. You are an earl. You cannot marry on a whim of lust!"

Intense laughter gleamed in his eyes. "I can. But it is not a whim, and it is not entirely lust. Don't you think we might have fun together?"

"Fun?" she repeated, frowning up at him in consternation. His fingers slid down her arm and clasped her hand, light, unthreatening, and yet his touch always unbalanced her, because she liked it too much.

"Have we not agreed we are friends?" Delicately, his thumb passed across her wrist, a faint, almost absent, caress. "Marriages have been founded on a lot less, yet it seems to me it is a basic requirement. We could be married friends. If you like."

She could not think for the stunning words spinning in her mind, for the distracting whisper of his thumb across her wrist, slow and strangely sensual, spreading sweetness through her veins.

"You…you want that?" she asked cautiously. "With me?"

She still could not read his eyes, but there was a softness in them that caught at her heart.

"Yes," he said. "With you." His thumb stilled, and he raised her hand to his lips. At the last moment he turned it and kissed not the backs of her fingers, but the inside of her wrist, which was already so sensitive to his touch that she gasped at the caress of his mouth. And then he released her. "The choice is yours, Sophia. Let me know when you are ready to answer. Either way, I stand your friend."

And suddenly, tears forced their way into her throat and she all but stumbled away from him. She wanted to cry, but she also needed to laugh and shout and run.

She could do none of these things here. So she pasted a faint smile on her lips and walked in a sedate fashion back to the house, while inside, her whole world was reeling.

CHAPTER ELEVEN

LADY FROSTBROOK WAS wound so tightly with fury that she was afraid the tension would shatter her.

How dare her son defy and humiliate her, and with such a nonentity? If, indeed, the Wallace girl was as wealthy as Judith had implied, then Lady Frostbrook might have been induced to countenance the match, despite his deliberate and public thwarting of her own plans. But the hoyden showed no shame, no humility or apology. She behaved as though she had every right to be here, every right to walk on the terrace by moonlight with her son, behaving like some lightskirt! If they had not been engaged, the girl would be ruined, a fantasy Lady Frostbrook would have liked to indulge, if only she had the time.

But she rarely hid from the truth. She was aware her son was less besotted than defiant. He imagined he was teaching his mother a lesson.

Let him think it, she thought with a curl of her lip as she strolled into the garden with a party of the dowagers who had remained behind while the young people went riding. In fact, she had no intention of allowing him to marry the Wallace girl, simply because it was quite clear that she would never be able to awe Miss Wallace, let alone overawe or control her. And Lady Frostbrook would never tolerate any such daughter-in-law. Standards must be maintained. *Her* standards.

Maintaining the pleasant conversation without even trying, she guided her guests to the pretty arbor where they could sit comfortably out of the sun or wander a little about the garden.

The countess chose to sit on one of the benches. Most of the others began to stroll along the paths, but she noticed that Mrs. West seemed to hesitate between joining her or following the others.

Mrs. West, who was a cousin, apparently, to Miss Wallace. And mother to Allegra who was, at the moment, joint second in Lady Frostbrook's list of suitable daughters-in-law.

She smiled invitingly, and Mrs. West came toward her.

"Such a lovely garden," Mrs. West said, sinking onto the other side of Lady Frostbrook's bench.

"I find it soothing, and a most pleasant respite from the demands of the Season."

"I imagine you might."

Lady Frostbrook smiled again. "I had not realized just at first that you are related to Miss Sophia Wallace."

"I am afraid I no longer speak proudly of the connection," Mrs. West said ruefully. "Indeed, I feel I should apologize. No one could be sorrier than I that she has got her claws into Lord Frostbrook."

Well! Here was plain speaking with a vengeance…

"Although I am not well acquainted with your son," Mrs. West added, "I can see immediately that he deserves better."

Lady Frostbrook hid her surge of triumph and instead allowed a trace of fear into her expression. "You must know something I do not, ma'am!"

"Many things regarding Sophia, sadly. Did you know, for example, that she jilted my son for yours?"

"No… No, I did not know that."

"She wishes to be a countess, of course, with all that attaches to your noble name, but even so, I would have said nothing, were it not for the fact that his lordship appears quite…smitten. I would not for the world have him wounded by her wiles."

"Neither would I," Lady Frostbrook said grimly. "I shall not hide from you my desire to end the engagement."

"Oh, thank goodness," Mrs. West exclaimed. "I could not have acted against your ladyship's wishes, but now that I know your views, I shall do my very best to exert family influence on her. I believe that between us, we might prevail."

Lady Frostbrook was no one's fool. She knew perfectly well that Mrs. West wanted Sophia out of the way to give Allegra a chance. But one took allies where one could find them.

"What influence might you have on such a wayward person?" Lady Frostbrook asked.

"I believe my son might be able to sway her by the time we leave Wellis Manor. He and Sophia were betrothed in their cradles, you know, and she was perfectly satisfied with the match until she heard Allegra praising Lord Frostbrook. I believe he can make her come back to him."

Lady Frostbrook blinked. "He would take her back? Would you?"

"For…reasons of my own," Mrs. West said demurely.

"Of course," Lady Frostbrook said, nodding. "Her fortune."

Mrs. West looked slightly surprised, as though she had not expected Lady Frostbrook to know about the fortune. But she replied only, "As you say. Between us, we should be able to detach Sophia from *your* son and return her to the disciplined care of mine."

"That would be perfect," Lady Frostbrook said. Though she knew something a little more solid was required. "I would, of course, be eternally grateful. Your charming Allegra would be a delightful addition to our family."

Mrs. West smiled. "I believe we understand each other, my lady."

SOPHIA FOUND THAT she did not need to avoid being alone with Lord Frostbrook for the rest of the day. He appeared to be doing it for her. He sat beside her at luncheon, but included others in their conversation, and neither then nor in the afternoon did he made any attempt to entice her on walks. The timing would have been perfect, too, for many people chose to rest during the afternoon in order to be fresh to enjoy the evening's ball. Not that she had much clue how she would answer his astonishing, not to say eccentric, proposal. Still, as she made her way up to her own bedchamber to change, she could not help feeling slightly piqued that he attached no urgency to her response.

Maybe he was afraid she would refuse him.

Which, of course, she should. She had nothing to bring to such a grand marriage. Her birth was merely respectable, she was completely penniless, and she was not used to the kind of august company kept by Frostbrook. She would make a terrible hostess and an embarrassing wife. And she disapproved of his politics.

And knowing all that, he liked her. He wanted her. Or said he did.

Why?

To annoy his mother even further? No, that was surely carrying the lesson too far for his own comfort. Besides, he was hard-edged, but he was neither wantonly cruel nor as cold as he pretended. They really did have some kind of rapport that she valued. They *were* friends.

Could they really be married friends as he suggested?

When she closed her eyes, she could almost envision such a life with him. A companionship not unlike that shared by Judith and Sir Humph. Long talks and arguments, laughter… And Frostbrook's kisses. The very thought turned her insides to liquid.

The intimacies of marriage, she could only imagine, but he promised them both pleasure, and she was undeniably curious.

No, curious was too mild. She was…aroused. She longed not just for his embraces, but for his company. For an end to loneliness. If he could only love her as she, poor fool that she was, loved him.

Did he? *Could* he?

A knock on her bedchamber door had her turning from the window, her heart suddenly hammering. Even engaged to her, he should not be coming here... Although, she blushed to remember, she had gone to his chamber at the Landrys' house.

"Enter," she said, a little too loudly. The door opened, and Cousin Amelia sailed through in a rustle of skirts. "Cousin." Sophia was too surprised to greet her with anything but courtesy. "What can I do for you?"

Amelia sighed and offered a tentative smile. "Come home."

"No thank you," Sophia replied. That was the one thing she knew with certainty. She would never go back to the Wests, however difficult her life became.

"My dear, we have never talked about this." Amelia came closer, as though she would take Sophia's hand, although fortunately, she stopped short of that. "Perhaps I have been foolish, and certainly not as observant as I should have been, but it never entered my head that you were not happy with us. I did not realize you had taken on quite so much. I am no housekeeper, as you know, and I had no idea what was involved until you left us and I spoke to Millie and Cook. But we miss you, Sophia." She held up her hand as though to stop Sophia from speaking. "No, not your work, my dear, your company. Come home with us and things will be different. No work but what you choose. And I would so appreciate your help in engaging more servants."

Amelia offered a tentative, sheepish smile, "I know I have been selfish, keeping you to myself. I thought you were still mourning. I did not realize you were lonely. You shall make calls with us, join us for dinners and parties. The whole neighborhood will see how we value you."

"Your offer is generous, cousin," Sophia said when Amelia paused for breath. "But I cannot accept."

Amelia sat down on the little sofa without being asked and caught Sophia's hand to draw her down beside her. It might have been the first time Amelia had ever touched her.

"My dear," Amelia said gently. "Frostbrook will not marry you. Judging by last night, his aim is merely to seduce you, and then he will abandon you. He is merely making a somewhat childish stance against his mother's interference. He will marry someone much more suitable, and you will be ruined."

Something twisted inside Sophia, catching at her breath. But it was not belief in her cousin's words, despite some of the truth contained within them. It was distaste that she should speak of him so. And the sudden, overwhelming realization that he truly *had* gone beyond their charade. He wanted to marry her.

Amelia misunderstood her silence. She leaned forward and took both of Sophia's hands. "What would you do then?" she asked. "I have to think of Allegra. I could not take you back if you were ruined. But I do not believe he has gone quite so far yet. There is still time. Come with us tomorrow, and all will yet be well."

Sophia withdrew her hands. "Thank you for your kindness, but I shall not go with you."

Amelia regarded her with something very like genuine pity. "You really do believe he will marry you? And when you find you are wrong, what will you do then?"

"Return to the Duchess of Cuttyngham, who employs me."

"To do what?" Amelia snapped. "She is not even here. And if you imagine she will keep a fallen woman in her household—"

"I am not a fallen woman," Sophia interrupted. "I am fortunate enough to be the betrothed of the Earl of Frostbrook."

"Poppycock!" That, at last, sounded like Cousin Amelia, impatient and assertive. But if she was truly angry, she took the trouble to hide it. "Remember what I have said," she advised more softly. "Do not allow yourself to be seduced by fine words and dreams of being a countess. And remember your home is with us."

With unexpected dignity, she rose and walked across the room. Sophia blinked when the door clicked shut behind her.

"Remember your home is with us." William had said something similar to her once, when she had first met him. In her grief and bewilderment, she had gone with him and accepted her fate. And over the following years, what would she have given for the kind words Amelia had just spoken to her?

My home was never with them. Could it possibly be with the Earl of Frostbrook? He could not be separated from his wealth, his estates, his position, but she could look at the complicated man beneath. Aaron, not Frostbrook. Outwardly cold and inwardly afire with passion. Outwardly haughty and inwardly lonely and riddled with self-doubt. It was Aaron, not the earl, who had kissed her and argued and laughed with her. It was Aaron, not the earl, who had offered her marriage instead of a fake engagement.

It was Aaron she loved.

Now, at last, the tears that had threatened in the stable yard spilled out of her eyes and ran down her cheeks. But she was smiling with sheer happiness.

"DELIGHTFUL." JUDITH BEAMED at her. "You will slay more hearts than Aaron's."

Sophia regarded her reflection in the glass with some doubt. The ball gown was undeniably gorgeous, a shade of creamy ivory that seemed much warmer than the pristine white worn by debutantes, and its shape was exquisitely clean and flowing from the high waist beneath her breasts. The gold net worn over it was gossamer thin and added both elegance and sophistication. Her hair was styled simply, too, thanks to Sillers, Judith's talented dresser. A gold clasp supplied by Judith held in place a small headdress of dark red roses and ivory ribbons. The only jewelry, also borrowed from Judith, was a gold necklace containing a single ruby worn close around her throat.

"I have never worn anything so beautiful," Sophia said. Long ago, when she had lived with her parents, she had not been very interested in clothes.

"You don't need beautiful gowns, you know," Judith said. "You shine without them, too."

Sophia blinked at her, but a knock at the door distracted them both.

"It's Humph," Judith said. "Time to dance!"

But as she followed Judith from the room, Sophia saw not only Sir Humphrey, but Lord Frostbrook, who stepped promptly around his brother-in-law to say, "May I hope you will wear these?" He proffered a small, bright posy of flowers tied with an ivory ribbon.

Sophia was so surprised that she gazed up at him rather than the flowers. "Thank you," she managed. There was a whole language of flowers she had never troubled to learn, and in any case, she had not even looked properly to see what they were.

Judith was tying them to her wrist with the silk ribbon. Frostbrook was silent, and Sir Humphrey radiated amusement.

Why was Frostbrook silent? Because he regretted his foolish words this morning? Because he could not be bothered with the nonsense of flowers and the lady's favor so publicly given by wearing them? Did he regret that too?

His gaze, which had been on her wrist, on her gown, rose slowly to her face. And for once, she read the uncertainty, the vulnerability in his eyes, reflected surely in hers. She smiled with such relief, such happiness, that Frostbrook's breath caught and Sir Humphrey stepped smartly out of the way.

Judith released her hand, and Frostbrook advanced, offering his arm. He still had not spoken, but he had himself in hand once more. His eyes were warm, and the faint smile lurking on his thin yet sensual lips was confident, almost predatory.

"Should you not be in the ballroom welcoming your guests?" she asked, laying her hand on his sleeve and hoping it did not tremble.

"That is where we are going. I wish I could ask the first dance of you, but sadly, tradition dictates I dance first with Lady Peabury."

"Don't worry, Aaron," his sister teased. "Sophia will not be short of partners."

"I know. I'm holding out for the first waltz. If Miss Wallace will condescend?"

"I believe she might," Sophia said with mock grandness.

"Will," Frostbrook insisted.

"Will," Sophia agreed, blushing. "Though you must remember I have not danced in years, and never the waltz except in practice for Allegra—and then I danced the male part."

"You will try to lead," Frostbrook said.

"I will try not to," she replied. "But I may well stand on your toes."

The four of them were laughing together as they entered the ballroom, which clearly irritated Lady Frostbrook, who was waiting impatiently for her son with a few of her houseguests already present.

"Mother. Dignity personified, as usual," Frostbrook greeted her.

Sophia released his arm, and he bowed to her with apparent gravity, although his eyes gleamed for an instant before he turned to stand beside his mother and greet their guests. Every inch of him was suavely, aristocratically handsome, from his fashionably brushed hair to his black silk knee breeches. He took her breath away, not least because she understood just a little of what lay beneath.

Although the ballroom was not huge, it was just the right size for the company, which Lady Frostbrook had clearly judged to a nicety. Gently born neighbors joined her houseguests for the event. Potted plants and fresh flowers lined the walls and marked the French doors onto a well-lit terrace beyond. Three chandeliers hung from the ballroom ceiling, spilling a warm glow and catching the glint of jewels.

Lord Frostbrook opened the ball with the stately Lady Peabury. His mother stepped a dignified measure with Lord Peabury.

"Miss Wallace, may I have the pleasure?" Lord Holden, one of Frostbrook's pall-mall-playing friends, was bowing before Sophia, and she was glad if nervous to accept. But it seemed she had not forgotten the figures of the country dance, and she soon began to enjoy it.

Afterward, Lord Holden swept her off for a glass of champagne, which was where Frostbrook found her in time for the next dance.

"Drat you, Frost," said Kilburn, another of the group around her. He sounded amiably disgruntled. "I was about to ask Miss Wallace to waltz."

"Betrothed's privilege," Frostbrook replied, and bowed to Sophia, holding out his hand.

As she laid her fingers on his, the moment seemed oddly symbolic. Perhaps he felt it, too, for a smile tugged at his lips as he led her on to the floor. She wondered a little wildly what they would talk about, what she should say, and then, after a moment, when the music began, she realized neither of them needed to say anything. Just like last night in the storm.

This was enough—just the beguiling music, the pleasure of his arm at her back, his hand clasping hers, the movement of the dance. His presence was everything, his loose embrace a delight. For several minutes, they waltzed in silence, and she didn't step on his toes once. Nor was she aware of the other couples dancing around them and past them.

Then, quite naturally, she said, "You really did mean what you said this morning, didn't you?"

"Of course. Is that why you ran away? Because you thought I didn't mean it?"

She shook her head. "I didn't run. I walked smartly." She met his gaze again with a rueful, suddenly shy smile. "Truthfully…I was confused, astonished, frightened. And happy."

He pounced. "Happy?" An answering smile touched his eyes.

"That is good. I want to make you happy. Very happy."

"Aaron?" she said a little breathlessly.

"Yes?"

"Will marriage to me make *you* happy?"

The glow in his eyes flared—a trick of the candlelight, perhaps. "Just hearing my name on your lips makes me happy. How can you even ask?"

"Because I don't believe you are a happy man."

His breath hitched. A hint of color seeped into his face. He was not used to such perception or to such admissions. His heavy eyelids sweeping down showed his instinct to hide. Yet a moment later, his gaze was wide and clear meeting hers. "At this moment, I am happy. With you, I have learned what it means, to hope for all it could be. We are taking a chance, a step into the unknown. But I want that chance. I want to take that step. With you."

Her heart melted. "And I with you," she whispered.

He glanced around him quickly and cleared his throat. "Don't look at me like that," he warned, "or I will drag you away and ravish you."

"What exactly does that entail?" she asked, not really to tease, but because she genuinely wanted to know.

A breath of laughter fanned her cheek. "Exactly? You will have to wait for that. But I can give you a hint, a small taste, if you allow me the supper dance. We can slip off during the buffet charge without anyone noticing."

"Two waltzes, my lord? Your mother will disown you."

"Three, for a I want the last waltz, too. It will be quite proper, since we are engaged."

"So we are," she marveled. "So we are…"

CHAPTER TWELVE

WHEN COUSIN WILLIAM asked Sophia to dance, it took her by surprise. She had actually stepped out of his way to allow him easier access to the other young lady in the group. But he moved after Sophia and bowed.

"Sophia. Would you grant me this dance? If you are not already spoken for."

His unexpected humility made her blink. But then, to her own astonishment, she had danced every dance, and had a choice of partners for most. She was, she supposed, what Allegra would have called a success. Which rather amused her.

But William had asked first, in this case, and it would have been impolite to refuse. "Thank you," she murmured, adding humorously, "though you are wasting a waltz on me."

"Let us waste it on each other," he said lightly.

He did not waltz with Frostbrook's easy grace or guide her with quite such confidence. In fact, he was a little stiff, even tense. But then, their last few meetings had been somewhat fraught, and now she was engaged to the nobleman he wanted for his sister. His expression betrayed no resentment or anger, however, although he clearly had something he wished to say. She hoped it was not to be a repeat of the offers his mother had made earlier. Either way, she chose not to help him, but waited for him to speak first.

"I think we have misunderstood each other," be said at last. "It is my fault, and I would like to put the matter to rights so that we might move forward."

"What did you misunderstand?" she asked. "My endurance? My tolerance?"

"The load we placed on your shoulders," he said quietly. "Mama has explained to me all that you did in the house, and I confess I had no idea. I never realized a quarter of the work that goes into a running a gentleman's home."

"Neither did your mother, which is odd, since she must have run one for years."

"With a housekeeper," William said quickly. "And rather more staff. The point is, I am as sorry as she is to have burdened you so and paid so little attention to your needs."

She detected no guile in his eyes, only seriousness. "Thank you," she said. "Your apology means a great deal to me. For my part, I was grateful for the roof over my head at a time when I really did not know what I was doing."

"The truth is, we always wanted you to feel part of the family, and you seemed to wish to be useful. I… We all relaxed too much into that as the months went on. For it was not long before I realized what I wished of you. And for that, it seemed only right that you learn to run the household."

She felt a frown of puzzlement begin to form on her brow and quickly smoothed it again. "What did you wish of me?"

He smiled, a little ruefully. "Marriage."

Her jaw dropped.

"I know," he said. "I gave you no hint of it. Part of me felt I would be taking advantage of one who was dependent on me."

You were. Somehow, she bit back the words, trying to make sense of this. Was it even possible? Why in the world would he lie?

"But the time has come to speak, Sophia, before you make an irrevocable mistake."

"I am over twenty-one, William. My mistakes are my own."

"Not if they hurt you and me. My family. Sophia, whatever your years, you are as innocent as a babe in arms. What could you possibly know of a man like Lord Frostbrook?"

"Enough," she said shortly, but he paid no attention.

"His type is not uncommon among the wealthy and privileged of the world. They feel entitled to anything and everyone they want, however passing the whim. It does not become me to speak ill of my host, but, my dear, the world knows he has abandoned a string of women from all walks of life, including well-born ladies much wealthier and more worldly wise than you are. I cannot bear him to abandon you."

"Then let us hope you are spared."

"Sophia, please," he begged. "Just think of what I have said. How likely is that the Earl of Frostbrook—handsome, influential, wealthy—would marry a nobody? An eccentric nobody who has bolted from her own family and taken employment with someone who has deserted her! No, don't speak now," he added as she opened her mouth to do just that, and in no uncertain terms. "Only think about it and consider. And remember that we all want you to come home. Then you and I can be married and comfortable."

Leaving the way clear for Allegra to marry Frostbrook, she thought cynically. However, she did not wish to begin a quarrel on the dance floor, so she swallowed the words and said nothing at all until the dance ended.

"May I take you to sit with Mama for a little?" he suggested, offering his arm. "I know she would love to talk to you."

"Thank you, no. Lady Landry is my chaperone for the party."

After the slightest hesitation, he offered his arm, and they moved together toward where Lady Landry sat amongst a small group of young matrons, most of them local gentry.

"How do you even come to know these people?" he asked a shade too abruptly.

"The Frostbrooks? Through the duchess."

"Another inexplicable connection. You must have been very

desperate, sneaking employment behind our backs." He could not quite keep the resentment out of his voice. She didn't tell him it was the duchess who had come to her with a very far-fetched tale that happened to be true. He frowned. "And when we met at the Coach and Horses earlier in the month, you claimed to be engaged to that rude officer. How does he feel about this new engagement?"

"He does not yet know of it," Sophia admitted. "But as I told you before, it was our parents who betrothed us. Giles was merely defending me. He has no desire to marry me." *Nor I him, thank God.*

They were almost at Lady Landry's side by then, so William contented himself by merely squeezing her hand, bowing, and leaving her.

Judith caught her eye, one eyebrow raised in silent interrogation as she flicked the briefest glance after William's retreating back. Sophia nodded reassuringly. She was not quite sure what her cousin was up to. She could never have considered marrying him, even before meeting Frostbrook, but she was more than happy to put all quarrels aside, if that was what her cousins really wanted.

SHE TOLD FROSTBROOK about the conversation after the supper waltz, when they did indeed slip through the crowd heading for the supper room and escape onto the terrace. From there, a set of steps led gracefully down to the formal garden, which was not lit.

Most of Sophia was remembering the earl's promise to give her a taste of ravishment, and the blurting of her cousin's words was a rather feeble attempt to distract herself.

"I am a modest man," he murmured at the foot of the steps, taking her hand in his, "but even so... What the devil makes him imagine his suit would be preferable to mine?"

"Your reputation, obviously, and the fact that you mean only to seduce and abandon me. But I suspect he was merely trying to make me realize how serious he was," Sophia mused. "He can't *actually* want to marry me, not judging from the way he treated me *and* spoke to me when I lived with them."

"Shall I thrash him for you?" The offer was casual, with just a hint of steel, and it made Sophia smile.

She squeezed his fingers and laid her cheek against his shoulder for an instant. "No, thank you, though I am more grateful than you can know for the offer."

He paused, turning her to face him and peering down into her face. The glow from the terrace lanterns did not reach them here, and in the pale moonlight, his expression was unclear.

"No one has ever stood up for you, have they? You have had no one to protect or defend you, or even show you any kindness."

She flushed in the darkness. "Not since my parents died, but you may have noticed I am quite capable of defending myself."

His teeth flashed white in the darkness, then he said, "Let me, Sophia. Let me protect and defend you."

She tried to laugh as his head bent slowly to hers. "But who will protect me from you?"

His lips smiled as they closed on hers, and she gave herself up to his kiss. His arms came around her, drawing her against him. His fingers held her nape, tenderly caressing while his mouth devasted her so sweetly. He tasted of wine and Aaron, sin and sunshine. The kiss deepened, or perhaps became another, spreading delicious weakness through her limbs. His hand stroked slowly down her back, over her hip and upward to the curve of her waist and her breast. Arousal blossomed into something much more breathless. Desire. Lust. And yet his touch was light, even where she felt the growing hardness against her abdomen.

"Are you ravishing me now?" she whispered into his mouth.

"No. But I'm hoping you'll like it enough to look forward to the future ravishing. Will you marry me, Sophia? In truth."

She could only kiss him for that, so long and passionately that her answer got lost, until he drew back to remind her.

"Well?"

"You know I will," she said shakily.

He smiled and kissed her lips and her fingers.

She touched his cheek. "Aaron? Will you be a faithful husband?"

"Yes. You are thinking of my reputation. Please don't." He drew her hand through his arm, keeping hold of it as they walked along a path she could barely see.

"Your reputation is part of who you are," she pointed out.

"Part of who I *was*. I would never so slight my wife. I would never want to."

"I might bore you," she pointed out.

"I might bore you."

She peered up at him, conscious of a deeper meaning to his words. "You believe in my fidelity, and I should believe in yours?"

"Exactly."

"I should not even have brought the subject up. It is a wife's duty not to notice when her husband strays."

"Strays? I am not a cat," he said tartly. "Do you not trust me?"

"I do," she whispered. "That is what frightens me."

His fingers tightened on hers. "Sweetheart, I will never let you down."

"I know," she said with new wonder. "I know."

⸙

THEY DANCED THE post-supper dance together, too, and then Frostbrook went off to perform hosting duties among the other guests, leaving Sophia with a glass of lemonade beside Judith.

She was surprised when, only a minute later, Allegra sat down beside her.

Allegra's gown was beautiful and new and must have cost a fortune. Sophia doubted Amelia would have any new servants for a while.

"I danced with him too, you know," Allegra said with quiet intensity.

"With whom?" Sophia inquired, although she knew perfectly well.

"Frostbrook, of course. So you need not look so smug."

"I shall try," Sophia said, for although she could not help this wild, new happiness, smugness was not a trait she wished to cultivate.

Allegra glared at her. "He won't marry you. Sneaking off with him and allowing him liberties will only disgust him in a prospective wife. Can't you see he is merely seducing you? And then you will be abandoned and ruined and no one will want you. Not even your family."

Sophia's temper rose, not on her own behalf but on Frostbrook's. Allegra had no right to regard him in such a way, let alone speak of him so contemptuously. She met her cousin's glare.

"Take care, Allegra. Vulgarity and the ill manners of slandering your host can also be ruinous. Cousin Amelia will be missing you."

Allegra's eyes widened. Her mouth opened furiously and closed on silence. Then she jumped up and stalked away.

Sophia felt an unworthy spurt of triumph. She was only human. And it seemed nothing could go wrong this night.

⊰※⊱

DESPITE NOT GETTING to bed until after three o'clock in the morning, Sophia woke just before eight, and stretched luxuriously, smiling as last night's events crowded back into her mind. Dancing with Aaron, kissing Aaron, talking with Aaron. Even in sleep, it seemed, the excited butterflies had never left her stomach.

In their last conversation before parting, he had asked her whether she would prefer marriage by special license or by banns.

She had thought about it, then replied, "Perhaps banns would be better. It might give your mother longer to get used to the idea."

"You are generous," he had said. "She has not been so considerate of you."

"I am spoiling her plans. She wants better for you."

"I will make sure she understands the situation," he said with a hint of grimness.

Lady Frostbrook, she suspected, was about to be routed. It would not make a pleasant beginning to their relationship, but fences could always be mended.

Daylight, but no bright sunshine, broke through the bed curtains. She sat up and drew them apart to see rain on the window and gray clouds in the sky beyond. But she did not miss the sun, or the singing of the birds. They seemed to be in her heart, whatever the weather.

What a strange turn her life was taking. Who would have thought this would happen when she had opened her cousins' door to Giles and Rosamund only three weeks ago? Her shock that he had not come to rescue her but to ask her to help the duchess seemed foolish now, and laughably unimportant. She had been holding on to an illusion, a fantasy that had no real basis in fact or even emotion. This relationship with the earl, with Aaron, this was real and wonderful and…

Rather to her surprise, she was interrupted by one of the housemaids, who knocked and entered, yawning and heavy-eyed.

"Excuse me, miss, most of the household isn't up yet, but Mrs. West asked me to give you this as soon as you wakened. I were going to leave it on your dressing table, but since you're awake…" She advanced across the room, a folded paper held out.

Sophia pushed the hair out of her eyes and took the letter with a word of thanks. The girl nodded and yawned her way from the room. Sophia's name had been scrawled across the note in what appeared to be Amelia's hand. Curious, she unfolded it and read:

My dear Sophia,

I hope you have considered my advice of yesterday and reached the only sensible decision, however difficult. Our dearest wish is, as I said, that you will return with us today. But either way, I would not quarrel with you. Please at least come down to wave us off when we depart this morning at nine of the clock. I shall wait for you until then at the front terrace.

Your loving cousin,
Amelia West.

Sophia blinked several times at the letter and read it again before letting it fall onto the bedclothes. What an odd missive! They had behaved badly to her, and she didn't truly believe either her excuses or William's. Even Allegra had been more honest.

On the other hand, they clearly regretted their behavior and Sophia had no desire to quarrel, let alone bear grudges. She was far too happy for unpleasant emotions. And so she would go and wave them off with all good wishes.

She pushed off the covers and slid out of bed. As she washed and dressed, she did wonder if they finally realized that she *would* marry Frostbrook. He would never have married Allegra, but the sponsorship of the new Countess of Frostbrook would certainly boost her on the Marriage Mart. The thought amused Sophia. But then, everything was amusing today, from the cold washing water to the contortions necessary to fasten her gown without help. In the end, she gave up on the latter, and simply threw a shawl around her to hide the few hooks still gaping apart.

By then, it was ten minutes to nine. She left the room and walked downstairs to the front door, which was not locked. Outside, the rain appeared to have gone off, though Sophia doubted it would stay so for long.

No horses and carriage waited on the front terrace. But

Cousin Amelia did, dressed in a familiar traveling dress and cloak.

She came toward Sophia at once, a faint, rueful smile on her lips. "Sophia, you came. That means a great deal to me, although it looks as if you have decided not to accompany us. Please, my dear, there is still time to run up and fetch your bags. Or are the clothes borrowed…?"

"The clothes were a gift. But you are right, cousin. I shan't go with you this morning, though I am happy to forget the past and remain friends."

Amelia's eyes fell. "You were always a good-natured girl. I'm afraid we might have taken advantage."

"Let us not dwell on that," Sophia said hastily.

To her surprise, Amelia smiled and took her arm. "Exactly. Will you walk with me to the carriage? I asked it to wait just around the curve in the drive. To give us a little privacy, and, I suppose, not to look as if we were taking your compliance for granted."

"I'm afraid I'm not really a very compliant person," Sophia said as they walked together.

"You will need to be, now, married to *him*," Amelia said with a hint of the old malice.

"He is not a monster, cousin," Sophia said, choosing to be amused—this time. After all, Frostbrook did his best to appear haughty, cold, and unbending. One had to work to find the man beneath.

"Of course not," Amelia agreed. "But you will keep in touch? Come and visit, occasionally?"

"Of course," Sophia said. She wondered if she had misjudged her cousins, somehow, if it was she who had been unreasonable in resenting earning her keep with them. Perhaps they truly had misunderstood each other. "And there is your carriage. I wish you a safe journey."

The blinds were down on all the carriage windows, as though the occupants had every intention of sleeping their way home. Everyone was tired after the ball.

Amelia stopped beside the waiting carriage but did not release Sophia's arm. "You are sure you will not come with us? It will not make you less engaged to his lordship."

"Of course it would not. But we have plans to make."

"Of course."

The carriage door opened, pushed from the inside to reveal William and Allegra on opposite sides.

"Goodbye," Sophia said to them, and received a blow on her back that pushed her sprawling against the step. She gasped at the sharp pain in her shin, but already William and Allegra were hauling her into the carriage. Amelia shoved her again from behind, and she landed sprawling next to Allegra, who seized one arm while Amelia seized the other.

On the opposite bench, William brandished a small, lethal pistol, pointing directly at her heart.

CHAPTER THIRTEEN

FROSTBROOK'S HEART WAS light and full of joy, his head full of plans for the marriage ceremony, the wedding journey, where and how they might like to live. He could not imagine Sophia losing herself in the social whirls of London and Brighton, and merely entertaining the local gentry when they stayed at Brookwood and the other estates. They had much to discuss, much to arrange, most importantly the calling of the banns.

Although it was merely ten of the clock when he sauntered into the breakfast parlor, he hoped to find Sophia there. Instead, he found his brother-in-law, Holden, and a couple of the younger men he suspected had not been to bed at all.

After bidding everyone good morning and filling his plate, he sat down beside Humph and reached for his coffee. "Is Judith up?"

"Yes, she's gone in search of Miss Wallace."

He nodded, wondering where Sophia would like to stay until they were married. He doubted she would wish to be with his mother. Judith and Humph would be happy to have her, though she might actually prefer to return to Cuttyngs. If the latter, he hoped Victor would not object to a frequent visitor. The new duke, previously barred by his controlling father from all administration of the estates, was stepping up to his new responsibilities with a vengeance. Frostbrook rather liked him.

Mostly, he watched the door, waiting for Sophia to join them, but when Judith eventually came in, she was alone.

"Miss Wallace must have gone off for a long walk," she said, sitting on Frostbrook's other side. "For she's not in the house or the garden. I hope you didn't upset her, Aaron."

So do I, he thought with sudden panic. Had he been too amorous, too passionate in his embraces? Was he pushing her to marriage faster than she wanted to go? Perhaps she didn't want it at all and was afraid to…

He set down his coffee cup deliberately. Sophia would never be afraid to tell him anything. Nor should he begrudge her time in solitude. And yet unease had crept into his new happiness, the nagging feeling that something was wrong.

When the guests began to leave, mostly for London, and she still had not returned, he sent Judith to see what clues were in her room, and, between waving off carriages, went round to the stables.

None of the horses were missing, and none had been saddled for Miss Wallace or anyone else. Not surprising with the weather being so wet. Nor had any of the guests departed before eleven o'clock, except the Wests, who had ordered their carriage for nine.

Unreasonably early after a ball. Breakfast was not even served at that hour. Most of the household, including servants, were still in bed. Unease tightened into anxiety, especially when Judith met him in the front hall and dragged him into the empty library.

"She didn't take her cloak," Judith said abruptly. "Why would you walk in the rain with only a shawl to cover you? All her clothes, apart from a morning gown and a shawl, are still in the room. The bed was slept in. But, Aaron, I found this. I know I shouldn't have read it, but I was worried."

She shoved a piece of paper at him, and he read it quickly with growing fear and anger. It took him five minutes to discover the maid who had delivered the note.

"Did she go to wave off her relations?" he asked her.

"I think so, my lord. I saw her go out by the front door when

I was carrying the mop and bucket up to…"

Frostbrook thanked her and walked away. It looked as if the Wests had *made* her go with them. But why?

He found his mother in her boudoir with her dresser, making the finishing touches to her perfect morning toilette.

She frowned at him. "I hope you have been doing your duty by our departing guests?"

"Religiously. The rest are clearly hoping for luncheon before they leave." He glanced at the dresser impatiently. "Thank you, you may go."

The woman was clearly outraged, but she did not dare glance at her mistress for confirmation. She left.

Frostbrook, ignoring his mother's icy fury at his high-handedness, asked, "What do you know of the Wests, Mother?"

"Respectable, a little dull, property in Essex and Cambridgeshire. Why?"

"Who told you that? About their property?"

"I can't remember. What does it matter? Are you thinking of Allegra? Beautiful girl. I saw you dancing with her last night. She would make a fine countess, although to be honest, I still favor Miss Brandon."

"Allegra being somewhat spoiled, petulant, and demanding," he said contemptuously.

His mother curled her lip. "I expect her cousin Miss Wallace told you that."

"She did. After Allegra had made her walk several miles at night in the rain to deliver a fan to a ball she was attending. Sophia was dressed little better than a servant, then, and treated no better, either. Why would such a wealthy family use an indigent cousin as a servant, do you think? Because they have no money to pay for one. The Wests are not wealthy, whatever they have told you."

"No matter. Allegra was very much my second choice."

He held her gaze, frowning. "Mrs. West does not know that, does she? Mother, do you have some kind of agreement with her?"

"What sort of agreement could I possibly have with Mrs. West? Even if you chose Allegra, it would be Mr. West with whom settlements would be discussed."

"There could be no settlements while I was engaged to Sophia," Frostbrook said. "I think you and Mrs. West conspired to part us. It would explain the cousin's sudden proposal of marriage last night."

His mother waved one dismissive hand. "Oh, that was not remotely sudden. They were betrothed in their cradles. Miss Wallace broke it to attach herself to you."

This was all making a nasty kind of sense. "No," he said slowly. "Sophia *was* betrothed in her cradle, but not to William West, to Giles Butler."

"Who on earth is he? Why do I know that name?"

Frostbrook had no intention of veering into the subject of the duel. "Why?" he demanded, staring at his mother without really seeing her. "Why are they so desperate to have her back? They kept her too poor and discouraged to leave them until the duchess came along. He took the trouble to track her down to Cuttyngs and try to force her return. Then they changed tactics to gentle persuasion, an offer of marriage, an assurance, no doubt, that I would be the husband from hell…"

"There is no call for such language, Frostbrook," his mother snapped.

He ignored it, focusing on her face. "Mother, have they *abducted* Sophia?"

"What on earth has got into you? I have never known you to be so foolishly melodramatic!"

"*Have they?*" He did not even raise his voice, nor take one step closer to her, but he made the tone of it as ugly as he knew how. He had cultivated the ability long ago, a defense against the world and his own hurts, but he had never before used it on her.

He saw the color drain from her face, the flash of unexpected fear, and he was not even sorry.

"I don't know," she said hoarsely. "I did not discuss means with Mrs. West."

"Only the end which suited you both." Abstractly, he rubbed one finger against his brow, thinking. If what he suspected was true, they would not physically harm her. But she might not know that. He turned on his heel, striding to the door. "I'm going to Essex."

"Frostbrook!"

He was fiercely glad of the desperation in her voice. How dare she treat *anyone* like this, let alone Sophia, who deserved so much more from everyone than she had ever received.

"Frostbrook, your guests!" his mother called after him. "Miss Brandon!"

"Who?" he flung savagely over his shoulder, and jerked the door closed behind him.

✦

As the shock of facing a pistol, held by her cousin, gradually dulled, Sophia realized he was very unlikely to shoot her. He could not risk any scandal, let alone a hue and cry for murder, if Allegra was to marry Frostbrook—which was, presumably, his ultimate aim.

"I will put this away," William said sternly at last, "if you promise not to struggle."

Sophia thought nothing of promises made under duress. Added to which, her choice seemed to be sitting where she was, squashed between Amelia and Allegra in the carriage, or throwing herself from a fast-moving vehicle into the road and risking almost certain injury or death.

"I promise."

William relaxed and slid the pistol back into his greatcoat pocket with obvious relief. "You must do exactly as you are told," he warned.

"Why? What do you want? Where are we going?"

"London," William said shortly.

En route to Dorwich? "You appear to want me there with you quite badly," she remarked.

"You were ruining everything!" Allegra burst out.

"Be quiet," William snapped, and Allegra's jaw dropped in such astonishment that Sophia let out a choke of hysterical laughter. Swiftly squashing it, she tried to sit back more comfortably, and thought with longing about Lord Frostbrook. Aaron. And knew he would be coming for her.

When they changed horses, no one got out of the carriage. Sophia's request for refreshment fell on deaf ears. Allegra sulked. Amelia looked grim, though behind that, Sophia thought she detected anxiety. William's manner was determined, and yet his quick, sudden movements betrayed excitement, especially as they entered London and he opened the curtains on one side of the carriage so that he could see where they were.

Inevitably, with all the town traffic, the carriage moved much more slowly and was forced to halt several times. Amelia and Allegra took tighter grips of Sophia's arms, and William stared at her in warning.

For Sophia, though, curiosity had replaced much of her fear. Though she had no intention of ever living anywhere with the Wests again, and every intention of marrying Aaron, she wanted to know what they were about and why. They did not seem inclined to hurt her or abandon her in some stew for spite. Instead, they crossed the river and moved northward.

She thought at first they were going to the fashionable area she had been in already, where both Frostbrook and the Landrys had their London houses. But it seemed not. The streets still seemed to be respectable enough, but she saw few ladies. *St. James* was carved into the side of an impressive building. They turned into a quieter street and the horses came to a halt.

"Two minutes and I will come back for you," William said. He frowned at Sophia. "Your promise, or do I have to give the pistol to my mother?"

"I see no need for that," Sophia said hastily. "Please, carry on with your business. I am fascinated."

The expression that flashed across William's face might have been admiration. At any rate, he merely nodded to his mother and got down from the carriage, closing the door quickly behind him. He ran up the steps to the nearest house, knocked, and was admitted.

Amelia and Allegra looked at each other across Sophia but said nothing. They too seemed excited now. Their fingers on her arms dug into her flesh painfully hard, but she doubted they noticed.

"Who lives in there?" Sophia asked. She didn't really expect an answer, but Amelia replied with some relish.

"The Reverend Lord Rupert Grande."

"Oh." Sophia felt none the wiser.

It was five minutes before William re-emerged from the house, and he did not look pleased.

Hurling himself back into the carriage, he said, "He's not there."

"Drat the man!" Amelia exclaimed. "When is he coming back?"

"They don't know. He's gone to Brussels."

"*Brussels!*" Allegra repeated, apparently appalled.

"Half the *ton* is in Brussels," Sophia said helpfully. "No doubt encouraging His Grace of Wellington to invade France and defeat Bonaparte all over again."

"Yes, but why would a dilettante clergyman go there?" William fumed. "He knew I wanted him *here!*"

No doubt your wishes were of no interest to him, thought Sophia, who could see no reason why they would be. Aloud, she said, "Is this Lord Rupert a friend of yours?"

"We knew each other at school. Before he went to Eton. He was amiable enough to keep in touch."

"Yes, but why do you want him *now?*" Sophia asked.

William regarded her with some bitterness. "To marry us, of course."

Sophia's mouth fell open. *"What?"*

They all ignored her. "Well, there's nothing else for it," Amelia said. "You must find another clergyman."

"I don't *know* any other clergymen!" Clearly harassed, William raked his fingers through his hair, upsetting his careful style.

"How hard can it be?" Amelia demanded. "This is London!"

William turned on her. "And while I am looking, trotting from church to church with my increasingly crumpled special license and a carriage full of women, what do you suppose Frostbrook will be doing? How far behind us do you imagine he is? Or are you so deluded that you think Lady Frostbrook can actually keep him in Surrey?"

Dismay pulled down their faces. But Sophia was clinging to the main point.

"Why on earth do you want to marry me?" she demanded. "You don't even like me, and it must be said that this start has hardly endeared any of you to me. What kind of a marriage do you expect to get out of it? You cannot be that desperate for a skivvy. And you should know, that even were I dead, Frostbrook will never marry Allegra."

Allegra's eyes spat at her. No one else troubled to answer.

"This is his territory," William said anxiously. "He has a reputation for knowing *everything*. Especially what you most want to keep from him. And we are too conspicuous." He drew in a breath. "We cannot stay in London."

"Dorwich?" Amelia said. "Our own vicar…"

"If I'm not mistaken, Frostbrook will go to Dorwich first," William snapped. "He could be there now." He paused with his fingers fisted in his hair and looked up. "Which is our hope. If he does not find us in London, he will go to Dorwich, and vice versa. While we will go south, to Dover."

"Dover?" Allegra repeated.

"From where we can sail to Ostend and go on from there to Brussels. Actually, it is perfect," William said with growing enthusiasm. "Frostbrook will never expect it. *We* will be in

Brussels among a lot of foreigners who care nothing for any of us, and Grande will be there to marry us."

"NO," SOPHIA SAID for the umpteenth time, before swallowing most of her second cup of tea in one furious jerk. "You are behaving like a madman. I will not leave the country, and I will not under any circumstances take vows of marriage with you!"

They were now in in the Charing Cross inn where they had been deposited with their luggage by the previous coachman. He, who had apparently been hired along with the carriage, had refused to take his vehicle out of London again. He had, he maintained, other commitments. Besides, it looked to Sophia as though he did not care for the behavior of his current employers. And so, with ill grace, he had dropped them, luggage and all, at the inn, where William intended to hire a post chaise to Dover.

While William gritted his teeth over the cost, Amelia had demanded refreshments and a private parlor in which to wait. Inevitably, the tea was disgusting. And Sophia had had enough.

She sprang to her feet so quickly that she felt dizzy. In fact, the day's events must be catching up with her, for she had to grip the table hard in order to make her mouth form the words.

"I am leaving now. You will not come near me again. In fact, don't even speak to me again. I shall not present Allegra at court." With that, she tried to stalk to the parlor door, but something was wrong. She weaved from side to side as she walked. Her feet felt too heavy, and for some reason no one was arguing with her. They had all fallen silent.

Only when she grasped the latch did William's hand close on her shoulder, hauling her back against him. He actually pinched her nose, and when she gasped in outrage, something vile and burning was poured down her throat. The world swam into nauseous darkness.

Chapter Fourteen

FROSTBROOK DROVE AT a cracking pace all the way to London. At each change of horses, he learned from the ostlers that he was catching up with the Wests. He was slightly surprised that they did not skirt around London but took the road into town. But, in fact, that suited Frostbrook, who had a few things to do there before dashing on to Dorwich.

He drove straight to his own house and commanded Bridges, his long-suffering valet, to pack a fresh bag and prepare to travel with him. He then summoned Bridges's various relations, his occasional employees, setting them to watch the Essex roads, and inquire of various posting inns and livery stables. He did not even pause to change his clothes before sallying forth to Lambeth Palace in order to remind His Grace the Archbishop of Canterbury of a favor owed.

Despite friendship and obligation that saw his business expedited much more quickly than usual, he knew he would have to spend the night in London after all. Accordingly, on leaving the palace, he called on his solicitors.

Naturally, despite the lateness of the hour, and the fact that the clerk was already wearing his hat to go home, he was ushered at once into Mr. Patterson's office.

"My lord, welcome, do please take a seat!" the elderly solicitor exclaimed, rising from his desk and waving him to the opposite chair. "I would have been happy to call upon your lordship if you had only sent word."

"I am in something of a hurry," Frostbrook said bluntly. "It is my intention to marry, and I suspect some…irregularities in the affairs of my bride-to-be."

Mr. Patterson frowned. "Then they will have to be resolved."

"Indeed. There is no question of the marriage not proceeding, you understand, but it goes against the grain to allow my wife to remain cheated, if cheated she has been."

"Perhaps you had better tell me everything you know."

Mr. Patterson listened, writing down odd notes, his frown deepening all the time. At last, he said, "The Wallace family were not my clients, but I have had occasion to deal with their solicitors. I shall, of course, make inquiries, but my understanding was that Mr. Wallace, who must be your Miss Wallace's late father, was well-to-do. The land was entailed and nothing could be done about that, but he had a good deal of money in funds. One of these funds was the cause of a dispute with a client of mine—a dispute resolved without acrimony in the end. But I did not get the impression Mr. Wallace was poor or struggling in any way."

"And yet he left his daughter nothing?"

"Unlikely," Patterson agreed. "Although obviously things might change suddenly for an imprudent investor. In fact, the exchange is growing volatile with matters abroad being so uncertain—Bonaparte, you know… There may have been a guardian involved in the supervision of Wallace's funds on his death, and he has already frittered it away." He straightened. "But that is speculation. I will make inquiries at once."

Frostbrook rose. "Thank you."

As he returned to Frostbrook House, he found himself increasingly uneasy. He was sure the Wests would not hurt Sophia, not if William intended to marry her, and yet his every instinct was to find her *now*.

He entered the house to be informed that John Bridges, one

of his valet's invaluable relations, awaited him in the office.

"Well?" Frostbrook said at once. He strode to the side table, poured two brandies, and shoved one glass toward John, who seized on it gratefully and downed it in one.

"I found the company who hired out the carriage and horses to Mr. West," he said in a rush. "Spoke to the coachman, Roberts. Roberts brought them into London to an address just off Piccadilly."

"What address?" Frostbrook asked, frowning.

John told him, and he slowly set down his glass.

"I found out who lives there," John told him.

"I know who lives there. Lord Rupert Grande."

"Oh. Well, he's respectable, isn't he?"

"Up to a point. In fact, by some miracle, he is an ordained clergyman. Did he go with West?"

"No, my lord, he isn't at home. He's in Brussels."

Frostbrook breathed again. "Thank God." It was a point, though. Did West actually have a special license, too? Would the archbishop's office not notice Sophia's name on an earlier license? Frostbrook had been urging haste, and now he had every reason to be uneasy. If his own license would not arrive in the morning, there was no point in waiting here overnight.

"There's more, my lord," John said. "Mr. West wanted Roberts to take them on to Dover, but he refused. Thought the fellow was havey-cavey and besides, he had other commitments. So, he dropped them at the Golden Cross Inn."

Frostbrook frowned. The public coaches to Dover left from there. "They meant to go by mail coach?"

"He thought they meant to hire a post chaise."

"And Miss Wallace?"

"Sailed into the inn with the other women while West saw to the baggage."

"I don't like this," Frostbrook said. "Are they still at the Golden Cross?"

"No, sir. En route to Dover."

"Dover." Frostbrook scowled. "Why the devil would they go to Dover?" Unless in pursuit of rakish clergyman, Grande, now in Brussels. Which almost certainly meant West *did* have a special license.

ALTHOUGH FROSTBROOK FEARED West's special license might prevent the production of his own, due to Sophia's name being on both, it apparently escaped attention, thanks, no doubt, to the archbishop's hastening of the process. The license was delivered by hand first thing in the morning, much to Frostbrook's relief, and he set off immediately, driving himself and taking Bridges with him.

He hated being so far behind Sophia, but even if they had already left Dover by the time he arrived, he had one other advantage over West. He did not need to wait for a packet or some other ship to take him across the Channel. He had his own fast yacht anchored there and ready to sail with the first tide.

SOPHIA BECAME AWARE of movement, a different kind of movement from the unspeakable rolling of the sea. This was more plodding and bumping. Someone or something was breathing loudly in her ear, and hard bands held her in place. No, not bands, human arms. She was being carried.

But she could still smell the sea. Her head hurt as if someone were squeezing it and hitting it with small hammers at the same time. She felt dreadful.

She had no idea how long she had been feeling dreadful for. The time since she had risen from her chair at the London inn had passed in a nightmare of sickness, terrible dreams, and more gin thrust down her throat, even when she had wept so weakly and cried for mercy. There had been moments she had woken alone with her stomach roiling and heaving. That was when she had seen the sea from the tiny, round window beside her bed. She had tried to rise, but her whole body shook and she barely had the energy to reach the door. It had been locked, and she slid back down into oblivion.

The next she remembered, she had been back on the bed. She remembered vague flashes of William, who did most of the gin dosing, though at least once Amelia and Allegra had been helping him. The fuzziness of her brain and her bodily weakness had terrified her. It still did, but with the slow, stumbling pace of whoever carried her, she found the courage to open her eyes.

It was a large, strong man she had never seen before, and she was being carried over sand toward what looked to be a town. But this was not William. There was hope.

She tried to gather her strength.

"Here, put her in the carriage," came Amelia's voice, and Sophia's heart sank. She closed her eyes hastily, because she had no idea if she could even walk, supposing she managed to wrestle her way out of the arms that held her.

She was deposited on a cushioned carriage bench with surprising gentleness and let herself flop. A clink of coins changing hands. Amelia's voice arguing, William's instructing, Allegra's whining.

They seemed to be discussing luggage, and the possibility of traveling on by canal boat, but William was adamant that having obtained two carriages, they should use them. Their voices droned on.

Sophia opened her eyes. The light hurt, but when she flexed her arms and legs, they seemed to work. Very carefully, she sat up. Her head spun for a moment into excruciating pain. But then she could see dimly out of the carriage window to a row of houses. On the other side was the beach, the sea, small boats and ships in the distance. Hastily, she looked away from the sea to the houses.

This must be Ostend, where William had wanted to go in pursuit of his tame clergyman. What a pity he had not left his bags in here so that she could rummage through them, find his special license, and tear it into a thousand tiny pieces.

On the other hand, if she allowed herself to be dosed with much more gin and whatever else she had been forced to swallow, she doubted she would live to find Frostbrook again.

Weak tears tried to clog her throat, but she swallowed them back. There was a door on either side of the carriage. The Wests' voices seemed all to be on the sea side, so, after testing her feet with a few gentle taps on the floor, she cautiously eased open the door on the other side. A cart laden with barrels swept past. She dared not push down the steps, but eased herself down to the road, stumbling but not falling, and softly closed the door.

She was shaking all over, but no one shouted, no one seized her. Forcing herself to pay attention, she let a horse and covered wagon pass going the opposite direction, and then flitted across the road. At least she tried to flit, though she staggered and weaved a little, like a drunk woman. Her mouth was dry, like sand before the tide comes in, but discomfort hardly mattered. She staggered along the side of the road, past the houses and around the first corner, out of sight of the carriage.

Only then did she hear the shout and Amelia's scream, which she recognized instantly. They had discovered her escape. In panic, she tried to move faster while peering over her shoulder in dread, and bumped hard into someone who shouted at her angrily.

"Please, please let me go," Sophia whispered, staring up at an old woman with a shawl round her shoulders, and hands like claws on her arms.

The woman scowled, looking her up and down with contempt. Sophia knew she must stink of gin. Her hair was unkempt, falling in tugs and tangles around her. She probably looked ragged, homeless, and demented. She tugged free, staring over her shoulder again.

"I have to hide," she muttered, though whether to the woman or to herself, she had no idea.

She stumbled on, but unexpectedly, the woman seized her elbow, firmly, but no longer angrily, then pushed her through a door, and Sophia all but fell into a tiny kitchen.

A man's voice spoke in surprise, and then two boots appeared in front of her. The woman helped her to rise, and she found herself face to face with a youngish seaman who looked from her to the old woman. They exchanged more quick, incomprehensible words, then the seaman caught her eye once more and said seriously, "You are English?"

Sophia nodded.

"Who are you hiding from?" the man asked.

"My family," Sophia replied, swaying. "I'm sorry. I reek of gin and I think I'm ill. I…"

Between them, the seaman and the old woman sat her on a wooden chair. The woman brought her a mug of water, which tasted divine, although she found she could only swallow with difficulty.

"I am Hals," the man said, touching his chest with his thumb. He pointed to the woman. "My mother, Inge."

"Sophia."

"What happened to you?"

An unhappy laugh tried to choke her. "You would not believe me."

"Try," he urged.

"My cousin wants to marry me by force. He has a special license and a tame English clergyman in Brussels. I was disinclined to come, so they forced gin and God knows what else down my throat. Their carriages are at the sea front where we landed, but I slipped away while they were arguing. They know I've gone and will be looking for me."

Her hand shook as she lifted the water to her lips once more.

"When did you last eat?" Hals asked.

"I don't know. Days ago, I think…"

Hals spoke to his mother, who was already bustling about the little stove. Then he looked down at Sophia once more. "I go and see."

She almost dropped the mug of water onto the table, where it splashed. "No, please!" she said, grabbing for his head. "Please don't tell them! I beg of you!" She even jumped to her feet, but she had moved too fast. The blood sang in her ears and the world went dark again.

WHEN SHE WOKE, she was in bed again. But the sheets were clean, and so was whatever she was wearing—a large, rough cotton nightgown. Her body felt clean, too, and someone had brushed the worst of the tangles out of her hair. She lay in a tiny room under the eaves. A single oil lamp burned on a wooden dresser opposite. She guessed it was nighttime. The curtains were pulled across the little window. The door was closed.

Had they given her back to William? Was the door locked? Could she escape again?

Not in a nightgown. Where were her clothes?

She could see no sign of them.

Her breath caught as she heard footsteps beyond the door. Then the door opened and Inge, the old woman, came in bearing a tray. Relief flooded her, hot and powerful.

Setting down the tray, Inge helped her sit up. She felt weak as a kitten. Then Inge gave her the cup of water beside the bed, urging her to drink, which she did. It felt delightfully clear and clean in her mouth, her throat.

"Thank you," Sophia whispered.

"You eat," Inge said, bringing over the tray and sitting on the edge of the narrow bed. "I help."

The broth in the bowl smelled delicious. Sophia managed to spoon some into her own mouth. Her hands no longer shook, but after several spoonfuls, she felt exhausted. Inge dipped a piece of bread into it and handed to her. Sophia leaned back against the pillows and ate it. She still felt odd, hot and uncomfortable.

"Fever," Inge said, touching her forehead. "But you get well."

"Your son, Hals," Sophia said with difficulty. "Did he find my family? Did he tell them?"

She repeated it several times, and then, with a flash of inspiration, tried it in French.

Inge smiled. "He see them," she replied in the same language. "He not tell."

"Oh, thank you! Thank you both."

Inge stood up. "You sleep now. Tomorrow is better."

WITH THE WIND behind it, Frostbrook's yacht made good time to Ostend. They arrived at dusk, and his efficient crew swiftly unloaded his baggage, horses, and curricle. He found lodgings for himself and his valet at a nearby inn, and it was there he first overheard the tale of the English girl who vanished.

Frostbrook paused, his foot on the first step of the staircase. Without a word, he handed his valise to the already weighed-down Bridges and turned back into the room.

"Her people set up a mighty yowling," said an English sailor.

"Where was she?" asked another. "Where did she vanish to?"

"Poof," said a French speaker, throwing his arms wide. "She was ill, apparently. They think God took her."

"Body and all?" Frostbrook interrupted mildly.

"Well, there was no body there," the first English sailor said by way of an argument clincher.

"How very curious," Frostbrook said. "Where exactly did this happen?"

He listened to the tale, still being so embellished that he wondered if it bore any resemblance at all to actual happenings.

Moreover, there was nothing to say that the vanishing girl was Sophia, and yet wasn't this what she would do? Wait her moment and flee?

"And the family?" he asked at last.

"Searched for her high and low, at every house nearby, along the beach, in every waiting boat," the sailor said. "Got the port authorities involved, too, but they couldn't find her either."

"I don't suppose you know where I might find this family?" Frostbrook said pleasantly, with murder in his heart. They had said she was ill, and she certainly hadn't been when he had last seen her. Perhaps she was just seasick. That would explain her abrupt recovery on land. But he blamed the Wests for that, too.

If the Wests were indeed the people concerned.

"They've gone on to Brussels," the French-speaking sailor told him contemptuously, "no doubt to seek sympathy from all their countrymen there."

Or because they knew Sophia would make her way there, to safety with the Duchess of Cuttyngham? Unless she got straight back on board a ship to go home... But she would have no money. In which case she could not get to Brussels either, unless she walked. She could not even eat except through charity.

Panic surged, driving him away from his informants and upstairs to think. He had to squash his urgent impulse to tear the town apart looking for her. It was dark. People would be reluctant to speak to a stranger, and he was more likely to get himself into trouble, from where his chances of helping Sophia were considerably less.

He tried to take comfort in the fact that she had clearly hidden herself. But had she? What if someone else had taken her? It would take a bold abductor to open a carriage door and steal someone from under the noses of their family, and the coachman and passersby. But such things did happen. And every moment he did not find her...

"You can do nothing until daylight," Bridges said quietly. "I'll wake you at first light."

BY FIRST LIGHT, Frostbrook at least had a plan. He sent Bridges to make inquiries, to see if she had been seen at inns, hiring a horse, or passage on a canal boat, or on any ship sailing to England. Frostbrook himself walked back to the shore and spoke to a few fishermen until he found one who had witnessed the strange disappearance and could tell him about it in a mixture of French and English, with the odd Flemish word thrown in.

"English sailor carried her ashore for them, laid her in their carriage, while they squabbled about nothing. When they finally decided to set off, she'd gone."

"Could you show me exactly where the carriage was?" Frostbrook asked, casually passing a coin into the gnarled hand, which grasped it readily enough.

The fisherman complied. "Carriage here," he said, spreading his hands. He moved along a few feet. "Horses here." He stepped back a couple of paces nearer the sea. "Gentleman and two ladies here. Coachman here."

"Thank you," Frostbrook said, distractedly passing another coin while he gazed about. The fisherman wandered off. If he was right, then Frostbrook was standing where Sophia had lain in that carriage, and then escaped. West had apparently rapped on doors up and down the street, but no one had seen her go inside any building. No one had seen her at all.

He tried to imagine himself in her position, looking out the window. Impossible to escape on the sea side, where her family would have seen her. So, she must have got out the opposite door. In one direction, an unbroken line of buildings. In the other, more buildings, and a narrow side street. He could see nothing of the street save for the gable of the first house. Which meant West could have seen nothing either.

After waiting for three laden carts to go by, Frostbrook crossed the road and strode up to the side street. It contained a row of small, narrow two-story houses opening directly off the street. The place was quiet at this hour. The fishermen would have gone out already.

He decided Sophia would not have risked the first house. She might have been seen there from the carriage. At the second door, a woman was scrubbing her front step.

"Good morning, madame," he said in French. "I am looking for a young English lady who might have come this way seeking help."

She looked at him as if he had grown horns, then shook her head vigorously and carried on scrubbing. There was nothing else for it. He went to the third door, knocked, and asked his question of several surprised or uninterested people.

It must have been the sixth person he spoke to—a wrinkled old woman—when he finally saw a flash of something like recognition, quickly hidden. Almost as if she had been expecting him. But she shook her head.

"No," she replied firmly, and would have shut the door except he said urgently, "Please, madame, it is important."

Her eyes were bold and fearless. "Are you her family?"

"Yes," he said, seizing on the lie with relief.

But a look of utter contempt filled her eyes. "There is no such person here. Just me and my son." And she shut the door in his face.

Found her. Sophia had to be here. The old woman knew damned well whom he was talking about. She knew to hate Sophia's family because Sophia must have told her. And she had taken the trouble to tell him she had her son as protection.

He tried to contain his excitement, for he could not barge his way inside without attracting the attention of the neighbors, who would at best deliver him to the authorities, at worst beat him to a pulp. He glanced at the windows. The shutters were open, but no one was watching him. How many rooms were there? Two? Three? Which was Sophia likely to be in?

In any case, he could not risk throwing stones at the window.

Perhaps the old woman would describe him to Sophia, and she would recognize him…

But he could not wait. If she was ill, frightened… He strode along the rest of the row, as if he had given up. But instead, he discovered what he had been looking for, a way round to the backs of the houses. Each had a tiny garden, some with hanging washing, some growing vegetables. He didn't really care. He counted doors until he came to the one next to where he was sure Sophia lay and jumped nimbly over the wall.

Both the shutters and the window itself were open in the upstairs room of "Sophia's" house. They were not tall buildings, and there was plenty to hold on to for someone who had grown up climbing everything from trees to ruined buildings. Without hesitation, for time was important now, he leaped for the windowsill and began to climb to the upper floor. No one yelled.

The hardest part was hauling himself from the upper windowsill to that of the house next door, but he managed it with only one stomach-diving slip that he quickly recovered from. Then, without pausing even to see what threats he faced, he forced the window wide open and climbed inside.

Sophia—a pale, thin, frail version of his Sophia—sat up in a narrow bed, staring at him.

"Am I dreaming again?" she said hoarsely. "Is it *you*?" Her arms lifted weakly, as if of their own volition, reaching for him. He threw himself onto the bed, and she collapsed into his arms with a sob of sheer emotion.

CHAPTER FIFTEEN

S OPHIA HAD LONGED for him so much in her nightmare that she couldn't believe it was actually him. And yet his arms around her felt blissfully real, strong and safe, and he *smelled* of Aaron. She clutched him, making tiny, desperate sobs, and he held her tighter, stroking her hair and whispering words of love.

"Oh, my sweet, I am so sorry," he said shakily at last.

"You found me." Everything was perfect now.

"I should not have lost you. It should not have taken me so long. I never thought they would—"

The bedchamber door burst open and Hals burst in, one step ahead of Inge, his fists raised.

"No!" Sophia cried, throwing herself to the side to protect Aaron, without actually letting him go. "He isn't the one. He isn't family. He is my betrothed, come to save me."

It sounded utterly ridiculous, so much so that she started to laugh. Hals frowned, his fists loosening and falling to his side.

Aaron's arms tightened around her. "I'm sorry. I could not make you understand, but I mean neither her nor you any harm. In fact, I am so far in your debt I will never be able to repay you."

She seemed to be incapable of letting him go. He was her world, everything that was good and safe. She could not quite believe he was here, and yet her heart was soaring with joy. She laid her cheek against his chest and breathed him in.

"Will you tell me?" Aaron said quietly. But he seemed to be talking to Hals. There was a scrape on the floor, as if Hals had moved the wooden chair from the corner and sat in it. Inge's footsteps clattered down the stairs again.

Hals said, "She all but fell against my mother, clearly distressed, ill, frightened, no idea where she was going. My mother thought she was drunk at first, for she reeked of gin and—"

"*Gin?*" Aaron said in disbelief.

"I think I drank it first in the tea at the inn," Sophia said, forcing herself to relive the nightmare now that Aaron's arms were around her. "The inn in London, I mean, without knowing. It certainly tasted disgusting. They had to make me compliant, I suppose, because I wouldn't go with them. I couldn't walk properly, and then he poured more down my throat and I—I couldn't do anything. Whenever I woke up, they would..." Her breath caught, and she buried her face in Aaron's throat.

"Dear God," he whispered.

"I don't think she'd eaten or had anything else to drink for days," Hals said. "And I suspect there was more than gin. Laudanum or something similar too. She has fevers, off and on. We were going to look for a doctor."

"I'll take her to Brussels. I know a good doctor there." Aaron caught Sophia's chin in his fingers, turning her face up to his anxious eyes. "Can you travel?"

"I can do anything with you."

He muttered something, cradling her face in his hand. Then he asked Hals, "What is the easiest way to journey to Brussels?"

"Canal," came the immediate answer.

Sophia's stomach protested, and she lifted her head. "No boats," she said firmly.

"A canal boat is different. No waves, just gliding along the water. Can you hire us one, with crew?" Aaron asked Hals, delving into his pocket. "There will just be the two of us and a manservant. And a curricle and two horses. Something comfortable if there is a choice."

"Sure," Hals said laconically. Rising, he took the proffered purse from Aaron and left without further discussion.

"What do you have to wear?" Aaron asked, as if he had just realized she wore only Inge's nightgown.

She wrinkled her nose. "What I stood up in the morning after the ball. Everything smells."

"No," Inge said, barging in with a tray of breakfast. "I wash."

ONLY WITH DIFFICULTY could Sophia persuade herself to stop clutching Aaron. It was harder again to let him out of her sight while Inge helped her to dress in the freshly laundered clothes she had arrived in. Inge even brushed out her hair again and pinned it up in a loose knot for her.

"Thank you," Sophia said, smiling with difficulty. "You have been so kind to me."

Inge patted her shoulder and draped the shawl around her. Surprised, Sophia realized she did not hate this gown or the rather beautiful shawl. Aaron had given them to her. They might have got soiled in travel illness, but they were clean now, and she would not let them become a symbol of her nightmare.

"Milord back soon," Inge said.

Panic surged. "He is not here?"

"He find the servant, the bags, come back."

Sophia tried to be sensible, to remain calm, but in truth, she only relaxed once Aaron had returned, with his valet and several bags, and a warm new cloak for Sophia. Inge smiled approvingly, and Sophia forced herself not to reach immediately for Aaron's hand. She would quickly become a burden being quite so pathetic.

"We are traveling incognito," he told Sophia with a wry smile, "since you will be entirely unchaperoned on the journey. In Brussels, I'll take you to the duchess and find Dr. Rivers."

She had no fault to find with that plan, providing he too stayed with the duchess. On the other hand, perhaps by the time they got there, she would have learned not to cling so.

The canal boat hired by Hals on Frostbrook's behalf was huge for three people. Only a week or so ago, such a vessel might have been impossible to hire, used as they were to ferry officers and men from Ostend to Wellington's mustering forces around Brussels.

Having said an almost tearful goodbye to Hals and Inge, she was carried into the curricle, and from the curricle to the canal boat.

"I'm sure I can walk," she protested.

"Small steps to start with," Aaron said sternly, and for once she did not mind being ordered around, not when it stemmed from a care so intense it made her want to cry. She didn't. Instead, she sat on deck, with her new cloak around her and her shawl over her hair, and watched the efficient loading of the horses and curricle.

Horses drew the boat along the canal in a smooth, dreamlike glide that soothed her spirit. Aaron sat beside her to watch to town go by and slowly give way to flat countryside, woodland, and farmland.

"William had a special license to marry me," she said into the pleasant silence. "I don't know why."

"I think I do."

She glanced at him in surprise.

"I don't know for sure yet, but I have set inquiries in motion. I don't believe your father left you unprovided for. I think he made West trustee of your funds. I suspect he has been embezzling them happily for years, while saving even more money on servants by making use of you. He thought to provide Allegra with expensive gowns and a London Season if necessary, in order to ensnare some simple-minded but wealthy aristocrat."

"They were certainly thrilled to pieces that you were to be at the Fairly Park ball," she recalled.

"My mother believes the Wests to be wealthy, and she is usually right about such things. But I suspect the wealth is yours."

She was silent for several moments while she digested that. "I would have shared it with them once. Now I would rather build a home for stray dogs with it than let them have a penny."

"That's the spirit," Aaron said. He pushed a glass of lemonade across the table to her, and obediently, she drank.

After a while, she rose and took his arm, and they went into the comfortable cabin. Although her legs felt weak, they supported her on the short journey, which pleased her inordinately. It was a pleasure to eat with Aaron, although she could not stomach the wine. He told her how he had found her, making it into a jest, but through the humor, she read his very real anxiety. His concern warmed her, even as she wondered at it.

The other cabin had been made into a bedchamber. So, they paused in the historic town of Ghent for the night, and Sophia enjoyed her first good night's sleep since the ball. In the morning, they carried on their way to Brussels.

WILLIAM WAS STILL furious to have lost his wretched cousin, after the considerable trouble he had taken to get her across the Channel. They had all been taken by surprise. But he was sure the right thing had been to come to Brussels. All the way along the road, he had asked about anyone resembling Sophia, and no one had seen her. The chances were she was either still hiding in Ostend or begging rides on slow carts off the main roads. She had no money for passage back to England, so her one hope had to be her precious duchess.

William held on to that certainty as he abandoned his mother and sister in a rather dingy hotel in Brussels.

"The first thing is to locate Grande," he told them, setting his hat on his head with a smart tap.

"The first thing is surely to locate the bride," Allegra said nastily. "Otherwise you will have no need of the clergyman."

"She will go to the duchess." William sounded obstinate to his own ears. "You must walk and mingle with the English visitors until you manage to scrape an acquaintance with her. A word about Sophia's sanity would not go amiss either. Judging by her appearance when she was carried off the boat, she'll be a complete wreck by the time she gets here. Which will favor our story over hers. And I shall be a saint for marrying her."

Allegra regarded him with a contempt he had never seen in her eyes before. Or, at least, not directed at him. "It has all come unraveled, hasn't it? And still you won't let it go."

"If I do let it go," he snapped, "you may wave goodbye to a Season, Frostbrook, or any other husband of fortune. Or even a new frock."

With that, he stalked from the room, leaving his mother to placate the increasingly strident Allegra.

Lord Rupert Grande was a prominent enough person to find quite easily, and in the end, William spotted him in a large public park, full of the fashionably dressed and English voices. The marquis's son, the most unlikely of clergymen, was flirting outrageously with at least one of his female companions, although as William strode up, he excused himself.

"Greetings, Westie!" he said with some surprise, holding out one amiable hand. "What are you doing here among the foreigners?"

"Looking for you, as it happens."

"Really? What can I do for you?"

"The same as the last time we spoke," William said, trying to hide his annoyance. "Marry me to my cousin."

"Happy to, old fellow. That will make the second wedding I'll have performed here in Brussels."

William's heart skipped a beat. Surely there had not been time for Sophia to get here and marry Frostbrook? "What was the first?" he asked.

"Lady Hera Severne to a Dr. Rivers. Decent fellow."

William sagged with relief. Of course the earl was still chasing his tail in England, and Sophia, surely, sleeping in a vegetable cart or the like somewhere on the road from Ostend.

"Lady Hera, the Duke of Cuttyngham's daughter?" William said.

"The very same. Beautiful girl." Grande kissed his fingers expressively. "Happy to marry you, too. Providing you have a special license, of course."

"Indeed—I showed it to you the last time we spoke," William said patiently.

"Just drop me a note, then," said Grande, extracting a card from his pocket. "Brussels address is on the back. You'll have to excuse me for now." The disreputable clergyman definitely winked before he loped after his own party.

⊰⊱

FROSTBROOK'S INVALUABLE VALET had very easily discovered the location and status of the Duchess of Cuttyngham.

"Her Grace is staying with a family called Edwards," he reported to Frostbrook and Sophia when he returned to the boat. "They're cousins of her mother or something. Although apparently, she is no longer the duchess, despite some people still calling her that. She is now Mrs. Butler."

Sophia's breath caught. Frostbrook was almost afraid to look at her, but there was no pain in her widened eyes, only wonder, and admiration, and something very like laughter.

Her clear gaze turned on Frostbrook. "She did it. She married him. Is she *shunned*, Bridges?"

Bridges shrugged. "I don't believe so, miss. Apparently, she doesn't go into Society much, but she has plenty of visitors."

"Then let us be among them," Frostbrook murmured, holding out his hand to Sophia to help her rise. She still seemed frail, although she stood with ease. Bridges fetched her cloak, which Frostbrook took and placed about her shoulders, drawing the hood carefully over her hair.

"You need a hat," he said ruefully.

A smile flickered across her face. "It has not been a high priority in recent days."

Frostbrook wanted to take her in his arms and protect her from all the ills of the world. He wanted to beat West to a pulp for what he had done to her. He contented himself with a gentle kiss on her lips, and was gratified by the way her mouth clung to his. But it was not the moment for passion.

He stood back and offered her his arm.

Half an hour later, they were admitted to the unimposing house of Mr. and Mrs. Edwards. "Is Mrs. Butler at home?" Frostbrook inquired. "In private, if you please."

The manservant took Frostbrook's hat and Sophia's cloak, and passed them off to a maid. "This way, milord, madame." He led them along the hall and opened a door on the right. "Lord Frostbrook, Miss Wallace," he announced, and stood aside.

Irritably, Frostbrook wondered which part of "in private" the servant could have failed to understand, for at first glance, the drawing room was full of people, all of whom stopped talking to examine the newcomers. The gentlemen stood politely. Two of the ladies sprang to their feet in astonishment. One of them was the duchess—Mrs. Butler. The other, to Frostbrook's considerable surprise, was her stepdaughter, Lady Hera Severne. Was Hera not meant to be staying with friends in Lincolnshire?

"Sophia!" Mrs. Butler exclaimed.

However, by then Frostbrook had taken in the rest of the company, which included Major Butler and a strange gentleman he had never seen before, two more unknown ladies, and the unmistakable person of Sabrina Hartley.

Immediately, his protective instincts closed around Sophia like armor.

"Mrs. Butler." He bowed, as low as he would have to any

duchess. "I hope you don't mind my escorting Miss Wallace home? I wished to pay my respects."

Despite the late Cuttyngham's occasional remarks to the contrary, Frostbrook had always found the duchess to be quick-witted. Her gaze clashed with his for a mere instant while her social mask never slipped. Indeed, her smile widened and her hand came out at once as if to an old friend.

"You are most welcome, my lord. I had not realized you were in Brussels. Thank you for bringing Sophia back. I don't believe she is quite used to the town yet."

Thus she implied Sophia had been in Brussels already, and so could not have travelled with Frostbrook. Frostbrook bowed over her hand gratefully. He glimpsed the warm smile she bestowed on Sophia. She even touched her companion's hand, a subtle gesture of welcome and affection that the others might not have seen, but which seemed to surprise Sophia.

"Lady Hera," he murmured, bowing to the late duke's beautiful daughter. There was something different about her, though he could not quite put his finger on what it was.

The one-time duchess was performing the courtesies. "Come and let me introduce you to everyone, my lord. First, here is our kind hostess, Mrs. Edwards. Ma'am, this is Lord Frostbrook, an old friend of my late husband's."

Frostbrook bowed to a pleasant matron, perhaps in her early thirties, who smiled and murmured a gracious welcome.

Mrs. Butler turned next to Sabrina. "Are you acquainted with Lady Hartley?"

More intimately than she appeared to know. "Of course. Lady Hartley, a pleasure."

Despite his words, he kept his face cool and expressionless, not least because he had caught the speculative gleam in her eye as she stretched out one languid hand. There was nothing for it but to take her gloved fingers and bow over them.

"You must know Lady Hartley is one of our most famous hostesses in Brussels," Mrs. Butler said, turning to the youngest woman in the room. "And this is Miss Merton, Mrs. Edwards's niece."

The girl, a very young beauty with dancing eyes, rose and curtseyed with perfect grace. "My lord," she said demurely, although her eyes raked him with interest that was too frank for a debutante and yet somehow too impersonal for a flirt.

Rosamund Butler had moved on to the gentlemen. "Sir Arthur Astley." She presented an amiable-looking man in a well-tailored coat, who was a few years older than the rest of the company, perhaps in his late thirties. Sir Arthur smiled, rose, and bowed, though without meeting his gaze. The name Astley was familiar, although Frostbrook could not immediately recall why.

"And I believe you know my husband, Major Butler," Rosamund finished. There was no defiance or pleading in her voice, though he did sense the sudden tension in the room, as she must.

The world knew that the last time he and Butler met had been at the duel that killed the late duke. And that Frostbrook had been the duke's second. Frostbrook's main memory of Butler was of a stunned, devastated young man confronted with something he had done that he could never put right. Although he had not meant to kill His Grace, he had most certainly provoked and accepted the challenge.

Butler was a handsome devil, in a casual kind of a way. Frostbrook knew him to be good company, amusing, fun-loving, and reckless. An attractive hothead. That Rosamund Cuttyngham, neglected and isolated, should have fallen for him was not surprising. That she should have married him against all convention and what was considered decent feeling was truly astounding. Frostbrook hoped the man was responsible enough to realize it.

Butler rose and bowed slightly, with a stiffness that did not seem natural. Of course, he had no idea how Frostbrook regarded him. A word from Frostbrook now could explode the scandal, especially considering Sabrina's presence. Butler's steady gaze flickered to Rosamund and back, asking, Frostbrook could have sworn, for his consideration for her. Not for him. Behind that was a certain steely warning that may have been to do with Sophia. After all, Butler had no idea why his old friend should have turned up here in such rakish company.

Frostbrook held out his hand. "Butler. I was hoping to see you here. Congratulations on your nuptials."

Surprise flickered in Butler's eyes and was quickly drowned in a grin. He gripped Frostbrook's hand. "Thank you."

Rosamund was introducing Sophia to Lady Hartley as "my companion," as if everyone else in the room must know her—which, of course, they did not. Frostbrook's heart warmed to the former duchess. Quick-witted indeed. And it was interesting that the Edwards ladies and Astley happily followed her lead.

Frostbrook held the only vacant chair for Sophia, and then, though Butler moved as if to bring over another, he perched somewhat outrageously on the arm of Sophia's, a fact that was bound to be known around the entire British population of the town by sundown.

Butler sat down again. Mrs. Edwards had poured tea, which the niece, Miss Merton, ferried to Sophia and Frostbrook. A moment later she came back offering sandwiches and cake. Sophia declined with a faint smile. Frostbrook helped himself to a sandwich.

"You must know we are gay to dissipation here," Sabrina informed him. "Almost like the Congress of Vienna, I'm told! When you came in we were discussing the Duchess of Richmond's ball, the most important event of the month. If you don't already have a card, Frostbrook, you must obtain one. I shall tell Her Grace you are in town. And, of course, I shall send you a card for my own Venetian breakfast this week. I have persuaded Mrs. Butler and Mrs. Rivers that they might attend without offending the mourning conventions."

Who the devil was Mrs. Rivers?

"What brings you to Brussels, my lord?" Sabrina asked. "How

unlike you to be following the herd."

Frostbrook ignored the dig and swallowed the last of his sandwich. "A little annoying business," he replied, "leavened, I have every hope, with a little pleasure."

Sabrina gave a delighted yet shocked little laugh, as though he had made some innuendo. "Let us hope you are in luck, my lord," she drawled. "But I must be off." She rose to her feet, clearly disappointed that the allotted time span of her call was up, just when more opportunity for gossip had presented itself.

Mrs. Edwards sprang up with a shade too much alacrity. Sabrina was obviously not quite as welcome as she imagined.

"Frostbrook," she said, as though a new idea had just struck her. "Perhaps you might give me your escort? It is only a step or two, but my wretched husband has let me down again."

Frostbrook, annoyed to be manipulated, could not in courtesy refuse, even though he had just arrived. He rose, allowing weary tolerance into his posture as he glanced at Mrs. Edwards. "If I may trespass on your hospitality immediately after, ma'am? I bear messages from Mrs. Butler's stepson, the duke."

"Of course," Mrs. Edwards said, gesturing them both toward the door. Clearly, she meant to see them out. Lady Hartley sailed after her.

Frostbrook glanced at Sophia, who had suddenly tensed. She did not look at him, but as though she had spoken, he knew she was appalled at his leaving. Pity for this change in her, renewed fury at West, almost consumed him.

Somehow, he managed to bow. "Excuse me," he murmured. Passing Rosamund, he bent nearer and added below his breath, "Take care of Sophia. She is very…tired." He had time only to glimpse the startlement in her face before he followed the ladies out and offered his arm to his one-time mistress.

CHAPTER SIXTEEN

S OPHIA TRIED NOT to stare after him in panic. Even her
instinctive jealousy of Lady Hartley, who clearly considered
her of no account, took second place to the sheer enormity of his
leaving her.

Instead, she tried to focus on Rosamund and Hera, whom she
was trusting a great deal and yet who were, in reality, strangers to
her.

Rosamund jumped up and came to sit where the earl had
been, on the arm of the chair. "Why is Frostbrook so concerned
for you?" she demanded. "For your health? Sophia, are you ill?"

"No, no," Sophia said. She tried to smile. "I have merely had a
bit of an adventure, and I...I find I am quite tired." She hoped
Rosamund would understand that she could not speak among all
these people, most of whom she knew nothing about.

"You are very pale," Rosamund said, frowning. "You *have*
been ill, I think. I have just the tonic to help. But first, let me
assure you that you are among friends here. We all know most of
each other's secrets and we are souls of discretion, even Izzy
here."

Izzy, who was clearly the youthful Miss Merton, smiled amiably. "Well, I will probably tell Tom, because I tell him
everything, but don't worry, he won't repeat it either."

Sophia looked around for Tom, but there was only Giles,

looking somehow absurdly contented behind the more immediate frown of concern he was aiming at her. The older man was Sir Arthur, not Tom.

"Tom is Izzy's betrothed," Rosamund explained.

"Informally speaking," Mrs. Edwards said with a hint of anxiety. "Nothing is settled between their families. And in any case, he is in England."

"Oh," Sophia said, inadequately.

"Sophia, what has happened to you?" Giles burst out, his frown suddenly deepening as if he could be patient no longer. His good-natured eyes darkened. She had never seen him look so…murderous. "Did Frostbrook…?"

"No, no," Sophia said in distress. "Never think it! Lord Frostbrook is everything that is kind and gentlemanly, and he s-saved me." She broke off, appalled by the emotion cracking her voice. She swallowed convulsively, aware of Rosamund and Giles exchanging quick glances.

Rosamund took her hand. "Saved you from what, Sophia?" she asked gently.

Sophia drew in her breath, mainly to be sure it would not tremble. "Do you remember my cousin, Mr. West? He accosted us at the Coach and Horses inn, trying to…*persuade* me to return with him. You and Giles helped me get rid of him."

"I remember," Rosamund assured her.

"Well, he did not give up. He came to Cuttyngs, where Lord Frostbrook sent him about his business, and then we met again at a party, and he abducted me and made me so drunk I was unconscious. For days."

"Dear God," Rosamund whispered. "Did he…" She had lowered her voice to little more than a breath, but Sophia, understanding, quickly shook her hand.

"He wants to marry me," she said. "I have no idea why, for he certainly does not like me, let alone respect me. Aar…Lord Frostbrook thinks he has been embezzling from my funds and wants to cover that up while spending the rest of it. I don't know.

In any case, I managed to run away at Ostend and hide with a very kind fisherman and his mother, who looked after me. I wasn't very well. But his lordship found me and brought me to you, and I'm sorry, Rosamund, you must have enough to bear. I did not know you were married to Giles already. You know I am pleased for you."

Rosamund smiled. "I know you were the one who gave me the courage to pursue my happiness. Very well, to pursue Giles!"

"I'm not a fox," Giles protested, but distractedly. His attention was still focused on Sophia. "I'm so sorry, Sophia. I never guessed, even after we took you away from these people, how awful they truly were. I should never have left you there so long without at least calling to see."

"It is done now, and to be honest, even I did not see how truly awful they were until…" Sophia broke off and swallowed. "But I am very glad to find you all here."

Rosamund said brightly, "We have lots more to tell you. You won't know yet that Hera is married too, to Dr. Rivers, whom you met at Cuttyngs. It happened barely two days ago."

That inspired Sophia to smile, even to crow. "I knew there was something between you! Where is he?"

"He will be here for dinner," Hera said, blushing. Sophia hadn't known she could blush. "Mrs. Edwards keeps the most relaxed and generous table ever. And I think you should consult him, Sophia, for you still don't look well."

Rosamund eased her hip off the chair arm. "Come to my room and rest for a little, and you'll be better prepared for dinner."

Sophia hesitated, looking at Mrs. Edwards, who said happily, "I hope you will stay with us, Miss Wallace. Would you mind sharing with Izzy? I'll have them make up the other bed in her chamber." She frowned. "If his lordship is in need of accommodation, he can have the study, or share with Sir Arthur, perhaps…"

Sir Arthur looked somewhat alarmed, but Rosamund was leading Sophia from the room into blessed quiet.

"It is actually quite fun living here like this," Rosamund said. "Once you are up to it, you will agree. Izzy won't plague you. She is actually very kind and understanding. Without her, Giles would never have got out of England, you know."

"Of course," Sophia said, suddenly remembering the unlikely tales she had heard. "She is *that* Izzy."

"We met again in Dover, and her aunt and uncle, Mr. and Mrs. Edwards, brought me here on their yacht. And then, bless them, they took in Hera and Sir Arthur. I'll leave Hera to tell you Sir Arthur's tale."

"And Dr. Rivers?" Sophia asked. "Is it good that she is married to him?"

"Very good, I think. He understands her, and she dotes on him... But you will see for yourself."

"And His Grace approved?"

Rosamund paused with her hand on a door handle. She looked surprised. "I suppose he must have, for the special license was in order. Victor is very unlike his father. He *trusts* people. Well, when he has reason."

They were in a pleasant little sitting room. Another door led to a bedchamber beyond.

"I have the best rooms in the house," Rosamund said guiltily. "It probably would make more sense for you to have this sitting room to yourself than share Izzy's chamber." Her face flushed. "I just thought... Giles stays when he can, and I thought you might not be comfortable."

"I would not," Sophia agreed. She sat with some relief, for she did indeed feel exhausted. Then she glanced up quickly. "Not because I begrudge you happiness with Giles, because if I ever did, I do not now, In fact, I am—probably...sort of...betrothed to Lord Frostbrook."

"Sophia," Rosamund uttered, awed. "How did that come about? You must know he is the bane of every matchmaking mama's life. He has been avoiding them for years. Even I know that much." As she spoke, she took a bottle from a cabinet and poured a decent measure into a glass, which she brought to Sophia. "It is not a marriage of convenience, is it?"

Sophia wrinkled her nose and accepted the glass. "It's not very convenient for him, even if I do end up owning property." She sniffed the contents of the glass. "What is this?"

"Harmless and nutritious. Drink it."

Since she smelled no alcohol or anything else that reminded her of the nightmare journey, Sophia drank it. It tasted neither pleasant nor unpleasant.

Rosamund smiled and sat down beside her. "Now, tell me about Frostbrook before he comes back."

FROSTBROOK OFFERED HIS arm to Sabrina, but he felt no compulsion to extend the courtesy to conversation.

"I'm thrilled you came, Frost," she said after a long silence, her voice warm and husky in the way that had once aroused him.

"I cannot imagine why."

Her smile was arch. "Can't you?"

"No. There appears to be a surfeit of congenial company."

"You mean my husband," she said brazenly. "He need not concern you."

"He does not. And I didn't mean him. We parted in a civilized manner, Sabrina. Let us keep it that way."

"God, you're a cold-hearted devil, Frostbrook."

"Actually, I am not. On the contrary, I am about to be married."

Emotional warmth had never been part of what had been a very physical relationship, so he was somewhat surprised to see a flash of hurt and jealousy amongst her anger. Then she was in control once more. She even laughed.

"Good God. Never tell me your mama finally caught you for one of her insipid little protegees! Which one is it? The grasping

Miss Brandon, or the desperate cit's daughter? Or did you fly in the face of the wagers, as you are wont to do, and take the unknown beauty instead?"

Frostbrook regarded her dispassionately. "I don't recall your being this vulgar."

Color tinged her cheeks, but she did not back down. "Not proud enough of your bride to tell the world?" she mocked.

"Why, you are wrong on all counts, Sabrina. I am immensely proud to announce my engagement to Miss Sophia Wallace."

"Who?" Sabrina looked genuinely baffled, then her brows flew up. "*That* Miss Wallace? The *companion?*" She might have been describing a worm he had picked up on his shoe.

"She is more of a family friend to the duchess. I should say, to Mrs. Butler."

Sabrina's lips thinned and twisted before she forced them back into a smile. "I hope you do not expect me to keep this joke to myself, Frostbrook?"

"What joke? That you care two hoots whom I marry?"

She stared at him. A small spasm running through her arm told him she had realized what he meant. That if she showed any interest, let alone unkindness toward his betrothed, *she*, not Sophia, would be the joke. Her affair with him, after all, had been an open secret.

"You don't need to invite me to your Venetian breakfast," he said. "I am, after all, newly arrived in Brussels."

"Oh no, you absolutely must come," Sabrina said with a hint of savagery. "Bring your little bride-to-be and let the debutantes weep with bemusement."

He let a moment go by. "It was never my intention to make anyone weep, Sabrina."

"Tell your bride that, not me," she drawled, withdrawing her arm. "This is my house. I shall not keep you any longer from your duties, my lord. Goodbye."

He bowed. "My lady," he returned, and walked away with considerable relief.

Returning to the Edwards's house, he was fortunate enough to encounter Rosamund Butler in the hall. She came at once to meet him.

"How is Sophia?" he asked.

"Tired, as you say. I left her resting. She needs feeding up a little."

"She does," he agreed. He hesitated, then, "More than that. You probably know she does not trust easily, but this was family who hurt her. It's as if...as if she has no trust, no confidence in herself."

Rosamund's eyes widened slightly. He had surprised her, perhaps by his perception, perhaps just by caring. "It will come back," she said gently. "She is a strong person. She just needs a little time, and kindness. Particularly, it seems, she needs you."

He felt blood seep into his face and could only nod.

Rosamund said abruptly, "Is that why you engaged yourself to her?"

"No." It wasn't enough. Rosamund didn't know him, except as a friend of her unpleasant late husband's. She had no reason to trust him. *I love her.* Had he even said those words to Sophia? He could not think right now, but surely she should be the first to know. He cast around for other words to reassure Rosamund of his motives, but she was already nodding.

"Good," she said. "Sophia has been a great friend to me. And to Giles, when neither of us truly deserved her friendship. I like her."

It seemed he could smile. "So do I."

"In that case, I shall take you to her. If she is not asleep, you may have ten minutes."

"Thank you," he said gravely.

Sophia was not asleep when he walked into the room, Rosamund watching from the doorway. She sat curled on the sofa, a blanket over her, and when she smiled at him in welcome, his heart seemed to disintegrate. He went and sat beside her, taking her hand in his. With perfect trust, she laid her head on his shoulder and closed her eyes.

The duchess closed the door.

GILES WAS RETURNING to camp before dinner, but his frown betrayed his concern. Alone with his wife in the hall, he tapped his hat against his knees and said, "Will he care for her? How well do you know him?"

"I know him hardly at all," Rosamund admitted. "He was Cuttyngham's friend, or at least acquaintance. He came to the autumn balls and took the trouble to dance with me when there was no need. I think he was sorry for me, although he never said so."

"I thought him a decent man at the duel incident," Giles allowed, "but a cold fish. Sophia could not be happy with a cold fish."

"She seems pretty devoted to him. Besides, can one be a rake and a cold fish at the same time?"

He considered. "Perhaps it's the only way to be a rake, by caring nothing for any of the women you are with. Why would he be friends with someone as awful as Cuttyngham?"

"Politics, I think. And I believe they shared an interest in boats at one time. But seriously, Giles, I do not think he is cold. His concern for her comes from more than gentlemanly decency, I swear. He took her hand, and she laid her head on his shoulder as though he were all she needed ever. There must be warmth in him we cannot see. After all, no one who met the Duchess of Cuttyngham knew what I was like."

The frown vanished from Giles's brow, and he wrapped his arms around her. "I knew."

"You met Rosamund, not the duchess," she argued, returning his embrace with enthusiasm. "Perhaps Sophia has met the man rather than the earl."

"He certainly did not give up on her when she vanished from his house," Giles said. "And I am prepared to give him the benefit of the doubt—at the moment!—since he did not treat me like the man who murdered his friend."

"You did not murder anyone," Rosamund said stoutly. "He probably already knows Justin Rivers's theory about poison killing Cuttyngham."

"Perhaps," Giles said, "though I doubt there will ever be proof of it. It might be enough to get me off at trial, though."

"It might be enough to save you from a trial," Rosamund said, hugging him tighter.

He stroked her hair and kissed her. "That's all ages away. I'm on duty pretty constantly for the next couple of days, but I'll come back when I can. I might even make this wretched Venetian breakfast with you. Take care of yourself and Sophia."

"I will."

"Send a footman with her whenever she goes out," he added, frowning as he released her. "Because the other thing I really don't like is that the vile cousin is very probably in Brussels, too."

SOPHIA DOZED FOR half an hour in Frostbrook's company, feeling all was right with the world. When she came to, his arm around her and her brow against his throat, a tide of sheer happiness washed over her.

She inhaled the distinctive, male scent of his skin before raising her head to look at him. Her heart seemed to turn over when his lips quirked. Butterflies soared as she waited for him to kiss her.

"Better?" he asked softly.

She nodded. "Much."

"Then shall we go and rejoin the others? There is much to discuss."

There was. And she could not step back and let other people look after her mess, however tempting it might be. She might have been slightly piqued by his eagerness to swap their solitude for company—without kissing her—but she appreciated the comfort he had given her. So she rose, tidied her hair, and accompanied him to the drawing room once more.

Giles had left by then, but Dr. Rivers, now Lady Hera's husband, had appeared, along with their host, Mr. Edwards, who seemed to be an easygoing, generous man approaching middle years. Mr. Edwards had apparently made a fortune in trade and married a gently born wife.

"You'll stay for dinner, my lord?" he said to Frostbrook as soon as they were introduced. He did not seem overawed by the title, but then, he already housed a one-time duchess, a duke's daughter, and a baronet.

"Thank you, you are very kind," Frostbrook replied. He glanced at Mrs. Edwards. "If it puts you to no trouble, I should be delighted."

"No trouble at all," Mr. Edwards assured him. "In fact, my wife tells me we can put you up, too, though not in the sort of comfort you will be used to."

"Oh, I shan't impose to that extent. I have already made arrangements, though again I thank you."

Had he? What arrangements? Sophia had no time to ask him, for Izzy Merton appeared, chatting to Sir Arthur about the play they were going to see that evening.

"You are off to the theatre tonight?" Frostbrook asked the company, as a servant brought a tray full of sherry glasses.

Sophia's stomach twisted, and she turned away from the smell. She shook her head when the tray was offered to her.

"Well, Sir Arthur is escorting my wife and Izzy, so I am off the hook," Mr. Edwards said with a hint of glee. "I am looking forward to a quiet evening at home for once."

"Rosamund and I are guarding our mourning reputations," Lady Hera said sardonically. "But Sophia, if you wish to go—"

"No, no," Sophia said at once. "I still feel I could sleep for a week."

"You probably need to," Dr. Rivers said, presenting her with a glass of lemonade.

"I asked Justin to take a look at you," Hera said. "I think it is for the best."

"Thank you," Sophia managed. She felt somewhat over-whelmed by the kindness surrounding her, and yet it was the perfect antidote to the nightmare.

Dinner was an informal and enjoyable affair. Sophia learned something about Hera's adventures in Lincolnshire, where she had again met up with Dr. Rivers, and encountered Sir Arthur, whom, for some reason, she called George. Rosamund suggested a little light shopping for the following day.

"You can't," Sophia said. "People always seem to be buying me clothes, which I keep abandoning for one reason or another."

"It may have escaped your attention," Rosamund said, "but I have not actually paid you any salary."

Sophia stared at her. "I have not actually done any work! I was your companion for about three days."

"Three very important days for me," Rosamund replied. "And I know you were working on the dower house. Don't misunderstand me, that dress is most becoming, but you need more than one."

A little later, they discussed Dr. Rivers's theory about Cut-tyngham having been poisoned before the duel. Sophia straightened suddenly.

"We found the mysterious lady who observed it all," she recalled. "Her name is Olivia Rainey, and she is Mr. Anthony Severne's natural daughter."

Rosamund and Hera exchanged glances. They were much closer now, Sophia thought, than those few weeks ago at Cuttyngs.

"Then she was only at the inn to see Anthony?" Dr. Rivers sounded a shade disappointed.

"Doesn't explain why she watched the duel," Sir Arthur pointed out.

"Curiosity," Sophia said. "I would probably do the same if I knew about a duel and could not prevent it."

Rosamund and Hera nodded thoughtfully.

"Then she saw nothing that would either confirm or deny that the duke was poisoned?" Dr. Rivers said.

"She never saw His Grace eat or drink anything at all," Aaron said. "But then, she was never in his company. She was only ever with Anthony. I do not even know that Cuttyngham was aware of her existence."

"We were not," Rosamund said.

"But Victor was," Hera said. "Though I doubt he knew her name. So perhaps my father did know of her. Not that he would have cared."

"Sadly, this does not aid Major Butler's cause," Aaron said.

Dr. Rivers frowned at him. "Did you believe her?" He looked from Aaron to Sophia.

Aaron shrugged. "I have no reason not to. She appeared to be a lady in every sense of the word."

"I liked her," Sophia admitted. "Besides, why would she lie?"

No one answered, although for a moment she thought Aaron was about to. Then Izzy squealed and declared they would be late for the theatre. She and her aunt sprang up and bolted for the door with apologies and excuses and promises not to wake Sophia if she was asleep when they returned.

CHAPTER SEVENTEEN

SOPHIA WOKE THE next morning feeling much more like herself.

Dr. Rivers had examined her after dinner the previous evening and asked her many questions before pronouncing her well on the road to full recovery. He approved Rosamund's tonic and bade her speak to him if she felt any further ill effects.

"And your state of mind?" he had asked quite naturally.

She had swallowed, for the admission was difficult. "I am tired. Nervous. Ever since he found me, I panic whenever Aar…Lord Frostbrook leaves the room, even though I know I'm being foolish."

"You are not panicking now," Dr. Rivers had pointed out.

"That is true," she had agreed, much struck.

And indeed, parting from Aaron last night had not been the terror she had expected. She was more annoyed that they had had no more time alone together, that he had left the company with no private farewell and no greater intimacy than a brief kiss to her fingers. So, she had retired somewhat disgruntled to the comfortable bed made up for her in Izzy's chamber, and almost immediately fallen asleep.

She rose in search of breakfast, leaving Izzy in blissful slumber in the other bed. She had not even heard the girl come in.

Rosamund and Sir Arthur greeted her in the little breakfast

parlor.

"You are looking much better," Rosamund said.

"I do feel stronger," Sophia said with a quick smile, helping herself to fresh bread, cold meats, and cheese.

"Excellent," Rosamund said. "Strong enough for the dressmaker?"

"I am happy to escort you, ladies," Sir Arthur said gallantly.

He was a strange mixture of courtliness and an almost childlike bluntness. Sophia rather liked him, and was as happy as Rosamund to accept his escort.

"Do we need the footman as well?" Sophia asked, when the servant followed them out the door.

"Yes," Rosamund said. "Your vile cousin could well be in town, and he probably knows you would come to me. I'm afraid my notoriety means everyone knows where I live."

A claw of fear swiped at Sophia's stomach, but she would not give in. She would not allow William to dictate her life one iota further than he already had.

When they emerged from the dressmaker's—Rosamund having ordered for Sophia two morning dresses, two evening dresses, a ball gown, and two hats—they were hailed by an acquaintance of Rosamund's.

"Ah, Your Grace!" The lady laughed at her mistake. "Mrs. Butler, I should say, of course! How are you? I hope I might still count on you to attend my musical evening?"

"I am looking forward to it," Rosamund assured her. "Are you acquainted with my friend, Miss Wallace?"

The lady smiled. "I don't believe so. How do you do, Miss Wallace?"

"Mrs. Kirkwood," Rosamund introduced the musical hostess. "I believe Hera and the Edwardses are going to Mrs. Kirkwood's party this evening, too." She turned back to Mrs. Kirkwood. "Miss Wallace is also staying with Mrs. Edwards."

"Then I hope you will come too, Miss Wallace," Mrs. Kirkwood said with a dazzling smile. "If the duchess can spare you.

Good morning!"

"You should come," Rosamund said as they made their way home. She glanced surreptitiously at Sophia. "Lord Frostbrook is bound to be there."

Sophia, who doubted that, hoped she would not have to wait so long to see her betrothed. However, it was well into the afternoon before he called at the Edwards's house, although he had sent a note to Rosamund first thing this morning, inquiring after Sophia's health.

Why to Rosamund? Why can he not write to me?

An answer hit her like a blow. *Because he longer wishes to be betrothed.*

But no, that was nonsense. She trusted him, and he had already gone out of his way to look after her, to care for her with every tenderness. If it was not quite love, she had reason to hope for that, too. She knew she was unique in his life, and she treasured that.

With her silly doubts squashed, she was delighted to see him when he walked into the drawing room that afternoon, all cool, aristocratic elegance. For some reason, she thought of the ride at Wellis, and those few blistering moments when he had snatched her in his arms and kissed her with such abandon. *That* was what she wanted now.

But though his eyes warmed gratifyingly as soon as he saw her, he made no effort to walk with her alone, even in the garden. He did not even sit beside her on the sofa, but on the chair next to it.

"Are you attending Mrs. Kirkwood's musical evening?" Rosamund asked him.

"I think she sent a card," he replied without much interest. He appeared preoccupied, a little distant, as he had been at Cuttyngs.

"You should go," Rosamund said. "Hera and Sophia and I will attend with the Edwardses. And Sir Arthur, of course."

His instant smile was balm to Sophia's anxious soul. "In that case, I shall be there as your betrothed."

To Sophia's relief, the first evening gown was delivered on time, duly altered to fit her perfectly. Not that she particularly wanted to be in any company but Aaron's, but she understood his need to make things proper for her. Besides, now that she felt more the thing, she was happy to be acknowledged as his future bride.

Accordingly, with the help of Rosamund's maid, the redoubtable Perry, who had turned much more human since Sophia had last seen her, she dressed in the newly delivered evening gown. The ladies were escorted by both Mr. Edwards and Sir Arthur. Dr. Rivers, who was busy preparing for the inevitable results of battle, did not go with them, but even so, they needed two carriages to travel, each with two footmen on the step at the back. It seemed a large number of men to deal with William, but Sophia was touched by everyone's care.

Mrs. Kirkwood's apartments were graced with a large drawing room, in which her guests gathered for their musical treats. When Sophia and her companions arrived, seats had been arranged in rows at the front of the room, with aisles between, but everyone was mingling in the back half of the room, enjoying glasses of wine with their chatter. The voices were loud, and yet faded as Sophia's party entered and nearly everyone turned to stare.

Were they staring at Rosamund, who had married her husband's supposed killer less than a month after his death? With the support of the Duchess of Richmond, and apparently of the Duke of Wellington himself, Rosamund's unconventional behavior was being tolerated in Society, though she was wary of drawing further attention to herself. So why was everyone staring now? Had Anthony Severne or someone else stirred up more trouble?

Suddenly Lord Frostbrook stood in front of them, bowing with incomparable elegance. Rosamund gave him her hand, as did Hera. The others, smiling in greeting, walked on, and Frostbrook turned to Sophia. The mask of his face, the cold correctness of his stance, told her he was aware of being observed. And as Rosamund and Hera moved on, she realized everyone was looking at *her*. Because she had captured that most elusive of marital prizes, the Earl of Frostbrook?

Heat flared into her face, but she tilted her chin and offered him her hand. A gleam of humor in his eyes relieved her tension, and she found she could smile back. He took her arm, guiding her through the throng, and helped her to a glass of lemonade. She was grateful, for she still could not tolerate alcohol of any kind.

"You look much better," he murmured. "In fact, delightful."

"Thank you. Is it normal to gawp at engaged couples in society?"

"I suspect S…someone has been stirring the pot," he said with a noticeable hesitation. "Refuse to be drawn, if you are questioned. Keep everything vague, as we discussed." His voice as well as his expression betrayed only fastidious distaste. It was not aimed at her, and yet she could not help feeling oddly deflated as he conducted her to a seat beside Rosamund and sat next to her.

The music began, provided first by a young violinist who played exquisitely, tugging at the heartstrings. For a time, Sophia managed to lose herself in the music. But as the piece finished and she turned impulsively to Aaron, his place was empty. Gazing around the room, she found him at the side near the door, leaning one broad shoulder against the wall as he spoke to Lady Hartley.

The lady touched his arm, a brief gesture, and yet somehow it betrayed intense familiarity. Intimacy.

Hastily, Sophia dragged her gaze free and tried to listen to Rosamund. Her world, suddenly, was in turmoil. She remembered Lady Hartley from yesterday's arrival at the Edwards's house, but she had been feeling too strange and unwell to pay a great deal of attention. Now, she remembered the woman's brief exchanges with Aaron, her somewhat insolent demand to be escorted home, and knew without doubt that this woman had been close to him. Closer than Sophia ever had—in a physical sense, at least.

Jealousy was a strange, ugly emotion. She had always been aware of women in his life, shadowy and unimportant to her because she knew he had not cared as he did for her. But this woman was not a shadow. Lady Hartley was possessive flesh and blood, and all Sophia's trust in Aaron, all her belief and serenity, flew out of the window when that woman touched him.

"Sophia?" Rosamund said, low. "Are you well? Is this too much? Shall we go home?"

And leave that woman in possession of the field? Absolutely not! Sophia tried to laugh at herself and couldn't quite manage it, though at least it brought some kind of smile to her lips while she wrestled the ridiculous emotions back under control.

Her shock was foolish. She should have been prepared to encounter in person women from his past. The important word was *past*. Sophia was his present and his future, as he was hers.

"No, I am fine," she said to Rosamund, and the sound of her own steady voice calmed her further. The storm of feeling had taken her by surprise, but she would be ready to weather it next time.

Rosamund, in her peculiar position of recent widow and new bride, did not rise to mingle with the throng, so Sophia remained with her. Izzy brought them each a plate of elegant nibbles and dashed off again with a smile. Other people sat down around them to exchange views of the violinist or discuss the latest rumors about Wellington's imminent advance on France, as opposed to the other rumors that Bonaparte had left Paris and was advancing on the allied army.

Rosamund introduced Sophia to each of them as Lord Frost-brook's betrothed, but though they all smiled at her and cordially wished her happy, Sophia had the feeling they already knew. One made a joke about the elusive earl finally being so sweetly trapped, which irritated Sophia more than it should. She did not want him trapped. She wanted him happy.

When she glanced about her at the larger crowd, she frequently caught other gazes. People were watching her, gossiping, which she should have been prepared for and could have ignored, if only she had not caught so many of the same look. A kind of curious amusement mingled with…pity.

Why should they pity her for marrying the Earl of Frostbrook?

None of it mattered, and she would not have cared if only Aaron had been beside her, but he was not. She didn't know where he was.

"Miss Wallace, I'm so glad you could join us tonight." Their hostess, Mrs. Kirkwood, glided into the chair beside Sophia's, which had only just been vacated. "What did you think of my violinist?"

"I think he is wonderful," Sophia replied honestly.

"He is, isn't he? Such a find. I hope you will like my soprano just as much. She has the voice of an angel."

"I look forward to hearing her."

Mrs. Kirkwood smiled. "I am sure you do. I had not realized when we met this morning that you are the brave lady who has taken on Frostbrook."

"I am not aware of any bravery," Sophia said as lightly as she could manage, for she had seen that flash of eager pity and veiled humor in her hostess's eyes.

Mrs. Kirkwood smiled back with sympathy. She touched Sophia's shoulder gently with her fan in a kind, encouraging way. "No, you wouldn't be. So charming. From the country, I gather?"

Why did that matter? Was she implying a bucolic ignorance, a lack of sophistication? Sophia pasted a smile on her lips. "Indeed. Aren't we all?"

Mrs. Kirkwood emitted a musical peal of laughter, as though Sophia had been wondrously witty. "Charming," she pronounced once more, rising to her feet. "Quite charming. But I must shoo my guests back to their places to hear my songbird. I hope you enjoy her!"

As Mrs. Kirkwood bustled off, and a general movement toward the chairs commenced, Rosamund murmured, "What was that about?"

"I don't know," Sophia replied.

"Gossip is inevitable. Especially in such an enclave of the English in a foreign land. Just smile and hold the line, as Giles would say."

Frostbrook slid into the seat beside her, large as life and sleek as a cat. "All well?" he asked, his voice cool, urbane as always in public. It annoyed her, and yet its very timbre aroused her too, as it always had.

"Of course," she replied, and though she felt his gaze on her face, she did not look at him. She did not want to ask him where he had been, what he had been doing. Fortunately, Mrs. Kirkwood was introducing the soprano by then, and there was no time to talk.

This time, she knew exactly when he slipped away, during the soprano's last song, but she did not follow him with her eyes. She did not risk looking until a few minutes later, when she turned her head toward the end of the seating row. She did not see Aaron, but a tall, good-looking young man who caught her gaze and smiled at her. There was no pity, no speculation, merely admiration and a certain beguiling mischief. For some reason, though she did not return his smile—they had not been introduced—it made her feel better.

The singer, who truly did have a beautiful, almost haunting voice, received rapturous applause. Then everyone began to mill about again. Sir Arthur led Rosamund, Hera, and Sophia to a quiet corner, and toddled off to find them wine and lemonade.

"Just think," Rosamund murmured. "I used to yearn to attend such events."

"I did attend them, by the score," Hera said. "But at least the music is good."

"Is that why you came?" Sophia asked.

A funny little smile, half embarrassed, half defiant, crossed Lady Hera's face. "Partly. Mostly, it passes the time when Justin is gone. I am an unfashionable wife."

I will be, too… And there was Aaron, at last, strolling toward them with his distinctive haughty grace that so drew the eye, even among those who were used to him. There was no sign of the vulnerability behind the social mask, but Sophia knew it was there, part of the whole complicated man whom she loved.

Her tensions, her foolish jealousies of a past that could not be changed, fell away. Her heart beat with anticipation, with gladness. And then from nowhere, Lady Hartley fell into step with him, taking his arm in a gesture far too familiar to be merely possessive. She had done so many times before, clearly, and he, equally clearly, had no objections to her presence. He inclined his head, and they changed direction, away from Sophia.

She swung away from the unbearable sight and almost bumped into a man. The same admiring man with the mischievous eyes she had caught watching her during the soprano's performance.

"Rupert Grande," he said.

The name seemed familiar for some reason, but her mind was much too full of Aaron to think of the context.

"And I know you are Miss Wallace," he continued. "I hoped we could pretend to be already introduced, since I am acquainted with your companions. How do you do?"

"Very well, how do *you* do?"

"Oh, excellently. Not a great admirer of these kinds of affairs, but the Kirkwoods' hospitality is legendary. Have you tried these pastries?"

Only then did she realize he held a small plate between them. She blinked at it. "Why, no, I don't believe…"

"Try one," he insisted. "Best to lean forward or the pastry will flake all over your beautiful gown. Someone else will sweep the floor, thank the good Lord."

There was something natural and insouciant about Rupert Grande that was appealing in this incomprehensible company. So, she took a dainty little pastry from his plate, leaned forward as advised, and bit into it. It was delicious. Crumbs of pastry fluttered to the floor.

"A master," Grande said. "Shall we walk?"

Sophia, swallowing the last of the pastry, glanced at Rosamund and Hera, who were talking to acquaintances, and then to the place she had last seen Aaron. He was once again alone and walking somewhat purposely toward her.

Some devil prompted her to turn away as though she had not seen him and smile up at Grande. "Why not?" she said, and laid her hand on his sleeve.

CHAPTER EIGHTEEN

WHEN SABRINA TOOK his arm so familiarly, Frostbrook exerted huge effort not to shake her off like a spider fallen from the ceiling. But he was only too aware of the avid eyes watching his every move. Sophia had seen his approach and Sabrina's intervention, and he cursed himself—again—for not having warned her.

"Just the man I wished to see," Sabrina drawled, just loudly enough to be heard by several surrounding people. "You will escort me to the table, will you not? I am dying of thirst."

In all courtesy, he could hardly refuse without causing precisely the talk he was trying to prevent, and so he turned away from Sophia, though not before he had seen the stricken look in her eyes.

Fury, as much at himself as at Sabrina's malice, surged within him. Only with difficulty did he keep the mask in place.

"The whole world talks of your engagement, Frost," she said fondly.

"Thank you for making sure of it," he returned, lest she imagine he did not know exactly what she had done. "Though it must be said, Sabrina, your world is very *small*."

A frown flickered on her face, though the smile somehow remained in place. "What on earth can you mean?"

"I thought you knew," he said, swiping up a glass of wine

from the table and leaning close to present it to her, "not to play games with me."

He was gratified to see the flash of fear in her eyes as her fingers closed automatically around the stem of the glass. He stepped back, inclined his head, and walked away. He needed to speak to Sophia at once, so he was glad to see she still stood in the same place, close to Rosamund and Hera. Then he saw Lord Rupert Grande right beside her, and the blood froze in his veins.

But she had seen Frostbrook, at least. She knew he was coming. She smiled, the bright, brittle smile of the socialite. Deliberately, she took Grande's arm and walked away.

Had Frostbrook not been so afraid for her, the pain in his heart would have devastated him. As it was, he could only see to her safety. Fortunately, as he approached Rosamund and Hera, they moved away from their companions toward him.

"Will you stand by the door?" he asked. "Don't let her leave with him."

"With whom?" Rosamund asked, peering around the room.

"Grande!"

"Lord Rupert?" Hera said. "Don't be silly. He won't hurt her. I know him."

"So do I," Frostbrook said grimly.

"No, seriously, my lord," Hera argued. "He only flirts—at least with gently born girls. He married Justin and me only a few evenings ago."

Frostbrook paused, frowning. "Did he? I didn't know that. My concern is—" He glanced around and lowered his voice further. "It was Grande whom West took her to in London to marry her by force, only Grande was here in Brussels. Grande is the reason West brought her here. They must have some kind of agreement."

"I can't imagine it," Hera said, though she was already moving casually in the direction of the door.

Sophia and Grande were at the other side of the room. She was laughing, damn him.

Rosamund laid her hand on his sleeve. "Wait, don't rush after them. I have a feeling there is enough talk in this room."

"There is," Frostbrook said with distaste.

"Do enlighten us, for I cannot help feeling Hera and I are the only ones who don't know."

He dragged his gaze back to them and curled his lip. "Apparently, it is the latest *on-dit*, and the greatest joke, that I have engaged myself to an innocent who has no idea that I am carrying on my affair with another, more sophisticated lady under her nose."

Rosamund held his gaze. "Are you?"

"No," he said savagely. "We had parted even before Cuttyngham died, but why let a little truth get in the way of spite? I would ignore it myself, only part of the joke seems to be to drop oblique hints to Sophia on the subject and see if she notices. I think she does."

"So that is what our hostess was up to," Rosamund murmured. "I did wonder."

"She is quite thick with Lady Hartley," Hera said, making it clear that she knew exactly who the mistress in question was.

"Could you not have intervened?" he snapped.

"Forgive me," Rosamund said. "But is it not *your* task to protect her from the consequences of your own past? Instead, you have hardly been near her, which has hardly squashed the rumors. And believe me, Sophia noticed that."

Frostbrook felt the blood drain from his face. "I was looking out for West in the vicinity, outside and in. And tracing the rumors. I did not—" He broke off and swallowed. It was a long time since he had felt like a badly behaved schoolboy. "It seems I am not as clever as I imagined."

Both women regarded him with more kindness than he deserved.

"When I first became mistress of Cuttyngs," Rosamund said, "I had to learn to delegate. You have marshalled your forces, Frostbrook. Now you must use them, not leave them kicking their heels in barracks while the enemy infiltrates."

Later, when he had made everything right, he thought he might be amused by Rosamund's use of military metaphors since she had married Major Butler. At this moment, all his concern was for Sophia.

"You are right," he said with difficulty. Near the doorway, he nodded curtly and walked away. Forcing himself to discretion, he circulated among the guests with bows and nods and the occasional greeting so that he could come upon Sophia and Grande as though by accident.

Once, what seemed a lifetime ago, he had told Sophia to believe in his fidelity. He thought she had, that she did, but he had to acknowledge his tactics this evening had been wrong. As Rosamund had pointed out, he should have used his troops—the Edwardses, Sir Arthur, even Rosamund and Hera—to reconnoiter, while he guarded his bride from the malice of his one-time mistress.

With perfect timing, he turned aside from a group of old acquaintances just as Sophia and Lord Rupert Grande were walking past.

"Ah, there you are," Frostbrook said blandly. "I was afraid I had lost you."

"Drat you, Frost," Grande said amiably. "And here was I trying to cut you out. It seems I must worship from afar after all."

"Not too far, I hope." Sophia sounded amused.

"Oh, so do I!" Lord Rupert grinned and took her hand to bow over it before sauntering on his way.

Frostbrook offered his arm instead. Did he imagine her slightest hesitation before she took it?

"You must be careful of him," Frostbrook said, the words coming out rather more coldly than he had intended. Where was his much-vaunted grace and confidence now?

"On the contrary," Sophia replied. "He is the first person I have encountered here who is both pleasant and natural." She shrugged. "He is full of nonsense, of course, but he is harmless."

He frowned down at her. "You do know who he is?"

"Of course I do," she said impatiently. "And you of all people should have some sympathy with exaggerated reputations."

He had no idea what to say to that, at least not where he might be overheard. His glacial mask slipped into place, protecting them both, and yet he was aware of some hidden, deep-seated panic, as though, inevitably, she were slipping through his fingers and he had no means of preventing it.

LORD RUPERT GRANDE was not best pleased to receive a visitor before eleven in the morning, but good nature prevented him from throwing the fellow out. They had been at school together for a time, though Rupert couldn't remember them ever being friends. At any rate, West seemed to imagine the very fact meant Rupert owed him favors.

Not that Rupert minded the odd favor, especially if it involved no exertion on his part. Though it seemed a lot of effort on West's part to have left England and come to Brussels simply to find someone who would marry him to his cousin.

"Dash it, old boy," he said, after dowsing his head in the washing bowl and shaking it like a dog, "I'm happy to perform the ceremony, but you haven't got the bride."

"Lady Hartley's Venetian breakfast tomorrow," West said impatiently. "I presume you will be there?"

Rupert picked a handful of unanswered cards of invitation of the mantelpiece and raked through them. "Got a card," he said, waving it at him. "Wasn't going to bother, though. Breakfast is not my thing."

"For once, I would be obliged if you could see your way to attending. I understand her ladyship has a large garden that would make a pleasant background for a wedding."

Rupert paused, dredging up the earlier part of the evening

before from his erratic memory. "I need to give up the brandy. Stick to wine. What did you say your cousin's name was again?"

"Wallace," West said with exaggerated patience. "Sophia Wallace. It is on the special license."

"That's what I thought you'd said. Met her last night." And it seemed to him that something damned havey-cavey was going on. Who would rather marry West than the Earl of Frostbrook? There was no accounting for women's tastes, of course, and Frostbrook *could* be a tad stuffy at times, but he had humor and Rupert rather liked him.

He'd quite liked the girl, too.

"Then you'll be there?" West said.

Rupert sighed. "Very well. But you might have to come and get me. Even if I have eschewed the brandy."

"That will be no trouble at all," West said with a rueful smile. "In fact, I was hoping you would take me as your guest. Along with my mother and sister."

Rupert gazed at him. "Not my party, Westie."

"You're a marquis's son, a charming fellow, and a known eccentric," West said impatiently. "My mother and sister are perfectly respectable, and naturally they wish to attend the wedding. And we shall need witnesses."

"Why doesn't Miss Wallace get them invited, then?"

West smiled, a lying kind of smile. "I don't believe Lady Hartley cares much for her."

She didn't, but the reason for that made no sense with West's plans. Something *very* havey-cavey was going on. Not that Rupert necessarily objected to havey-cavey. On the contrary, it piqued his erratic curiosity.

"So you'll do it?" West nagged.

Rupert scratched his head and rubbed at the back of his neck. "Unless you hear from me before, come and get me tomorrow morning," he said at last. "Lady Hartley won't mind a few extra guests, especially new people. Now please do a fellow a favor and shab off while he deals with his sore head."

IT WAS NOT Lord Frostbrook but Rosamund who explained the strange atmosphere of Mrs. Kirkwood's party to Sophia. Frostbrook had looked so cold and forbidding for the rest of the evening that Sophia had refused to ask him, not from intimidation but from pique. Which meant she then spent a miserable night regretting her behavior and worrying that Frostbrook truly had changed his mind and heart.

So the following morning, she bearded Rosamund in her sitting room and asked her outright what had been going on at the party. And Rosamund told her.

Sophia gazed at her in astonishment. "But that is childish, spiteful, and ridiculous. What on earth does Lady Hartley expect to accomplish?"

"A great deal if Frostbrook went along with it, whether from inertia or amusement."

Did he? The words stuck in her throat, because she knew he had not. It was his silence that hurt, the fact that he had not even discussed the matter with her.

"Of course not," Rosamund said, as though she had spoken aloud. "He was furious with her."

"Then why did he walk off on her arm?" Now it was she who sounded childish.

"To tell her so, no doubt. At any rate, he left her fast enough, by which time you had swanned off with Rupert Grande. Talking of Lord Rupert—"

"He hardly came near me all evening."

Rosamund knew she did not mean Grande. "That was a mistake," she allowed. "But he was trying to look out for you, searching for any sign of your cousin or any spies or bravos he might have hired, and then tracing the source of the rumor about him and Lady Hartley. Besides, once he realized the damage, he stayed with you until we left."

He might as well not have, for he had been so stiff and haughty that her only course had seemed to be to present a similar front to him.

Rosamund said, "I think…I think this is new to him, too, Sophia. He is not used to looking after anyone but himself. He is not used to caring, to loving as he loves you."

Tears started to Sophia's eyes so quickly that she had to spring up from her chair and walk away to hide them. "I know this," she said unsteadily. "And yet I let him behave as he did, and I made it worse. What if he—"

"Women are not helpless," Rosamund interrupted. "It was a revelation to me, and you reminded me of it when I needed the push. I am returning the favor."

Sophia swung back to her, frowning.

Rosamund smiled. "This has happened to you both very quickly. You are bound to face misunderstandings and bumps in your journey. But if you love him—"

"I do," Sophia whispered. "Oh, I do…"

"Then I think you know what is in his heart, too. Don't waste the knowledge."

With a breath of laughter, Sophia sat down and pressed her knuckles against her eyelids. "This is idiocy."

"Yes. When he calls, you may tell him so. And no, you can't go barging off to his hotel."

"Because someone will see me?" she asked with contempt.

"And because your cousin might. You need a gentleman escort and a footman wherever you go, remember?"

Sophia subsided. She had no wish to encounter William again. The nightmare was still too close.

On the other hand, pacing around the house and garden waiting for Aaron to call grew quickly intolerable. Her hope that he would come before luncheon was dashed. Nor did he come after. Was she going to have to wait for the *damnable* Venetian breakfast at that woman's house tomorrow morning before she could speak to him?

After luncheon, Hera went off with Dr. Rivers. Izzy and her mother were making calls, escorted by Sir Arthur. Mr. Edwards was nowhere to be seen, and Rosamund was busy in the kitchen with evil-smelling herbs and potions. Sophia could have screamed with frustration.

The sounds of voices in the hall at last brought her drawing room pacing to a halt. One of the occupants of the house returned? Or a caller? *Aaron?*

Hastily, she smoothed her hair and draped herself gracefully on the sofa, snatching up the book she had been failing to concentrate on all day.

The servant appeared, presenting her with a card. "Milord requests your company to walk in the park."

Not Milord Frostbrook, she saw with a sinking heart as she blinked at the card. Lord Rupert Grande.

Where are you, Aaron?

She could stand this no longer. Perhaps he would be here when she got back.

"I will come now."

FROSTBROOK, HAVING FINALLY tracked West and his family down to a very second-rate hotel on the outskirts of the city, beyond the old walls, debated whether to give in to his instincts and beat the man to a pulp now. Or whether to wait for news from England and simply ruin him. As far as Frostbrook was concerned, West deserved both for what he had done to Sophia, for what they had all done to Sophia, and his fists itched to punish.

Curiously enough, it was also thoughts of Sophia herself that stayed him. He doubted she would approve of the barbarity of his instincts. She certainly would not like the ensuing scandal if he were charged with assault or even murder. There would be no easy House of Lords trial for him here.

No, he would watch and protect.

"Here." He summoned an urchin in French and dropped a coin into his filthy paw. "Do you know an English gentleman staying at the hotel?" West and his family would surely stand out in such a place.

The boy nodded vigorously and drew himself up in a recognizably good impression of West in full pride as Frostbrook had seen him at the dower house in Cuttyngs, trying to justify his actions.

Frostbrook smiled. "That's the fellow. Well, if you keep your eye on him and tell me exactly where he goes and whom he talks to, even who visits him if you can, I'll give you another coin for each name and place."

The child looked awed. "No problem, monsieur. When will you come back?"

"Tonight or tomorrow morning. Or it might be my servant who comes, but he will pay you just as I would."

On that understanding, he left the boy staring at the hotel as though willing West to emerge, and returned to the town via the nearest gate. Frostbrook drove himself straight to the Edwards's house and alighted, conscious of hunger and an overwhelming need to see Sophia.

Annoyingly, there was no sign of Bridges, who was supposed to be watching the house. He knocked sharply on the door, asked for someone to take care of his horses and curricle, and to be shown to Miss Wallace.

Someone immediately darted out to hold the horses. The remaining footman said, "Miss Wallace is out with an English milord."

Fear spiked through his heart. "*Which* English milord? Mr. Edwards? Sir Arthur?"

"No, no." The footman frowned. "Milord…Rupert."

Oh dear God. "Where did they go?" Frostbrook demanded. "Think, man! Which direction? When?"

"Ten minutes ago. That way," the footman answered, clearly aggrieved by Frostbrook's manner. "And they go to the park."

"Why aren't you with them?" Frostbrook said between his teeth.

"Because Francois went instead."

Thank God for that, at least. He nodded curtly, turned on his heel, and strode smartly off in the direction of the park.

It was not far. The main trouble was the size of the park and how to find two people among the throngs who tended to walk there. And since it was full of British people, he could not walk too smartly or look too worried as he scoured the paths.

At last, he saw them strolling toward him, arm in arm.

Frostbrook found himself short of breath and almost incandescent with fury, all spiked with some other fierce pain he could not name.

Yes, he could. It was jealousy.

He had never been jealous in his life before, but seeing Sophia so comfortable and friendly with an attractive young man was like an open wound. Only his astonishment at the strength of his own emotion held him in check.

He felt his whole body stiffen and tense as they both caught sight of him. Sophia did not smile, but neither did her feet falter, and as she came closer, he saw something desperate in her eyes that might have been hope or gladness.

Or was he deluding himself?

"Cutting you out again," Grande said amiably.

"Not any longer, I'm afraid," Frostbrook managed without even glancing at the other man. "I've come to escort Sophia home."

Her eyes changed at once, and he knew he had been too high-handed. He had not meant to, but he recognized he was treating her like a naughty child, and in public. Mistake upon mistake upon mistake...

She would insist on returning in her own time, and he was miserably aware that she was quite right to do so. Would some kind of mitigating explanation or apology work? He had to get her away from Grande, and yet the steel in her eyes told him she would not give in.

Until, entirely unexpectedly, Grande took the wind out of both their sails.

"Excellent," he said. "I was hoping for a word with you, Frost. Got something important to discuss."

Sophia, looking outraged, dropped Grande's arm. Frostbrook used the moment to place her hand on his arm instead, holding it in place with a gentle, pleading caress as they walked back the way he had just come. He was aware of her staring at him with incomprehension, but at least she did not withdraw her hand.

Grande ambled along beside them, making odd bits of small talk until they reached the Edwards's house. Rosamund, white-faced, met them in the hall, her gaze flying to each of them in turn.

"Thank God," she said.

"As you say," Frostbrook agreed. "Do you suppose Grande and I could use the breakfast parlor? Just to be private for a few minutes. We'll join you afterward in the drawing room, if you permit?"

"Permit?" Rosamund said dryly. "I insist."

Sophia looked furious, which hardly calmed Frostbrook's anger against Grande as he all but shoved the unlikely clergyman into the breakfast parlor and closed the door.

Quite casually, Grande left him the place at the head of the table and sat in the chair next to it.

Frostbrook remained standing, gazing down at him. "How might I help you?" he asked with cold courtesy.

"I find myself," Grande said ruefully, "in something of a moral dilemma."

Frostbrook raised one eyebrow. "Is that not more your area of expertise than mine?"

Grande wrinkled his nose. "Hardly. The world knows I'm a terrible clergyman and would never have been ordained at all if my father's blood didn't run in my veins. Still, I like to help out, if I can." He met Frostbrook's gaze. "Only a few days ago, I tied the knot for Lady Hera and Rivers. They had a special license and seemed in a hurry."

"So I believe."

"I helped another friend obtain a special license several weeks ago," Grande remarked. "He probably would not have been granted it without my intervention."

Frostbrook sat down slowly. "West?"

Grande's lips quirked. "West. Known him a long time. We were at school together at one point."

"And you like to help," Frostbrook repeated.

Grande nodded. "Did my good deed and forgot about it. I forget quite a lot."

"That will be the brandy."

Grande's eyes lightened. "Exactly. Going to stick to wine."

"Clearly, you will soon be a model clergyman."

Grande grinned openly. "No, I won't. Thing is, West turned up here in Brussels because apparently I'd promised to marry him to his cousin once he'd received the special license. Bothered me. Unless he was coming here in any case, why would he be so keen on *me*? Lots of clergymen in England."

"Perhaps because the lady in question did not consent and he could not rely on a clergyman who was not a friend."

"Well, even I'm not *that* big a friend," Grande said with a hint of indignation. "No consent, no marriage. Thing is, whether she consents or not is a different dilemma. I recognized her name last night, at the Kirkwood party. I was sure it was West's cousin's name, only this Miss Wallace appears to be engaged to you."

"She is."

Grande held his gaze. "Does she consent to that?"

Frostbrook felt his fists clench, but in the circumstances, it was a reasonable question. "We can ask her," he said shortly,

"I already did."

Frostbrook had never been so aware of the beating of his own heart. *What did she say?* The inevitable question stuck in his throat, for fear of the answer. How much had he annoyed her?

How difficult to live with did she think he would be? *Could* she still love him?

"She said she did," Grande said. "Consent, I mean."

Only with considerable effort did Frostbrook manage not to close his eyes with the force of his relief.

"The thing is," Grande said seriously, "what do we do about it?"

Frostbrook rose to his feet. "To begin with, I think we should join the others in the drawing room."

CHAPTER NINETEEN

T HE SUN CHOSE to smile upon Lady Hartley's Venetian breakfast. William West's rather battered hired carriage, containing himself, his mother, and his sister, actually drove past the Hartleys' house on his way into the town to fetch Lord Rupert. The sunshine cast a pleasant glow over the building, the open gates, and the small part he could see of the busy gardens behind.

"The house is not as large as I had imagined," his mother remarked.

William shrugged. "It is only a hired house, and compared with the few rooms people like the Duchess of Cuttyngham are forced to lodge in—"

"Well, she isn't the duchess anymore, is she?" Allegra interrupted. She was growing tiresomely petulant these days, dissatisfied with everything, from their admittedly rather dingy hotel to the dullness of Brussels in general. "So, she hardly needs a palace. Yet somehow, she has managed to find room for Sophia!"

"Well, she appears to *employ* Sophia, or at least so I have always been told."

His mother sniffed. "How much further to Lord Rupert's establishment? Really, would it not have been more sensible to meet him at Lady Hartley's house? The carriage will be terribly crowded."

"He doesn't appear to have a manservant to wake him up," William said unwisely.

Both his mother and Allegra stared at him.

"You mean we're to wait in the carriage while you wake him, dress him, and shave him, for all I know?" his mother said wrathfully. "I wish to be among the first to arrive, so that we might appear established in Lady Hartley's circle of friends. At this rate, we shall arrive just as everyone else is leaving! Sophia might even have gone. I really don't see why we can't simply call on her where she lives, bringing Lord Rupert with us!"

William sighed, for he had considered this possibility. "I looked into it, Mama, but in a small household the necessary privacy would be difficult to manage, especially if she proves reluctant again. And she must have the duchess and Lady Hera under her thumb somehow. Plus, aside from Mr. Edwards and at least three burly footmen, there is a baronet residing there, and frequently both the duchess's husband and Lady Hera's."

Allegra glared at him. "And will all those people not be at Lady Hartley's?"

"Probably," he said patiently. "But not all squashed into a small drawing room and standing guard over our cousin. Here, people will be more spread out, mingling, and we may pick our moment. Before Lord Rupert joins us, let me remind you of our plan and your place in it."

Allegra yawned rudely. "When we have all charmed our hostess, with Lord Rupert's help, you will find a quiet corner for the wedding, either inside the house or out. Mama and I will seek a quiet word with Sophia and bring her to you and Lord Rupert, where you will be married and then we can all go home and have a decent carriage and new clothes and I will have a rich husband."

"In a nutshell," William said grimly, as the carriage came to a halt outside Lord Rupert's lodgings. "And mind your tongue, Allegra, which grows unfemininely waspish."

With some satisfaction, he closed the door on her complaints and strode off in search of the erratic clergyman.

SOPHIA UNDERSTOOD THAT they had a point to make. So, although they could easily have walked the short distance to Lady Hartley's temporary residence, she was happy, for any number of reasons, to be driven in Lord Frostbrook's curricle.

His very nearness moved her. And even while the tension between them remained only partially resolved, she managed to enjoy civil and even witty conversation with him. When he looked at her, his eyes were not hard or cold, and that gave her hope. And when he drove the curricle through the gates to Lady Hartley's house, she was grateful that he troubled to make her laugh, for Lady Hartley herself stood welcoming her guests at the head of a path round the side of the house to the surprisingly large garden beyond.

It might have been because she could see them that he lifted Sophia down with such care, his hands lingering at her waist longer than they properly should. But she felt their warmth, and surely the hitch in her breath was echoed in his? At any rate, she smiled up at him, and he drew her hand through his arm.

By then, the carriage containing Rosamund, Hera, and their husbands was arriving.

"How charming," Lady Hartley greeted them. "A pleasure to see you so domesticated, my lord. Miss Wallace, so good of you to come."

"Not at all," Sophia said, smiling back as she dipped a slight curtsey. "I am looking forward to it."

Frostbrook drew her on up the path to the main part of the garden, where a marquee had been set up with a few small tables and chairs, and a vast array of food and drink was being brought out and placed on the larger tables at one end. Blankets for the younger people to sit on had been scattered about the pretty garden, in the shade of various trees.

The Edwards family and Sir Arthur were already present and acknowledged their arrival with waves. Sophia waved back and looked around for the Wests. In spite of her renewed courage and her knowledge of so many friends to protect her, her stomach twisted painfully at the thought of seeing them again.

"They're not here yet," Frostbrook murmured, bowing slightly to an acquaintance.

"I'm not frightened," she said ruefully, "at least, not in my head. There is just a dread in the pit of my stomach that I cannot reach, a revulsion…"

"Let me take you home," he said once with unexpected intensity. "I will deal with this in a different way."

"No, no." She squeezed his arm and cast him a quick smile. "Everyone is here to protect me. And I *need* to do this. I need to face them."

He nodded as though he understood. She thought he probably did, and her heart warmed. One good thing was that she did not see any of the same smirking glances she had intercepted at Mrs. Kirkwood's. Either that joke was old now, or her arrival with Frostbrook had given it the lie. Or, more likely, she was too concerned about other things to notice. Such as the arrival of her cousins.

With the entry of the Duchess of Richmond to the garden, along with one of her daughters and a very smart hussar, the breakfast was declared open by their hostess, and the milling around for tables, blanket space, food, and drink commenced.

Unusually for her, Rosamund had chosen a place in the center of things, a large blanket on the lawn. By prearranged plans, Sophia and Frostbrook sat beside her and Hera, while Giles and Dr. Rivers went to fetch food. It was a fine, shaded spot beneath a chestnut tree, and parasols were not necessary. Other people, whose names Sophia could not remember, joined them from time to time. In the background, a trio of musicians played quietly, which was a charming touch.

"Maybe they are not coming," Sophia murmured to Frost-brook.

"Unlikely. But either way, this situation ends today." There was a grim certainty in his voice that was both a comfort and an excitement. Now, she *wanted* them to come.

As it happened, she had to wait another half-hour before Lord Rupert appeared at the foot of the path with Allegra on his arm. She was wreathed in smiles, as was her mother, only slightly behind with William.

Something seemed to claw viciously at Sophia's stomach, a hopeless mixture of fear and hatred, anger and a wild desire to hit back.

"Don't even look at them," Aaron murmured. "I'll tell you where they go, what they do."

But she found she did not want to look away just yet. Lady Hartley hurried to meet her late guests, and playfully struck Lord Rupert's arm with her fan—his punishment, presumably, for being so late. He grinned in his usual engaging way and presented his guests. Lady Hartley, clearly, made them very welcome, without a trace of irritation at having uninvited guests foisted upon her. But then, the Wests were well turned out, William's tailoring perfect, the ladies fashionable without being ostentatious. Allegra, in fact, looked the perfect debutante in simple white muslin, her smile modest as she walked forward on Lord Rupert's arm.

Sophia turned her gaze away at last before they noticed her.

Hera, who had seen the direction of her gaze, spoke quietly on her other side. "So, *they* are your cousins? They have definitely noticed you—they all looked directly over here—but they are walking well to the left of us toward the Duchess of Richmond."

Major Butler glanced at Frostbrook, then stood up. "Excuse me," he murmured, and wandered off in vaguely the same direction.

"Her Grace is suffering introduction," Rosamund reported, leaning forward over the plate of fruit in the center of the blanket.

"She is tolerating them, no doubt, for Lord Rupert's sake…"

"They are moving on to the marquee," Dr. Rivers said. "But West is peeling away from them…strolling around the garden as though the flowers interest him. Grande is helping the ladies choose breakfast."

They were in no hurry, but suddenly Sophia was. She wanted this to be over. She wanted something to happen quickly, so that it could be. Her nerves seemed to stretch to breaking point, yet her cousins went through the motions of sitting down at one of the marquee tables with their food. Amelia even waved to Sophia, as if she had not watched her son pour quantities of gin down Sophia's throat. As if she had not helped by doing the same with laudanum and locking her in a cabin with no food or water…

With an effort, Sophia dragged her mind back to the present and noticed that there was no sign of William rejoining his family.

"Where is he?" Sophia asked tensely.

"I don't see him," Aaron replied, accepting a cup of coffee from the servant. "He may have gone inside, or around the other side of the house. But Butler is on his way back to us."

Sophia had to turn aside then to greet a young lady she had spoken to at the musical evening, who joined them on the blanket for a little. Sophia, smile firmly in place, was forced to contain her impatience until the girl had gone, although she saw Giles murmur something to Frostbrook, who nodded once.

When, finally, there was an instant's privacy, she turned at once to the earl. "What is happening?"

"West is in the house, a reception salon for visitors where, of course, no one will be this morning. I suppose he discovered the garden has no private nooks for his purposes. He is waiting, clearly, for the others to bring you into the house."

But Sophia had finally had enough of waiting for other people's decisions. She jumped to her feet, and, of course, the gentlemen all stood with her. More interestingly, Amelia and Allegra suddenly rose from their table.

"Sophia?" Aaron breathed. A faint frown marred his handsome brow, but it was quizzical, not commanding. And suddenly, as though understanding, he smiled—a brilliant smile that nevertheless held something of the predatory. "What an excellent idea!" He raised his voice and offered Sophia his arm. "Shall we join him?"

Rosamund and Hera were helped to their feet, and suddenly the Edwardses were in amongst them too as Sophia and Aaron led the way into the house. Further away, Allegra was all but dragging Lord Rupert out of the marquee, Amelia trotting behind them in some alarm. And suddenly, it was all fun. People were watching them with surprise and amusement. Some even joined them as if they formed some bizarre Polonaise. She glimpsed Lady Hartley's face amused and baffled and then suddenly worried, and a breath of laughter escaped her.

"Are we spoiling her party?" she murmured as a servant with a large teapot leapt out of her way.

"I can't help hoping so," Aaron replied, walking with her through the back door.

"Straight ahead, past the kitchens," Major Butler guided them cheerfully from behind, and they all trooped along the passage. Through the windows to the kitchen, cooks and scullery maids stared at them, open-mouthed.

They emerged into a hall.

"Second door on the right," Major Butler advised, and Sophia and Aaron veered obediently across the hall.

Aaron threw the door wide and walked in with Sophia still on his arm. William had been pacing toward the fireplace and now turned eagerly toward the door. His mouth fell open at the sight of Frostbrook with Sophia, and then his eyes widened in alarm as people began to troop in behind them.

"Good day, West," Frostbrook said. He even smiled, the most wolfish smile Sophia had ever seen. "I have been looking for you."

Sophia was only vaguely aware of the crowd jostling behind

her, their avid attention as they spilled around the room. Mostly, she felt Aaron's calm strength beside her, his air of contemptuous amusement as he came to a halt a couple of yards in front of William. She knew, without looking, that they were flanked by her true friends Rosamund and Giles, Hera and Dr. Rivers.

William's face had whitened, his eyes darting in alarm around his unexpected companions. Lord Rupert eased his way to the front, Amelia and Allegra behind him, and William's gaze latched on to them with relief.

Only then did he appear to see his hostess, for his pale face became suffused with color.

"My lady," he managed in the expectant silence. He bowed. "Please, forgive my intrusion. When I saw that my cousin, Miss Wallace, was your guest, I hoped for a private family discussion. Of course, I should have asked your permission rather than making free with your house, but I'm afraid family feeling overcame me. I can only apologize for my presumption and throw myself upon your mercy." He tried a smile. "Lord Rupert will reassure you of my character."

"Indubitably," Grande drawled.

William stared at him for several charged seconds, clearly willing him toward more practical help. When it remained unforthcoming—Rupert seemed more interested in some flaw in his fingernails—he was forced back on his own devices.

"My lady," he began again.

"There is no need for apology, Mr. West," Lady Hartley said, her voice amiable and amused. "My hospitality is well known, and any friend of Lord Rupert's…"

He might not have understood why, but clearly William sensed an ally in Lady Hartley, and seized his opportunity. "You are kindness itself. Might I therefore crave your assistance in this family matter? My mother and sister wish only to resolve certain issues with our cousin, Miss Wallace. Lord Rupert, in his role as clergyman, has agreed to help and guide us."

"Lord Rupert never ceases to surprise us," Lady Hartley said with a smile. "What do you say, Frostbrook? Shall we leave Miss Wallace to resolve her private issues with her delightful family?"

"You must do as you wish, ma'am," Aaron said coldly. "I shall not be leaving Miss Wallace anywhere."

His voice, even without the disdainful stare, should have frozen Sophia's cousin in his shoes, but from somewhere, William found the courage to brazen it out.

"You misjudge your authority, sir," he said, not without dignity. "Miss Wallace was left in my care by her late father."

"I am not sure you really wish to discuss the legalities of that matter in public," Aaron said. "But allow me to remind you that your cousin is of age, and any authority once recognized by the law is now actually mine."

William even managed to dredge up some pity into his eyes. "My lord, you might imagine yourself betrothed to Miss Wallace, but the truth is, she was engaged to me first, a promise I fully intend to hold her to."

"Just do it, William!" Allegra instructed. "The more witnesses, the better!"

A flash of irritation showed in William's eyes. Sophia was not surprised. But he turned to her, his expression wondrously soulful and pleading. "You cannot deny it, Sophia. Come now, this silly defiance must end." He gave her a smile that most present would no doubt consider sweet and understanding. It turned Sophia's stomach. He held out one hand to her. "We must keep our promises, marry, and have done with these playful charades before they hurt you any further."

His gaze was locked to hers, and she read every unspoken threat in his eyes. That if she did not accept this now, then she would again be taken by force and subjected to the same assault and humiliations as had brought her across the Channel. In spite of the company present, her friends behind her and Aaron's hard arm beneath her finger, she felt those threats in the pit of her stomach, churning up the memories of helplessness, fear, sickness, and pain.

And with the surge of memory came anger.

She met his gaze and smiled. "You are ridiculous, William. Leaving aside that I never promised to marry you, and never would, the law would not allow it."

A quick frown drew down William's brow. "You cannot know what you are talking about."

"Of course I do," Sophia said calmly. "I cannot marry you or anyone else because I am already married to Lord Frostbrook."

CHAPTER TWENTY

L ORD RUPERT HAD performed the marriage the previous evening, before the entire Edwards household gathered in the drawing room. To Sophia, still swirling with uncertainties and anxieties, the simple ceremony had taken on an air of unreality. The man to whom she was committing herself had remained calm and cool throughout, as though his only reason for marrying her was the one he had stated.

"Short of killing West—and believe me, I am tempted," he had said, "the only way to be certain he will not try to abduct Sophia again is to remove any possibility of her marrying him. Therefore, she should marry me now, for her own safety."

All eyes had turned on her, and for a moment she had felt she could not breathe. So many things lay unresolved between them, not least of them his past in general and Lady Hartley in particular. Yet these were things she had known, in a vague kind of way, when she had begun to fall in love with him. Her own advice to Rosamund, what felt like a lifetime ago, to follow her heart, had come rolling back to her. She did not know the depths of Aaron's feelings for her, but care was surely there, and she would never stop fighting for his love, because her own for him was so great.

That alone had shone through the last couple of days of turbulence and doubt and petty jealousy. None of these things could alter her ever-growing love for Aaron.

Everyone had been looking at her. Aaron had worn his usual mask, and yet she had seen the tightness of his grip on the chair back in front of him. His knuckles had been white.

Giles had said, "Sophia, if you are not ready to—"

"I am ready," Sophia had interrupted him. "Lord Rupert, would you be so obliging?"

Lord Rupert had indeed obliged, with the aid of a prayer book Mrs. Edwards' maid had dredged up from among her private possessions, and in a very few minutes, Sophia had found herself the Countess of Frostbrook.

Not that anyone would have known.

After a quick toast in sherry, they had dined and planned, and Frostbrook had departed with Lord Rupert, saluting his bride with no more than a kiss to her hand. A kiss she had cradled to her damp cheek when she finally lay alone in her bed that night.

As wedding nights went, it had hardly been auspicious, but the wedding itself was undeniable.

Now, in Lady Hartley's reception room, her announcement was greeted in stunned silence.

The color drained once more from William's face. Amelia and Allegra goggled at her. And Sophia was fiercely delighted.

"*What?*" Lady Hartley exclaimed, and then seemed to wish the word unsaid, judging by her sudden, ferocious frown.

Obligingly, Sophia repeated, "Lord Frostbrook and I were married last night."

"Nonsense," Allegra said petulantly. "He would *never* marry you! The engagement was all a sham to annoy his mother."

It won her a ripple of laughter, none of it from her own family. In fact, Amelia snapped, "Oh, be quiet, Allegra."

Still, Allegra's outburst seemed to have given William fresh hope. "Ah, I see how it is. I warned you about him, Sophia. A fake marriage and a willing lover. You are not the first innocent girl to fall for such tricks, and I daresay you won't be the last. You are lucky I forgive you." With that, his arm shot out and he seized

Sophia by the shoulder, jerking her physically away from Aaron.

Even as she wrenched herself free, a roar of pure rage split the room. Aaron's fist crashed into William's face, sending him staggering backward to collapse prone into Lord Rupert's hold.

"You are wrong," Lord Rupert told him conversationally. "I married them myself."

But Aaron had followed his prey and reached down, hauling William to his feet by his coat, his fist already swinging back for another strike.

Sophia's heart overflowed with emotion, but while everyone else fell back, she sprang forward and seized her husband's arm. His face jerked toward her, his mouth twisted in fury, his eyes positively murderous. Because William had touched her. Because he had hurt her.

"Don't, Aaron," she said gently. "He is already punished."

After the tiniest, tensest instant, his eyelids swept down. He breathed out and dropped William. This time Lord Rupert didn't stop him hitting the floor.

"If I were you," Aaron said, his soft voice dripping with contempt, "I should keep traveling. There are several lawyers awaiting you in England, where you will be charged with embezzling from your cousin, who, I believe, now owns the clothes on your back in recompense for what you stole. The rest of your crimes will not be forgotten, so pray—pray damned hard, West—that I never see you again."

He turned on his heel, offering his arm to Sophia, who took it without thought. "I believe it is time to go. My thanks," he flung in the general direction of Lord Rupert, the Butlers, and the Rivers.

In silence, he strode to the door, so quickly Sophia was almost trotting. All the same, Lady Hartley was before them, in the doorway.

"Frost," she said, her voice soft, pleading.

Don't stop, don't speak to her, Sophia begged silently.

He stopped. "Forgive my manners, Sabrina. Thank you for

breakfast, but I hope you won't trouble with further invitations."

As though he had struck her, Lady Hartley stumbled aside and Aaron stalked out and across the hall to the front door, which an avidly listening footman ran to open for him.

"WHERE ARE WE going?" Sophia asked breathlessly.

Frostbrook's furious pace had not slowed. Nor was he bothering to hide his still-raging passion. It made her stomach clench and dive, for she did not believe it was all anger, or all aimed at her cousins or Lady Hartley. On top of that, he had made his position publicly plain to Lady Hartley. Her cruel tricks against Sophia had deprived the woman of his friendship, and even his consideration.

She had never seen him so angry, so uncontrolled. It was a little frightening—and yet curiously exciting.

Since he did not answer, or even seem to hear her, she gave his arm a little tug. "What of your curricle and the horses?"

"Butler will drive them back," he said impatiently. "And we are going somewhere we can talk in private."

They were hurrying along the road toward the Namur Gate, and then over the bridge spanning the banks of the canal. A large, solitary boat was tied up, a hundred yards from the bridge. Something about the vessel looked familiar, although the curtains were drawn on the cabins and it appeared to be deserted.

"Aaron? Is that not the boat we travelled in from Ostend?"

"I hired it for a week. I still have the keys." Turning, he stepped aboard as easily as if entering a friend's house and held out his hand to her.

Her heart skittered, but she took his hand without hesitation. "What are we talking about? William's legal position?"

"I don't give a monkey's curse for William's legal position," he said savagely, ramming a key into the lock of the main cabin door. "Or even yours, if the truth be told."

She followed him inside, and when he closed and locked the door again behind her, her stomach dived. He stood facing her, his chest rising and falling with the speed of his agitated breath.

"Sabrina Hartley and I parted some weeks before the duel," he said carefully, although his eyes were anything but calm. "Even if I had never met you, I would never have gone back to her. I was always in search of novelty, easing a boredom that was bone deep and nothing to with her or with any other woman I have known. It was to do with me." He swallowed. "In your presence, I am never bored."

Her lips twitched, even while a new warmth began to seep up from her toes. "As romantic declarations go, it is quite weak, but I'll take it as a compliment."

Light gleamed in his turbulent eyes. "You should," he retorted. "Sophia, I don't deserve you, but you are my wife, and I *will* make you happy."

"How do you propose to do that?" she asked, her voice trembling only slightly.

His eyes devoured her. "Come here."

Her heart was thundering. "Now?"

"Right now."

"Whatever made you think," she asked with a tilt of her chin, "that I would be a dutiful wife?"

"God, I hope you never will be. Of everything between you and me, there should never be mere duty. Come here, because I ask it, because you want it. Or should I come to you?"

"There is not so much space between us," she managed, taking a step toward him.

He took the other, closing the distance, and snatched her up into his arms.

"I love you," he said intensely, as though the words were wrung out of him. "I adore you, only you, for as long as I live and probably beyond. Say you could love me, Sophia—say it…"

She could not, for his mouth came down on hers so fiercely

that she could barely breathe, let alone talk. But it seemed she could speak without words, throwing her arms around him and yielding, opening her mouth wide to his invasive, all-consuming kiss. She pressed even closer to him in some primal need to be one with him.

"I do love you," she whispered between wild kisses. "I have always loved you, and you are the only one who doesn't seem to know."

Somehow, her bodice was drooping and his hands were hot on the naked flesh of her back, her waist. He lifted her in his arms, swinging around to kick the cushions off the nearest sofa, and when she landed on them, with him leaning over her, she was completely unclothed and he had lost his coat. He tore at his cravat while kissing her, and she helped him push his shirt up over his head.

For an instant she felt all his glorious weight, and the bliss of his naked chest pressed to her breasts. And then he levered himself up, breathless, his eyes all turbulent passion as she had never seen them. They were hidden again as he kissed her throat, his fingers gentle and knowing on her breast, reducing her to helpless need.

His hunger must have matched hers, but he had much more idea what to do with it. His pantaloons were kicked off as he worshipped her flushed and trembling body with his mouth and his strong, sensual hands. She could only gasp and stroke the masculine flesh undulating beneath her caresses, and then he gave her what she didn't even know she wanted, sliding into her welcoming body with a soft, blissful groan.

It was a new, wondrous caress, and she reveled in it, eagerly responding until his control seemed to slip and the reckless passion was back, throwing her into unimagined convulsions of ecstasy. Where he joined her.

Her joy was complete.

"THAT IS WHY," Aaron said softly, tracing lazy patterns across her breast with one delicate finger, "I did not stay with you last night."

"You prefer the daylight?" she guessed, watching the sunshine come and go around the hems of the curtains. She liked the patterns they made on his golden skin as he stretched sleek and naked on the bed beside her. Male bodies, she had discovered, had their own beauty. Or, at least, Aaron's had. Everything about him moved her.

"I preferred not to make love to you for the first time in a house packed to the gunnels with concerned people and far too few lockable doors. I still prefer it."

She let her arm settle across his waist and smiled. "I prefer it, too."

He kissed her for that. "Did I hurt you?" he asked, his eyes steady though rueful. "I meant to be gentler…"

"Oh, you were gentle," she whispered, hugging him close, "and sweet and wonderful, and I feel as if I shall never recover."

"I hope you will," he murmured in her ear, "because I thought we might move you and your things to my hotel for tonight. They are pleasant rooms, and big enough for two."

She smiled into his neck. "What an excellent idea."

"Then shall we rise and dress, and broach the matter with Mrs. Edwards?"

"Not yet," she said, reluctant to leave the intimacy of the cushions and the faintly rocking boat. And her naked husband. "Just another few minutes."

"As many as you like," he said softly.

IT WAS AN hour before they rose and dressed. She straightened his cravat, and he helped her pin her hair and secure her new hat. Then they left the delightful cabin, and he handed her off the boat. She took his arm, and they strolled together along the canal, through the Namur Gate and the streets leading to the park and, eventually, to the Edwards's house. The spoke of various things, and often of nothing. Just being with him, holding his arm in the sunshine, gave her a special kind of contentment.

When, finally, they reached the house, it was late afternoon. Izzy saw them first and dragged them toward the drawing room, declaring, "My lord, you were magnificent! If I did not already love Tom, I assure you I would be quite madly in love with you!"

"Izzy!" Mrs. Edwards exclaimed, clearly appalled. "Seriously, you must not say such things!"

Rosamund laughed. "Forgive her this once. After his lordship's performance at the breakfast, I think we are *all* a little in love with him."

To Sophia's amusement, a little color seeped into her husband's cheeks.

Giles offered him his hand, grinning. "I include myself. Sophia was masterly, but I own to particular admiration for your strike and for the deadly warnings. And, I own, for the set-down to Lady Hartley. Both she and Sophia deserved that."

Aaron shook his hand and inclined his head in acknowledgement. "They did. Though I still think the Wests got off lightly. Particularly William."

"Perhaps it was as well there were ladies present," Rosamund mused.

"What happened after we left?" Sophia asked, taking the seat Aaron held for her. "Did the Wests try to plead their case and insult me?"

"Absolutely not," Rosamund said with relish. "Lord Rupert gave them the cut direct, and there was nothing they could do but slink off. Oh! And an hour ago, a small urchin appeared with a message for you, my lord. Apparently the Wests left their hotel with their luggage and drove out of the city, traveling south."

"Good," Aaron said. "Perhaps they'll run into the French."

Rosamund nodded, as though she considered that a fitting punishment, before she recalled what a French invasion would mean, and hastily moved on with her tale. "Lady Hartley carried on as though nothing had happened, merely told Lord Rupert to keep better company and not to fight his battles in her house again. Actually, in her own way, she is quite brave." Rosamund glanced from Aaron to Sophia and back. "She might not invite you again, but you are still bound to see her, at the Duchess of Richmond's ball if nowhere else. But I don't believe she will dare say another word about you, Sophia."

Sophia thought about it. "I don't mind if she does. It was all so much foolishness. Mrs. Edwards, you have been kindness itself, but I shall remove myself to Frostbrook's hotel now."

Mrs. Edwards's eyes danced. "Quite right. Very wifely."

"Besides, we shall need the space," Rosamund said. "Mrs. Edwards wants to offer Victor the breakfast parlor."

Victor? "The duke is coming?" Sophia asked, astonished.

"Apparently so."

"Good for him," Frostbrook said, and murmured to Sophia, "It seems all the late duke's caged birds are spreading their wings." And it seemed they were both glad of it. "I wonder if he has discovered something more about his father's death?"

"I think we would be clutching at straws to hope so," Giles said ruefully. "I always meant to stand trial for what I did. It is right that I do."

"You will stay for tea before you leave us?" Mrs. Edwards asked Sophia quickly, before Rosamund could respond.

"If we may," Sophia replied, rising. "But first, I shall go and pack my things. Your things, really," she added as Rosamund followed her from the room.

Rosamund waved one dismissive hand and held Sophia's gaze for a moment. "All is well?" she asked with a shade of anxiety.

Sophia glanced back through the half-open door. She could see the earl, relaxed, smiling quizzically at something Izzy was saying, and her heart turned over.

"Oh yes," she said softly. "Everything is very well. Very well indeed."

EPILOGUE

Six months later

I N EARLY DECEMBER, on a fine, cold day, the Earl and Countess of Frostbrook returned to Brookwood, the earl's principal seat in Lincolnshire.

Sophia had her first glimpse of the house as the luxurious traveling coach swept around the bend in the drive. Her breath caught. She had expected splendor, but this seemed more daunting than anything she had imagined. It was like Cuttyngs. A vast stone pile, mixing the styles of the centuries as it had been added to over the generations. And yet the overall effect was gracious and beautiful.

"Oh my goodness," she murmured. "How will I ever become mistress of such a huge house? Such a massive estate?"

"I would like to say with my mother's help," Aaron said ruefully, "but you won't need it. In truth, she is here to welcome us home, but she has spent the six months since our wedding preparing one of the lesser country estates for her own use."

"At your...advice?"

"At her own wish. I merely suggested the house. You can do whatever you like here, change the purpose and decoration of any rooms, any space you want to. Though I am available for consultation." He took her hand, caressing her wrist in the way he knew aroused her. "And distraction."

She smiled. "I know."

There had already been many, many distractions. In the aftermath of Waterloo, they had finally set off on a wedding journey that encompassed Austria, Hungary, and Italy. For Sophia, even with the tragedies of the war behind them, the trip had been wonderful. Coming home had felt a little more like returning to face punishment for absence without leave.

But when the coach clattered into a large courtyard, the first person she saw was Judith Landry, rushing out of the house to welcome them, and her heart lifted with pleasure. Judith and Humphrey had been so kind to her that she genuinely looked forward to knowing her new family better.

"Aaron!" Judith squealed, enveloping him in a hug before he was properly down the steps from the coach. She pushed away from him, searching his face, and then she beamed. "Good God, you look wonderful! Is this Sophia's doing?"

"Absolutely," he replied with no trace of embarrassment, and turned to help Sophia down. She held out her hand to Judith with a shy smile, but immediately received the same treatment as Aaron.

"This is wonderful! Just wonderful!" Judith almost dragged them into the house, calling, "Humph! Wake up, you lazy creature! Aaron and Sophia are home! Twins!"

Aaron's eyebrows flew up. "The twins are here?"

"They could not wait to meet Sophia…"

"Judith, must you scream and shout like a fishwife?" came the voice Sophia had been dreading.

But Aaron took her hand, and they went forward together to greet the dowager countess. Regal and unbending, she waited for them to approach.

Sophia curtseyed. "My lady."

The countess nodded in return, her face glacial, and turned to her son. "Frostbrook."

"Mother." He kissed her proffered hand and her cheek.

"Thank you for coming to welcome us."

The countess sniffed. "Someone has to make sure that your…wife knows how to go on."

Why? Do you think I will break wind and put my feet up on the table at dinner parties? Sophia bit back the words, which were hardly conciliatory, and merely smiled.

"What on earth possessed you to marry abroad, Frostbrook?" the countess demanded. "None of the Lomans have ever married abroad."

"They have now," Aaron said peaceably.

"After the way she behaved at Wellis, I am surprised she allowed you to come home and face me at all," the countess said quite audibly as she turned away.

"I am surprised she wanted to," Aaron shot back. "But it seemed appropriate that our heir should be born at Brookwood."

The countess swung back like a weather vane in a sharp gust of wind. "What? *Heir?*"

"Well, possibly," Aaron amended. "Certainly, we are expecting a child in the spring."

To Sophia's amazement, the countess's frigid eyes softened. "Why the deuce didn't you say so?" she demanded. "Sophia, my dear, come and sit down after such an awful journey. There will plenty of time tomorrow to see the house…"

Alarmed, Sophia allowed her arm to be taken, glancing back at Aaron in panic. He raised one eyebrow and grinned. Judith laughed.

"I TOLD YOU," Aaron said, some hours later. In the interim, Sophia had enjoyed tea with the whole family, renewed her acquaintance with Sir Humphrey, met Aaron's mischievous but highly engaging schoolboy brothers, and been marched smartly around on a conducted tour of the house. Or at least a large part of it. Finally, they had reached the private apartments that were

Aaron's, and they were alone. "My mother will never be warm and affectionate, but you will now receive all the respect due to the countess."

"She won't stay to look after me, will she?" Sophia asked uneasily.

"Good God, no. She has not changed that much. She is still my mother! What do you think of the house?"

Despite his frequent jokes on the subject, she knew her opinion was important to him. In the months since their marriage, she had learned many of his odd vulnerabilities, and yet he had become the rock on which all her trust rested. This great house, his family home for hundreds of years in one form or another, was part of his heritage, part of *him*, and he wanted her to like it.

But she could never spoil their relationship with easy lies.

"As a home, it is…daunting," she said frankly. "I did wonder if I could ever feel comfortable in such splendor. It is a little like Cuttyngs, is it not? But there is something more about Brookwood that I like. Parts of the house are beautiful, and I love the sense of history. It will take me some time to adjust and learn to manage everything, but I have ideas to make the house into more of our home, especially once we have children."

There was relief in his smile. His shoulders relaxed. "And these rooms?" he asked in quite a different voice. "Will you be happy to share them with me?"

"I love them because they are yours," she said, walking into his arms. "And truly, I will love everything about my new life." It was true. She was ready to be the countess. *His* countess.

"So do I," he whispered in her ear. "Shall we see if you like the new bed?"

She only smiled, and it seemed no other answer was necessary.

About Mary Lancaster

Mary Lancaster lives in Scotland with her husband, three mostly grown-up kids and a small, crazy dog.

Her first literary love was historical fiction, a genre which she relishes mixing up with romance and adventure in her own writing. Her most recent books are light, fun Regency romances written for Dragonblade Publishing: *The Imperial Season* series set at the Congress of Vienna; and the popular *Blackhaven Brides* series, which is set in a fashionable English spa town frequented by the great and the bad of Regency society.

Connect with Mary on-line – she loves to hear from readers:

Email Mary:
Mary@MaryLancaster.com

Website:
www.MaryLancaster.com

Newsletter sign-up:
http://eepurl.com/b4Xoif

Facebook:
facebook.com/mary.lancaster.1656

Facebook Author Page:
facebook.com/MaryLancasterNovelist

Twitter:
@MaryLancNovels

Amazon Author Page:
amazon.com/Mary-Lancaster/e/B00DJ5IACI

Bookbub:
bookbub.com/profile/mary-lancaster

www.ingramcontent.com/pod-product-compliance
Lightning Source LLC
Chambersburg PA
CBHW070338200726

48294CB00003B/705